Yellow Hair

**Center Point
Large Print**

**This Large Print Book carries the
Seal of Approval of N.A.V.H.**

Yellow Hair

WILL HENRY

CENTER POINT PUBLISHING
THORNDIKE, MAINE

This Center Point Large Print edition
is published in the year 2004 by arrangement with
Golden West Literary Agency.

The text of this Large Print edition is unabridged. In other
aspects, this book may vary from the original edition. Printed in
Thailand. Set in 16-point Times New Roman type.

ISBN 1-58547-460-6

Library of Congress Cataloging-in-Publication Data

Henry, Will, 1912-
    Yellow hair / Will Henry.--Center Point large print ed.
        p. cm.
    ISBN 1-58547-460-6 (lib. bdg. : alk. paper)
    1. Custer, George Armstrong, 1839-1876--Fiction. 2. Indians of North
America--Wars--Fiction. 3. Arkansas River Valley--Fiction. 4. Large type
books. I. Title.

PS3551.L393Y445 2004
813'.54--dc22

                                                    2004001607

HISTORICAL FOREWORD

. . . The energy and rapidity shown during one of the heaviest snowstorms known to this section of the country, with the temperature below freezing, the gallantry and bravery displayed, resulting in such signal success, reflects the highest credit on the 7th Cavalry . . . and the Major-General Commanding expresses his thanks to the officers and men engaged in the Battle of the Washita, and his special congratulations to their distinguished commander Brevet Major-General George A. Custer for the efficient and gallant service opening the campaign against the hostile Indians north of the Arkansas . . .

Text of General P. H. Sheridan's communique
announcing the Battle of the Washita,
November 27th, 1868

Custer's "signal success" along the Washita may indeed have reflected the "highest credit" upon his "distinguished commanding." But the tongue of White Man's history can be crooked. And the pens of Generals do not always travel in straight lines.

What actually happened that snow-shrouded, shameful dawn along the Washita has not been told.

Not the way Moxtraveto, the trusting Black Kettle of the Southern Cheyenne, would deeply mutter it. Not the way Axhonehe, the sinister Mad Wolf of the Cut-Arm Dog Soldiers, would angrily snarl it. Not the way Monaseetah, the legendary South Plains tribal princess, would hauntingly smile it. And certainly not the way Joshua Kelso, Custer's Indian-killing Chief of Scouts, would soft-spokenly remember it.

It has been told only in Brevet Major-General George Armstrong Custer's self-hallowed, heroic way.

Now it will be told in another way. Scarcely self-hallowed. Hardly heroic. Surely not distinguished. Nor highly creditable.

Now it will be told in *Yellow Hair*'s way.

W. H.

1. Plenty Kills

THE BIG DUN GELDING picked up the weary rhythm of his shuffling gait. His rider tensed, restless eyes quartering the darkened prairie beyond the nervous flick of his mount's ears. Shortly he relaxed, the softness of his voice belying the grimness of the nod which accompanied it.

"There she be, Wasiya. Broad as a squaw's bottom and twice as welcome. I allow we won't have no trouble makin' the fort by moonset now."

Ahead lay the Arkansas. Its broad trace glimmered ghost-white in the moonwash, bringing the smell of the first water since sundown. It had been a long, dry forty miles from Fort Larned back there on the branchwaters of the Pawnee Fork, and the gelding was thirsty. Black nostrils belling gratefully, the big dun went forward.

When the horse had watered, the man turned him to grazing, set himself to packing the bowl of his stone pipe with the bright shags of longcut Burley, alternating the precise slowness of the action with snakefast glances into the outer prairie darknesses. Apparently reassured, he struck the pocket flint to the shagcut, sucked the Burley into soul-satisfying life and settled on his heels to stare along the westward track of the wagon road down which, some forty miles now, lay his destination, Fort Dodge.

Although he was still those forty miles short of hearing Custer put it in his own words, a man already had a fair prime hunch what the palaver down there at

7

the fort was going to be about. And why the "General" had sent that Osage scout to summon him to it. In his total years as a man grown on the short grass, he'd never seen so many warpaint hostiles as he had in his past week's ride. It figured to be sudden hell on the South Plains, mister, and nobody but naked red devils stoking the furnaces.

The tall rider shook his head, knocked the emberless dottle from his squat Sioux pipe. The quick, good sound of his laugh echoed strangely, lifting Wasiya's curious head from the belly-deep graze of the river swale. With the laugh he was on his feet, moving with all the noise and effort of a six-foot cat.

At his mount's side he paused, his hand checking swiftly beneath the cinch-loosened saddleblanket to see that the gelding was cooled out. Satisfied, he grinned knowingly.

"Sure as sin's for sale in St. Louie, Custer's aimin' to run them redguts off the Canadian once and for all, come summer again. Once he's did that there's them million skinny cows south of the Red River dyin' for a mouthful of good grass. And them ten million fat Yanks east of the Big Muddy dyin' for a mouthful of good beef." He paused again, letting the grin sober with the final nod.

"Old son, I figure any Texas boy with half a belly and no brains can get rich bringin' them two appetites together!"

The gelding grunted to the sudden cinching of the girth, skittered playfully to the mounting weight of the rider. "Leastways," the thoughtful voice continued, "I figure you and me can do it—"

He broke his words sharply off as his body stiffened to the westward swing of his narrowed gaze. Straight down the line of the wagon road, five, maybe six miles west, the prairie sky was pinpointed by the rising stain of a freshly lit nightfire. Grim-lipped, he heeled the gelding into a hammering gallop.

"Leastways we can, happen a few hundred South Plains Cheyennes don't meanwhile lift our hair higher than the stink of a stick-poked polecat!"

Big Coon Creek was ordinarily a decently dark and quiet stream. But at 2.00 A.M. of the morning of November 13, 1868, it was anything but dark and quiet at the confluence of the Big Coon and the Arkansas.

The bushel-sized blaze of the fire booming so cheerily on the south banks of the Coon lit up the Santa Fe wagon road for hundreds of feet in either direction, limning the four figures squatting to its broad glow. It bounced ruddily off the high-sided army freighter whose corded load of stovewood and three-span hitch of patient mules formed the backdrop for the fireside group. Nor was the unwonted illumination without its fit complement of heartily raised human voices. The four soldiers were making oral sign enough to be picked up by a stone-deaf squaw listening eight miles off the trail and dead up-wind.

First Sergeant Ben Henderson, Company B, Seventh United States Cavalry, graciously passed the glazed clay jug of Taos Lightning to his immediate inferior, Corporal Willy Hardermann. Having done so, he felt the time was right for a rousing chorus of the "Battle

Hymn of the Republic."

Privates Toland and MacDougal fought valiantly, if six keys sour, for the tenor lead while Corporal Hardermann took what was left, making the least of his coonhound bass in the effort. The harmony had struggled to the point where the Lord was about to take a prodigious, whack at the wicked "with his turrible swift sword," when MacDougal, the least saturated of the South Arkansas Woodhauling and Choral Society, broke off his bid for first-tenor supremacy to gape up the firelit eastern reaches of the Santa Fe Trail.

The sight which dropped MacDougal's jaw easily warranted the dislocation.

Take six foot-three and one hundred and ninety pounds of bone-gaunt mountain scout clothed in grease-blackened Cheyenne buckskins, add a slab-rock face bristled with half an inch of hogwire beard and a gimlet-mean brace of eyeholes bored alongside a nose as horn-sharp as a bald eagle's, then blanket the net results in a coating of alkali trail dirt deep enough to be turned with a moldboard plow and there'd be a middling idea of what MacDougal's jaws were ajar about. Especially if that apparition were mounted on a seventeen-hand giant of a Sioux gelding, unclipped since the past winter and wild-eyed and wicked-looking as a bull elk whistling up six strange cows.

The scout slid the lathered Wasiya into a stiff-legged stop that had his hocks burning horsehide. Without a word or look for the startled soldiers, he stepped off the gelding and went for the wood wagon. Seizing the five-gallon water keg, he lifted it from its leather moorings as easily as though it had been a backstoop dipper. In less time than it took MacDougal to get his molars back together, the offending blaze was drowned out.

"Don't you jackass jaspers know no better than to build up a bonfire in the bellyhole of Injun country?" The question hissed in over the angry spit of the drenched coals. "Happen I couldn't see you was new to the country, I'd swear you was some of Custer's outfit!"

"Yeah?" MacDougal's long legs were coming unwound. "And if we couldn't see you was all buckskin and no bath since last spring, we'd swear you was Custer hisself. The way you come bustin' in here with your fancy mouth flappin' a mile a minute—"

With the suspended observation, the bear-sized private stepped around the steaming firebed.

Fancy-mouthed or not, the newcomer knew when to stop talking. He came into MacDougal with a twisting cat turn. The first sensation the big soldier enjoyed was that of his right arm departing its shoulder socket. Followed a three-second flying journey through the Arkansas night air. Terminating his impromptu nosedive with a five-foot furrow of jaw-turned creek sand, MacDougal came to his feet fighting mad and fanning for his holster.

"Hold up, soldier." The flat warning came from behind the skinning knife which had appeared in the right hand of his adversary. "Right now I ain't gettin' paid to fight white men. You savvy?"

MacDougal, like all salt-worth fighting men, never bucked the tiger. Not when it was nine steel inches long and trained squarely on his favorite navel. "All right, laddie buck, you're callin' the tune, suppose you strike up your fiddle. This here's a wood detail for Fort Coon, yonder up the crick there. Who the hell are you?"

"Joshua Kelso—"

"Joshua Kelso! Oh, sure!" The angry soldier's face relaxed to the sudden spread of the sarcastic grin, his accompanying nod going to his three companions. "Josh, I want you should meet Jed Smith, Jim Bridger and Charlie Bent. Of course you know me, Kit Carson!"

"I ain't goin' to straddle out here arguin' birth certificates with you." The big thumb slid suggestively along the edge of the skinning blade. "I'm Kelso and you'd best believe it. I'll tell you something else you'd best believe, too—"

"Sure. You can trust old Kit, Josh!"

"Shut your damn mouth, Jock." First Sergeant Henderson, moving forward over the smoking debris of the fire, was sobering fast. "He's Kelso, all right. I remember him from last summer when Hancock had him out Injun-huntin' with Custer. How you been, Kelso? What's up? You had Injun trouble up the trail?"

"I ain't had none and I ain't aimin' to have none. But *you're* goin' to. How far's this Fort Coon and how soon can you make it?"

The soldiers were no longer questioning the scout's identity. They were, in fact, doing considerable mental foot-shifting under the nervous impact of their new-found conviction.

Joshua Kelso, for his later day and time, had no less a name than the hairiest of the old Rocky Mountain

12

Rough Brigade. Indeed, it had been Jim Bridger himself who, in recommending the young mountain man as a scout to Custer, had described him as "the Lew Wetzel of Wyomin'." When Old Gabe went that far and fancy in labeling a fellow fur trapper, a man didn't forget it. And as for becoming the enlisted man's hero of any garrison from Fort Huachuca to the Bozeman road, the surest method was that employed by Joshua Kelso—killing Indians.

"About six miles, Mr. Kelso." Private Bates Toland, the teamster, furnished the respectful answer while the others were still wrestling with the reality of meeting the shadowy Ota Kte, face to face. "We can make it, come daylight."

"I allow you'd best make it *come daylight.*"

The faint chill of the emphasis wasn't wasted. Privates Toland and MacDougal, with Corporal Hardermann, grabbed their stacked carbines and scuttled for the wood wagon. Sergeant Henderson, half a jump behind them, boarded his tethered mount and kicked him back toward Kelso. The scout shot him a quick look, for the first time noting the familiar red and white regimental insignia on the issue saddleblanket.

"I might have knowed you was with the Seventh." There was that in the disgusted grunt which went a full set of ricepaper encyclopedias past the bare count of the words themselves. "Beginning with Custer there ain't none of you in that outfit that's ever learned to smell a redskin with your nose less than six inches shy of his stinkin' shirttail."

"Yeah?" The sergeant's little bid for dignity faltered

under the drive of the dark eyes. "Well, you civilian scouts can't seem to quit smellin' them. Not even if they're a hundred miles off."

"I wouldn't let that hundred miles comfort you none." The grin was bobtailed as a bay lynx. "I just seen Mad Wolf and three hundred Dog Soldiers not six hours ago. Maybe forty miles north of where we set."

"Naw! You sure it was Mad Wolf?"

The big scout ignored the question, asked pleasantly, "Sergeant, you got any good idea why them Injuns calls me Plenty Kills?"

"You mean them wholesale yarns Custer tells about how you've killed more of them than the smallpox?"

"Somethin' like that." The voice was still easy. "It's been overdid by Custer, like most everything he puts his hand or mouth to. I ain't took to killin' squaws and kids yet, like you army boys."

The trooper set his jaw to the old service insult, wisely chose to give it passing room. He let his question come as his uneasy glance divided itself between the towering scout and the disappearing tailgate of the wood wagon. "What's that to do with you seein' Mad Wolf and them Dog Soldiers?"

Kelso shrugged the answer as quietly as though he'd been asked the time of day. "Somehow Mad Wolf found out Custer had sent for me again. Right off, he tooken himself a personal pledge to put me under before the new grass comes. That's next spring the way they figure things, the same time they allow the Seventh will start after them again."

"Well, them Injuns is always talkin' big."

"Not this one, mister."

"Damn it, Kelso, I sure hope you're wrong."

"I ain't." The noncommittal grunt came as the scout reined Wasiya around. "You'd best get along after your boys. I allow Mad Wolf hisself will foller me. Anyhow, I'll do what I can to lead the main pack of them off'n you. See you downtrail, soldier."

"Cripes Amighty!" the trooper's delayed realization checked his departure. "You mean to say him and *all* them Dog Soldiers is follerin' you personal?"

Once more the dry flick of the grin kicked up the dust track of its passage across the dirt-powdered jaw. "If he ain't, and if he ain't been since first I snuck out'n the Bayou Salade six days gone, I been seein' double a hundred and fifty times over."

Before the sergeant could begin to unravel this bit of prairie arithmetic he found himself staring into nothing but South Arkansas darkness, no longer hearing either the fading clip-clop of the Sioux gelding's unshod hoofs or the hurrying trot-jangle of the wagonmules' trace chains. He was suddenly and unquestionably alone, alone with the muttering Arkansas and the muddy swirl of Big Coon Creek—and maybe three hundred of Mad Wolf's Cheyenne Dog Soldiers.

With a startled imprecation which echoed more of present Cheyenne panic than prior Indian-proof conviction, First Sergeant Benjamin Franklin Henderson, Company B, Seventh United States Cavalry, surrendered the field and fled without shame or evident shred of regimental regret toward the dubious sanctuary of sod-roofed Fort Coon.

2. Mad Wolf

THE EMBERS OF THE wagonfire still fingered the Arkansas night air with the wan tendrils of their blue-wet woodsmoke when the quiet of the Big Coon confluence was disturbed for the second time within the hour.

This time the noise was not so easily catalogued. Not at any rate by a white ear. It was in fact a sound seldom heard by fair-skinned settler or soldier lucky enough to live to report it: the savage, animal-grunting sound of three hundred Cheyenne war ponies slashing at a flat gallop through the shallows of a South Plains tributary.

The greasy cloudfront of a storm building rapidly to the southwest rolled the Arkansas moon in its leaden wash, cut the light short off and made a nebulous blob of the close-packed Cheyenne horsemen. There was still, however, enough light to distinguish the faces and figures of the four Indians who rode forward to the soldier's fire.

The leader was of medium height, lean as a sun-dried bone, dark-skinned as the smokehole of a Sioux hunting lodge. His slender body, naked but for a doe-skin breechclout and wolfskin shoulder robe, was as muscle-writhing as a prairie rattler's. His axe blade of a face was as high-cheeked as a Mongol Khan's, the tight leather of its skin entirely free of paint or charcoal. He wore none of the usual adornments of the horse-Indian warrior, his sole personal ornament being a gleaming

16

Sun God medallion of Apache silver, pendant from a massive throat chain of the same metal. This was Mad Wolf.

Contrariwise, the first of his three henchmen was bedizened with every war-trail accoutrement: white eagle-feather bonnet, dyed horsehair shirt and leggin tassels, bear-claw necklaces, hawk-bone hair skewers and the like. He was a brute-faced giant, dwarfing the others with his great bulk, and his name was Etapeta, Big Body.

The third Cheyenne, Yellow Buffalo, was squat and pale-skinned. Also flashily beaded and feathered, he affected as his personal Big Medicine a war bonnet fashioned from an ocher-daubed buffalo skull.

The fourth horseman was very old. Dressed in the simple elkskin shirt and breeches of the rank-and-file Dog Soldier, he wore three black eagle feathers down-hanging at the rear of his head—the ominous trademark of his illfamed lodge.

The dark-skinned chief signaled to Yellow Buffalo, who spoke gently to the old man. The latter swung down off his pony and as he did, the animal backed away, revealing the lead rope which attached it to the cantle ring of Yellow Buffalo's cavalry saddle. He, too, dismounted now, took the old man's arm and guided him carefully, toward the fire's bed.

"Hovahan hoesta!" snapped the chief, the guttural bark of the Cheyenne tongue stinging like a lash. "Never mind the fire, you fool! I can see that from here. Take him to the tracks over there. Those are the marks of that yellow demon Ota Kte rides."

17

Heovhotoa, the Yellow Buffalo, nodded his horned skullpiece and led the old man quickly to a line of hoofprints clearly etched in the damp day of the creek bank.

"*Hehe!*" Yellow Buffalo's shout was triumphant. "These are his prints, all right. A blind man couldn't miss them. Not with that crooked right forefoot!"

"*Nenano ononistahe,* shut your mouth and let a blind man see them, then." The dark-skinned chief snarled the order with a lip-lifted grimace which would have identified him even if his next words had not. "Mad Wolf is followed by nothing but fools. Tell me, old one," the ugly sound went out of the voice, "am I not right? Are we not very close to him?"

Hokom-ooene, the Blind Coyote, let his thin fingers run lightly over the rim of Wasiya's hoofprints. He rubbed and blew upon the delicate members that they might serve him yet more faithfully and felt, once more, the inch-deep impressions of the Sioux gelding's prints.

"*Hehe,* Axhonehe is right. Ota Kte was here."

"*Etoneeso?* How long ago?"

"A very short time. *Onehetto.* There were soldiers here, too. I smell the iron on their mules' feet. *Vehoemap,* the smell of white man's whiskey is here on the ground as well. *Hehe!*" the old man's cackle picked up interest. "Maybe they left it behind. Maybe I can find it. Let me smell around here—"

"How many soldiers?" The blunt question came from the silent giant, Etapeta.

"Three, no wait, four. Yes, four." His answer came from Yellow Buffalo. "One a big man like you, Etapeta. They've gone up this stream, one riding a horse. The

18

other three in the wagon. *Hee-ahh,* father?" the anxious query turned back to Blind Coyote. "Have you found that whiskey yet?"

Mad Wolf scowled, whirled his roan pinto hard around. "You go," he directed Yellow Buffalo. "Take Etapeta and the old man with you. Many thanks, father," he called to Blind Coyote, accompanying the acknowledgement with the quick touch of the fingers of the left hand to the brow, which was the Plains Indian's sign of highest respect. "*Zeo notaseas,* I go from this place now!"

It was Big Body's turn to scowl. "You are going after Ota Kte some more now? Without Etapeta?"

Big Body was as simple of mind as a child, though hardly as innocent. He was a chief by virtue of his one talent—splitting white skulls with his four-foot war club, a piece of bois d'arc thick as a man's wrist and crotching a six-pound Navajo silversmith's anvil in its forked end.

Mad Wolf turned on him. "I'm tired of telling you. *Naseintamo,* I'm sick of you. Now hear it once more—" He threw his pony into that of the hulking brave, his words grating like a Conestoga axle long without antelope tallow.

"You were with us when we caught that Osage of Yellow Hair's. You heard him talk. You heard him tell us Ota Kte was ordered once more to guide Yellow Hair against our people.

"Then you heard my vow. You were there at the Sun Dance, remember, Emptyhead? I pledged myself to kill Ota Kte before the new grass came. Before he could

19

again lead Yellow Hair into our camp. Well, that's where I'm going now, to kill him. *Ononistahe!*"

"Oh, Yes. Good, good!" Big Body was virtually slobbering through the loose-lipped disfiguration which passed for a smile in Dog Soldier circles. "I'll go along with you. I want to see you do it. I want to work on his head with this, after you've taken his hair."

With the words, the big brave whirled the misshapen war club in a giant swing which came perilously close to decapitating his enraged leader.

"*Nonotovetto!*" Mad Wolf rasped at Yellow Buffalo. "Get this idiot away from me. Take him and leave in a hurry!" The Dog Soldier chief raised his rifle. "*Onehetto!* Go at once or I'll kill him where he sits."

Yellow Buffalo knew the sound of his chief's voice in terminal earnest. He knew that when Mad Wolf's ordinary snarl dropped into that deep growl, the time for tarrying was long past.

"We go," he signaled, hurriedly. "How many braves do you want us to take?"

"Take a hundred. Beat the ponies with your gun butts. You can catch the soldiers easily."

Yellow Buffalo hesitated, looking skyward. As he did, the last quarter of the moon foundered in the engulfing tide of the thunderhead, and the first fat spatters of rain exploded in the dust of the trail.

"I don't know, Axhonehe. It is pretty black now. How will we follow them with any certainty if we beat the ponies and go fast?"

"Follow the little stream," growled Mad Wolf. "Like I'm going to follow the big one. A white man will always ride along water when he can. *Nataemhon,* good hunting, brother."

With an impatient gesture, Mad Wolf wheeled his roan and raced down the Arkansas. Behind him, the hammer of eight hundred unshod pony hoofs drummed the deepworn ruts of the Santa Fe Trail.

The sound died aborning in the sudden cannonading of the South Plains thunder. The moon was completely covered before the first volley of the thunder echoed away across the Arkansas.

Thirty seconds later, the rain was sheeting down in a driving blackness six shades deeper than the pit.

3. Lieutenant Colonel Custer

MAD WOLF'S TERSE prophecy to the contrary, there *were* white men who did not "always ride along the water when they could," and Joshua Kelso was one of them.

It took a man fifteen miles out of his way to cut inland from Big Coon Creek to ride the dry route down Onto Dodge. It was harder on a tired horse than the straightaway wet route along the river and tougher on a weary rider's saddle-aching seat.

But it sure saved wear and tear on a man's hair.

It was 5.00 A.M. when he topped out on the rearing bluffs which gave the first view of the Arkansas from the dry-route approach. The storm which had cut his tracks out from under Mad Wolf's Cheyenne trailers had grumbled on off toward the South Platte, leaving the prairie clean-washed and brilliant.

A mile south and east lay the straggling compound of

21

board-and-batten barracks, Sibley tents and sutler shacks that was Fort Dodge. Another mile south, the rising smokes of the daybreak coffee fires, ash-gray against the dirty mushroom cluster of Pittsburghs and Conestoga freighters, located the Santa Fe teamsters' wagoncamp which always marked the spot where the wet and dry routes of the Trail came together.

It struck him that the freighters' spread was nearly ten times the size it had been last year, in spite of the fact it was late fall and past the peak of commercial travel along the old South Road.

Well, a man could figure that quick enough. Nobody but a slickbrain idiot would be staying out on the plains now. There looked to be no less than five hundred people shantied-up down there below the fort and it didn't take a set of mountain eyes to see they were ninety per cent of them sod-hut farmer families driven onto the River by the Indian stir.

These things his slant gaze recorded in one compass-swinging glance. After that he let his eyes linger on a sight which always took a High Plainsman's heart no matter he'd seen it so many times before.

He nodded. The tension of his jaw muscles, tooth-set for the better part of the past week, eased.

If there was a God, and somehow a man didn't always feel for certain there was, this would be his country. Born to it, as he had been, he had still never been able to describe it until the past summer.

And even then it was a simple-souled Negro woman who gave him the proper words.

Custer had just come on from Fort Riley with his

omnipresent body servant, Eliza, an ageless colored woman who struck Kelso as being nearly as old as God and anyway half as smart. He and the little officer had taken the round-eyed woman to the bluffs atop which he now paused, and Custer had jokingly asked, "Well, Lize, what do you think of Kansas?" expecting her to protest the emptiness of the vast lands.

He smiled as the woman's answer nudged his memory.

"Well sah, General sah, when de Lawd made dis hyar world he found out dat he'd made one mistake. Dat was dat he hadn't made hisself no garden. So he jest went to work and made hisself a garden and I allow we just calls it Kansas!"

He shrugged off the brief picture and jammed his moccasined heels into Wasiya's ribs. The smile was gone, the alkali mask resettled in its place.

Three minutes later he was loping past an indignant brace of maingate sentries, advising them if they didn't like his precipitate entry they could take their troubles to Captain Custer—with Josh Kelso's compliments.

The gate detail was still untangling these instructions as he stepped off Wasiya and handed the sweat-stained hackamore rope to a third trooper inside the compound. The latter was the prompt recipient of some further sentiments along the same salty mountain line.

"Rustle up a groom for this hoss, soldier. And see you put him in a box by hisself. He'll kill another hoss quick as he'll look at him."

Turning to stride down the raw dirt street marked "Hq. Co. 7th Cav.," he flung a parting crumb of advice to the mouthhanging recruit. "And see you don't crowd him none yourself, happen you enjoy army life in the Far West. He ain't famous for limitin' his hostilities to, hossflesh."

Custer's name caught his eye at the third quarters.. But it wasn't the name which held him, frowning thoughtfully. The last he'd seen of the "General" he'd been operating under his permanent rank of captain and having hell's own time holding on to that. Then word got into the mountains he'd been court-martialed and suspended from rank and command for one year. Some tomfool business about having left his command bad fed and busted up in Fort Wallace while he traipsed off to Fort Riley to catch up on his homelife with Mrs. Custer. And getting himself waylaid en route by old Satanta and a flock of his Kiowa badbloods and losing a sergeant and two men.

That had sounded like Custer, all right. But now, so did that neat new sign pegged up there alongside his office door. By damn, you had to hand it to the little rooster. Rank-broke from brevet major general to captain, two years ago. Then busted from captain to plumb nothing less than ten months gone. And now there it was, fresh as porchswing paint and twice as sassy.

"Lt. Col. G. A. Custer, Cmdg."

Josh turned into the little path, so precisely bordered with its whitewashed creek stones. It was perhaps thirty feet long, no more. But when a man's mind wants to, it can move a long ways in a short spell.

Especially backward.

As he walked, he was balancing his surprise at the General's five-grade promotion against the growing total of his own doubts.

Adding what he'd heard all summer about the South Plains tribes being out to what he'd seen of the big drift of warpaint hostiles he'd just ridden through, a man had to allow there must be close to seventy-five hundred warriors camped astride the Santa Fe Trail and daring the whole army to come along out of Fort Dodge and move them off of it.

Given that much of a fill-in, a man didn't need to be any redskin genius to reckon what was in store for him beyond that office door yonder. Not if he knew Custer the way Josh Kelso knew him.

For all the long-haired cavalryman had a War-Between-the-States reputation second only to Little Phil Sheridan's, a man who'd scouted for him had to admit that when it came to Indian-savvy the "Boy General", wouldn't have ranked a chevron higher than a two-stripe corporal. Naturally, you couldn't help liking the crazy-eyed little devil. He was a sure enough he-coon for all his buckskin fringes, cowboy gauntlets, red silk sashes and special-made big black hats.

But he-coon or no, to Josh's careful way of figuring such things Custer was always a sight too quick to set his dandy foot into the buffalo chips before looking to see if they were still fresh-wet.

The backsweep of his thoughts tightened his jaw, slowed his hand as it started toward the weathered door panels. A moment, only, the hand hesitated, then descended with plank-bouncing force.

"Come in, come in! That door will open quite readily, sir! You don't have to beat it through. It's equipped with excellent hinges."

Josh grinned. That was Custer for you. It made no never-mind to him *who* was knocking. It could be Private Jed Jones, General Sherman, Mad Wolf or God Almighty. The idea was, come in, state your business and don't slam the door on your way out. The "General" was a busy man. No matter that if he was as busy as usual it would be in scribbling one of those ten-page, two-a-day letters to his precious "Libby," or to old General Walter Scott Hancock, running on about how come he hadn't quite got around to shagging Black Kettle and Satanta and the whole Cheyenne and Kiowa Nations clean into the North Canadian.

He lifted the latch and stepped in.

Custer was at his desk writing furiously. He didn't bother to put a comma to the galloping scrawl, much less look up from, it. All the scout got was a head-jerked, "Be with you in a minute, Sergeant. As you were—"

He took the "sergeant's minute" to eye the Colonel's new quarters and found them a faithful tintype of the studied bareness of the ones he'd had as a Captain at Fort Riley.

The same tired pictures backed the big desk: his much worshiped wife as "Elizabeth Clift Bacon, age 14," prim and schoolmarm—pretty in a French lace kerchief and starched Pilgrim collar; "Brigadier General G. A. Custer, 1863," left hand jammed Napoleonwise into the double-buttoned dicky of his Union dress tunic; "Eliz-

26

abeth, Custer and Tom Custer (standing)," with the great man as a two-star major general and young Tom as a one-bar second lieutenant.

The same Spartan row of straightback chairs stood at attention along the wall siding the desk. On another wall were the familiar big-framed chromos of Sherman and Sheridan, the Boy General's patron saints in the War Department. And there on the floor was the same mangy white buffalo robe—the one Satanta, the White Bear of the Arkansas Kiowas, had given him as an eternal peace offering last summer—two weeks before ganging up with the Cheyenne Dog Soldiers to knock loose his boyish backside down on the Cimarron.

Coming to the General himself, a man couldn't see he'd changed much.

Maybe his hair was a mite longer and not so yellow. Maybe his forehead had gained another inch in pushing back the skirmish line of his scalp against his famous curls. Maybe, too, his jug-handle ears stuck out more than ever and his needle-long nose twisted itself more and more to the left. But his twitching, woman-small mouth still hid under a sunbleached droop of haystack mustache and the little ambush of beard on his chin still did its damndest to make him look like he wasn't weak-jawed as a pocket gopher. Top all that with the fact that his varmint-close eyes were as wild and coyote-looking as ever, and a man had a fair idea of the way the "Boy General" sat that present morning of November 13, 1868.

"Joshua, by Heaven!"

The expletive, strongest in a vocabulary religiously

disciplined to the proper desires of Mrs. Custer, broke with the quick, friendly flash of the widely spaced upper teeth which hallmarked the famed Custer grin. It came backed with a catlike step around the desk and the firm grip of his small hand.

"I hadn't an idea in the world you would make it before the fifteenth. But it's good you did, sir, it's good you did! Sit down, sit down. What on earth were you riding, Joshua, a Cheyenne relay?"

"Well uh, nope, General, same old hoss—"

He found himself floundering in the backwash of schoolboy awkwardness this man always set up in him. He stood there grinning and arching his back like a tabby-cat getting her tailroot tickled. Damn it all, anyway. A man could sit around all winter hating the little game-cock's innards and vowing he'd never cinch a saddle in his service again. Then the minute he grabbed your hand and broke out that peg-toothed grin, you were dead. You'd not only follow him to hell and back, but kiss his foot for the chance.

"Do you mean to say that same scabrous yellow monster?" Custer was galloping on. "That slab-sided, slat-ribbed Sioux Percheron? That spavined excuse for a misbegotten jackass with which you won every enlisted dollar in Kansas Territory last summer? What was it you called him? Blizzard Boy? Snow King?"

That was Custer for you again. Talking faster and fancier than a hardshell Baptist preacher unselling a flock of sodbusters on sin. Asking six questions a second, before a man could get a civil answer in sideways.

"Winter Giant," Josh managed. "*Wasiya,* in Sioux."

"Ah yes, that's the horse—Winter Giant. Well, no matter, Joshua. You've won your last wager with him in my command!"

The big scout smiled. He couldn't remember the General ever having called him Josh or Kelso. Always "Joshua."

"No sir, by Heaven," Custer thundered on. "Not another dollar for you and that Prairie Pegasus! I've just got an Arab racer from Sheridan. Most magnificent buffalo horse mortal man ever sat to. I'll match you either on a killing run or a marked mile. Yesterday, Major Coates and myself—you remember Coates, my assistant surgeon? Well, yesterday Coates and I ran twelve straight in the afternoon alone! All bulls, mind you. No cows or heifers. Ah, you'll see, Joshua, you'll see—"

"Beg pardon, General," he fumbled the interruption, "but I'm bound to report a mite of trouble downtrail before we get onto old times. You've got a sergeant and three men standin' hipdeep in Dog Soldiers down yonder to Fort Coon."

"What the devil, Joshua?" There was the second choice in the General's aseptic selection of strong language. "Why didn't you say so instead of standing there baiting me about buffalo horses?"

Josh cut the inner grin loose once more. Trust Custer. He didn't mean it to be that way but he could lie himself off any spot you could corner him on and swear over signature he'd trapped *you* there!

"What's the trouble down there? That was a wood detail, eh? Let's see—Fort Coon—ten men and a sergeant there—plus Henderson and my three—" He broke the thought abruptly. "What Indians, Joshua? How many? How long ago?"

Josh rattled it to him not forgetting a moccasin print of what had passed since he received Custer's message, his own mind as sharp for "red" soldier incident as was the officer's for white. He concluded his report with a jawthrust postscript for the Osage scout.

"That's about it, General, savin' for one thing. You better bury that infernal Osage of yours pretty deep in the woodpile. I mean the one you sent out to bring me in."

"How's that, Joshua? He found you, did he not?"

Custer's voice showed the nettle it always did when the question was called on him or any under his orders. The tall scout took the nettle in stride, not even wincing as he stepped on it.

"He did, and quick."

"Well, sir?"

"Well sir, he found Mad Wolf a shade quicker."

"What the devil do you mean, man?"

That "man" was another tip for you. The General was bridling for sure now. He had a temper shorter than a stepped-on polecat's patience and nobody had better reason to remember it than Josh Kelso. But for the moment his own store of restraint was tolerably short-stocked.

"Them damn Dog Soldiers got wind of me comin' back to work for you. That's how come Mad Wolf tooken hisself that lodge oath to put me under. You can bet I didn't tell them!"

Custer frowned, his keen mind prying at the full sense of the scout's words. "I see. You're saying that Short Bear did then? Is that it?"

"Whatever his name is, yeah."

Custer nodded, temper subsiding with the soft agreement. "Well, perhaps he did at that, Joshua. He isn't back yet."

Josh's eyes tightened. "Sometimes I talk too much," he grunted. "The poor devil. I allow I had him wrong." He paused, then added grimly. "Well, he talked anyhow. But likely he done it with his feet in a fire and his face in the flashpan of a pistol."

The officer's pale eyes flared. His tongue flicked the surface of his lower lip. "What's this 'flashpan of a pistol' business? Something new?"

"Not for Mad Wolf. He's got one of them old single-loadin' Henry Derringers, with a primin' pan big enough to drink coffee out'n. He piles her up with Du Pont and triggers her off in your ear. She spits flame enough to roast a rack of hump ribs and belches loud enough to jar a ten-pound rock off a shelf. Time he's cut loose with that dose enough times, a man would tell the devil where God lived."

Custer swung to the door, whipped it open, bellowed for the corporal of the guard. When the wide-eyed trooper had raced off down the company street with the orders for Fort Coon's relief, he turned on Josh, dismissing him as curtly as he had greeted him effusively.

"All right, Joshua, I'm glad you're here in time for the fun. You'll excuse me now. Check with Captain Benteen after you've cleaned up. He'll bring you up to

31

date. We've got a fine red fish due in Dodge tonight. You can watch me fry him!"

"What you aimin' to fry him in, General?"

The question, for all its apparent innocence, was not lost on Custer. His answer came with the obvious relish of high confidence.

"A kettle, sir! A splendid, big *Black Kettle!*"

Josh chucked his head, threw the little half salute he reserved for Custer. "All right, General. Any special chef's directions for me?"

"I told you, man. Check with Benteen. Check with Benteen—"

Custer was at his desk scribbling again, the pen scratching across the rough paper at a hell-for-leather clip that would have done full justice to a rush call for all the reserves west of the Big Muddy, his thoughts as far from Joshua Kelso and Mad Wolf's Dog Soldiers as the distance by express courier from Fort Dodge to Fort Riley—and Mrs. Custer.

Josh watched him a moment, then eased out the door to stand with his broad back to the closed panels. Shortly he shrugged, and moved quickly down the rock bordered path.

All right. If Custer wanted to have himself a Cheyenne fish fry, that was his business. But when it came to dropping a High Plains lunker the size of Black Kettle into the greasepot, a man better stand plenty far back from the fire.

He'd better, happen he didn't want to get splashed his sudden death of hot Indian fat.

32

4. Bad Medicine Night

CAPTAIN FREDERICK W. BENTEEN, Custer's executive and fifth in command, was a plain-faced, quiet man and as cautious and head-steady as his illustrious senior was rash and flighty. He received Josh, not as an old buffalo-hunting or horse-racing crony, but as an officer of the United States Army briefing a hired civilian professional.

"Come in, Kelso. Glad to see you. You've talked with Colonel Custer, I gather."

Josh took the proffered hand. "Thanks, Captain. Yeah, I seen him. Didn't learn nothin' though, savin' what a peecuttin' new buffalo hoss he's got. He don't change none."

"Unfortunately." The officer's agreement was meant just the way it sounded. "I suppose you've been sent to me for the bad news."

"Somewhat, I reckon. All I know is he called me in. I allow he wouldn't have, happen he just wanted to race buffalo hosses."

"You 'allow' right, Kelso. Here, sit down, man. Have a cigar. We might as well be comfortable."

"By damn, they're pure Habanas!" The scout removed the big Corona Corona from the cedar box with a reverence reserved to a breed brought up on Burley, buffalo chips and broomstraw. "Lookit the color of that baygold leaf!"

"The Colonel's compliments." The officer's smile broke a little wearily. "General Sherman keeps sending them to him though he knows as well as you and I that Custer never smoked in his life."

"Nor chawed, nor swore, nor guzzled," added the scout. "He's sure enough a rare-clean bird, ain't he, Captain?"

"Yes, Kelso, I really believe Colonel Custer is the most moral man I ever knew."

"Uh huh—" The fleeting sunbreak of the grin winked at the stolid cavalryman over the edge of the Habana's blue cloud. "Maybeso, Captain. All the same I'll wager Missus Custer's got her work cut out for her!"

"I beg your pardon, Kelso?"

Benteen wasn't sure whether an *entendre* had been doubled or not. Was taking no chance on the distaff side of the Seventh having been insulted.

"No offense, Captain. I was just thinkin' the General's got a bad eye for three things. Two of which is fancy hossflesh and flashy women. A man's got to do somethin' with his talents."

Benteen nodded, satisfied the honor of the Colonel's lady was secure.

"What's the third thing you say he's got a bad eye for, Kelso?"

"Walkin' into *wickmunkes,*" growled the big scout, the smile long gone from his dark eyes.

"That's an Indian word of some sort—"

"It is," said Josh. "It means 'traps.'"

"Indian traps, eh?" Benteen shook his head slowly. "I know what you mean, Kelso. My God, I know what you mean." The hopeless feeling of the gesture was compounded by the tension in the tired voice. "He'll get us all killed, one day."

"Not while I'm scoutin' for you, Captain."

The denial was flat and quick. It held no hint of boast or joke. It was just a proud, child-simple statement of professional fact.

"I appreciate that, Kelso. And I'll remember it." Benteen played the cards of his confidence face up, embarrassing the scout.

"Uh, sure, Captain. I know. Thanks. Uh, what's the details on this here thing?"

Benteen stubbed his cigar, leaned quickly forward, once more the impersonal executive officer.

"The situation here has altered rapidly since you left. This spring General Hancock was relieved and Sheridan succeeded him in command of the Department of the Missouri. That's us, Kelso."

The big scout cocked his head attentively, and Benteen continued.

"Last January, prior to his dismissal, Hancock negotiated a good treaty with the Indians at Medicine Lodge Creek, guaranteeing them, through the Indian Bureau, one million dollars for immediate relief as well as arms and ammunition for the spring buffalo hunt. It looked to most of us here as though the worst was over.

"However, the minute Sheridan took over he had the appropriation cut in half and its administration turned over to the War Department. In direct treaty violation, he withheld all arms and ammunition from the Indians and, since Hancock had burned their main camp and all their supplies the previous fall, they were soon desperate.

"At this juncture, Agents Wynkoop for the Cheyenne and Leavenworth for the Kiowa succeeded in forcing the Department to grant them discretion in issuing limited arms—"

The officer paused as Josh frowned and spat disgustedly. He relaxed and continued only when the scout's lancing spittle rang the bell of the office spittoon.

"On August first, Wynkoop made the first of his issue, not to his Cheyennes, but to Little Raven's Arapahos; a matter of one hundred Lancaster Rifles, two hundred pistols, fifteen kegs of powder and twenty thousand caps. Bear in mind now," Benteen pointed the emphasis with his frayed cigar, "that not one weapon was issued Black Kettle's Cheyenne, the principal belligerents, you will recall, of last summer."

"I never thought so," said Josh, levelly. "Black Kettle ain't a *bad* Injun, and never has been. Them buzzards give us all that hell last summer was old White Bear's Kiowa and Mad Wolf's Dog Soldiers. You boys ain't never learned to tell a regular Cheyenne from a Dog Soldier."

"We won't argue that point again, Kelso."

Benteen's too-quick reprimand deepened the scout's frown.

By God, they would never learn. Let a hundred hottail bucks hit the warpath and the army would jump the nearest meat camp full of friendly squaws. Let that damned White Bear or that hatchet-headed Axhonehe get out a few-score renegade Kiowa or three-feathered Dog Soldiers and go to killing settlers along some outprairie stream, and Custer would pile his cavalry into the closest big village of peace-treaty Indians, killing everything they caught in their sights, down to and including kids and camp dogs.

No man hated a bad Indian better than Josh Kelso. But every time you killed a good Indian you made ten bad ones. Nobody knew that better than Josh Kelso, either. But the damned army—

The angry scout's thoughts were checked by Benteen's continued briefing.

"Now, then. The night of August seventh, Black Kettle came into Fort Hays to protest his great friendship. I have here the transcript of that masterpiece if you'd care to see it."

Josh nodded and Benteen passed him the document. His wide lips moved haltingly as he deciphered the precise army penmanship:

A LETTER OF TRANSCRIPT, FROM MOXTAVETO, BLACK KETTLE, CHIEF OF THE SOUTHERN CHEYENNE, TO THE OFFICER COMMANDING:

> Fort Hays, Kans. Terr.,
> 9:00 P.M., Aug. 7, 1868

COPY TO:
A.A.G., F. B. Weir,
Fort Harker, Ind. Terr.,
Hq. Dept. of the Missouri,
P. H. Sheridan, Lt. Gen. Cmdg:

. . . Black Kettle loves his white soldier brothers and his heart feels glad when he meets them and shakes

*their hands in friendship. The white soldiers ought
to be glad all the time, because their ponies are so
strong and because they have so many guns and so
much to eat. All other Indians may take the war
trail but Black Kettle will forever keep friendship
with his white brother . . .*

M/SGT. J. EDWARDS,

CO. A,

SEVENTH CAV.

A. J. SMITH, COL. CMDG.

"Well? That sound like a bad Injun to you?" The big
scout returned the pathetic paper to Benteen's desk and
sat back to draw on his faltering cigar.

"Well!" echoed the officer sarcastically, "three days
later the Cheyenne began to kill on the Solomon. Fifteen settlers killed and five women carried off. There's
no question in our minds that it was Black Kettle, and
no question that he got the guns from Little Raven. *Sic
semper Moxtaveto!*"

It was clear from the little hand flourish with which
the officer signaled his conclusion that he was pleased
with his success at phrase-turning. Josh wasn't
impressed.

"What's that 'sick simper Black Kettle'?" he drawled.

"Latin for 'never trust a Cheyenne.'"

"My sentiments, precisely," grunted the lean-faced
scout. "Providin' you know what Cheyenne you're
talkin' about. What else you got?"

"That's about it. When Sheridan got the report on that raid, he moved his headquarters to the terminus of the Kansas Pacific at Fort Hays. He has been there since September building up his command and setting up a big field depot about one hundred miles south of here—place called Camp Supply."

Josh had never heard of the place, reckoned he never would again. That he would, indeed, hear of it again, and in fact live to wish he never had heard of it in any way, shape or form, was naturally beyond his knowledge of the moment.

"Looks like they mean to make an end of it once and for all. That it, Captain?"

"That's it. Custer's pushing Sheridan for immediate command, and of course he'll get it. I don't have to tell you where that leaves us."

"Nope. You follerin' him and me leadin' him," grimaced Kelso. "And seventy-five hundred hostile Injuns waitin' for him to waltz us into their blue-ribbon *wickmunke,* come spring and the new grass."

Benteen stood up, signaling the end of the interview. "Right, with one small exception."

Josh caught the inflection, returned the officer's steady gaze. "So? How's that?"

"You recall last year Custer pooh-poohed your warning not to try fighting a summer campaign?"

"Naturally. You can't catch an Injun, much less kill him, when his ponies is grass-sassy and his own belly and the whole damn prairie is full of fat cow."

"Naturally," Benteen echoed. "Well, three weeks ago I transmitted Custer's request to Sheridan for the winter

39

campaign you insisted on last year. Sheridan and Sherman have both approved it."

"Good, by damn!" His first reaction was genuine, his last, hard-grinned. "Of course the General gives me full credit for the idea?"

Benteen, never one to multiply a meaning, no matter how obvious, ignored the knowing grin. "I really don't know, Kelso. It wasn't in the transcript I prepared. Suppose you ask him?"

"Thanks, Captain." He slid his bone-weary buttocks off the split-oak seat of the office chair, headed for the door, then paused thoughtfully.

"Say, what's old Black Kettle comin' in again for? Make another peace spiel?"

"Undoubtedly."

"Hang it, what's the matter with the General that he would leave him do it? Can't he see he's never goin' to get anyplace talkin' to them one day and killin' their women the next? Is he plumb blind?"

"Just in *one* eye."

The officer's quiet emphasis caught and held his narrow stare. He let the little silence fatten ahead of his short challenge.

"Which eye, Captain?"

"One of your 'three bad ones,' I'm afraid."

"Such as?"

"There's a girl—"

"Not an Injun, for hell's sake?" The scout's question leapt with the quick denial of its own statement. "By God, I don't believe it. It ain't possible!"

"It is with this girl, Kelso."

40

The sober-faced officer paused, mustering his inadequate vocabulary reserves for the effort.

"Kelso, she is the most fantastically beautiful woman I have ever seen!"

The scout watched him, suspicious he was essaying a clumsy sally outside his accustomed fort of stodginess. He decided, short quick, that he wasn't.

"You been away from white women too long, Captain." The knowing headchuck put the smile to the words. "You know what they say when the squaws start lookin' good to you."

"I beg your pardon, Kelso!"

"Sorry, Captain." He respected this officer and knew the feeling was mutual. He intended it should stay that way. "You figure the General will actually give the old chief another chance to talk tonight?"

"In a manner of speaking, yes. You know how he loves to display that bright mind of his. He's been drooling over the prospect for the past week. He'll let the old man talk himself out, then he'll cut him to pieces, Custer-style."

"Maybe, maybe not," Josh shrugged. "Pretty hard to chop up a good Injun kettle when it's as old and smoke-black as Moxtaveto."

"We'll see. Leave the door open, Kelso."

"She's open. See you downtrail, Captain—"

With a nod, the scout was gone. His gaunt, high shoulders hunched nervously to the swift, loose swing of his narrow-hipped gait, leaving the officer to stare after him and wonder how a man could sound and talk so like a man—yet look and walk so like a wolf!

41

• • •

Josh finished his inspection of the quarters granted Wasiya in the officers' stableyard. Finding them superior to those furnished the men in the enlisted barracks, he promptly chose to sleep with his horse in preference to Custer's troopers—a not uncommon selection for his soldier-sensitive breed.

He slept like a six-foot sawlog, awakening eight hours later to the eye-squinting demand of the sun slanting over the sill of the boxstall door. After saddling Wasiya, he swung up and guided him across the parade yard toward the sutler's store, his refreshed mind once more taking up the backtrail to his present position.

He had come down to Dodge expecting a repeat of Custer's performance of last summer. After all, it was standard army procedure. There would be five winter months of rest at the respectable scout-pay rate of seventy-five dollars a month. Then a pleasant six months of Indian-chasing and buffalo-hunting across the friendly plains of the South Arkansas. A man would wind up with his hair a year longer and as safe as money in the Mastin Bank of Kansas City. He would, too, have had a government-guided tour of the best rangelands in the Indian Nation. And could have taken his own sweet time to pick out just the stretch of grass suited to his personal cow-purposes, protected all the way by six troops of prime grade U.S. Cavalry. Plenty of chance and to spare, any way you figured it, for a half-smart Texas boy to set himself up in the North Canadian cow business.

That was the picture that had popped into his head the

minute the General's Osage had found him over in the South Park country. But what Benteen had just slapped to him was a horse of a far-off color. The way the wind set now, a man would be damn lucky to collect three measly months' pay and save his cussed hair.

He turned Wasiya in at the hitching rack in front of Bob Wright's Store. Seeing the half-dozen horses standing, rein-looped at the sun-blistered hitching rail, he grunted his satisfaction. Good, by damn. Those were mountain horses, and they meant that inside there would be at least four or five sons who could give him more information in a minute than Custer and Benteen could in a month. He recognized Bill Wilson's broken-down bay, Jim Hickok's fancy black Morgan, Apache Bill's glass-eyed calico stud and that stringhalted crow-bait of California Joe's. Good again, by God. Boys like that could fill a man in quicker than a cat could wink.

So, all right. Maybe the situation wasn't as bad as it looked.

In the ensuing half-hour with his fellow professionals and in the clay jug of Taos Lightning always party to any such gathering of the curdled cream of the frontier, he found his hopes well justified. The situation *was not* as bad as it looked.

It was a hell of a lot worse.

The whole short-grass country from old Fort Harker to Fort Lyon at the mouth of the Picketwire where it emptied into the Arkansas had been a battleground all summer. The Kiowa, Comanche, Arapahoe, Cheyenne and Apache were out, and making like they aimed to stay out. Charlie Bent, the two-timing Cheyenne breed, was keying-up the whole mess by running guns and powder to Mad Wolf and the Dog Soldiers who, as Josh knew, were spearheading the rebellion.

The Barlow Sanderson Stage Line, running from Kansas City to Santa Fe, had abandoned its route in early May. Come late June, the Butterfield outfit had had to close out its Smokey Hill run and route its California traffic through southern Texas. All told, counting in close to two thousand northern Hankpapa Sioux and Wind River Arapahoe who had drifted down to help their southern brothers run the last of the "white buffalo killers" back to St. Louis, Apache Bill and the others figured there were some eight thousand hostile bucks swarming the plains south and west of Dodge.

Josh scowled bitterly at this estimate, backing as it did his own guess of seventy-five hundred, and countering Custer's confident claim that he had no more than twenty-five hundred of Satanta's Kiowas and Black Kettle's Cheyennes to put down.

He was still scowling when, an hour later, his head full of red figures and his belly full of raw white whiskey, he door-banged his way out of Wright's emporium to climb on Wasiya and head him for the council grounds, word having just come from Benteen that Colonel Custer requested the presence of his scout corps. The approaching Indian column had been sighted winding up the Arkansas.

It was 7.20 P.M., Friday, November 13—a wineglass-clear, dead-quiet fall evening. The yellow of the departed sun still eerily lamplit the floor of the broad valley. Long shadows backed the endless ranks of the ridges stretching south from the fort to the far horizon.

It was the kind of an evening a mountain man didn't like. Too quiet. Too clear. Too smoke-still. The pure hush of it put a man's nerves on edge. Kept his eyes working the prairie constantly, and his ears straining for the first sound that would read Indian trouble.

It was a Bad Medicine night, and Josh Kelso could smell it just as sure as he could the stink of a sick dog.

5. *Bright Hair*

BY THE TIME JOSH, with Apache Bill, California Joe and the rest of Custer's regular scouts, reached the main gate, the Colonel was already mounted up and sitting impatiently at the head of his reception committee.

Josh's disturbance increased the moment he saw the nature of that committee—Captain William Thompson's Troop of the Seventh, fully armed with booted Spencers and heavily belted with regular field issues of ammunition.

Damn the General anyway. The way Indians saw such things a man didn't come to a peace palaver with his weapons polished. Not if he was a white man and his heart was really big for peace. Of course it was only natural for an Indian to bring along *his* war tools, but that was another matter. An Indian lived by his gun and would no sooner appear in public without it than without his breechcloth.

Custer, however, gave no opportunity for debate, and waved Thompson the "forward ho!" when the scouts rode up.

Minutes later, the command was drawn up on the level plain midway between the fort and the river, awaiting Black Kettle's mission. The nature of that mission served only to deepen Josh's scowl. For a solid half-mile the far bank of the Arkansas was clouded with the rising dust of the Indian cavalcade.

Moxtaveto was coming in force.

As the white forces watched, and while the enemy caravan was yet a mile distant, a single horseman detached himself from its ranks and spurred his pony toward them.

He drew up before Custer with a flourish of South Plains horsemanship and a shower of Arkansas sod for the indignant Colonel that brought a hard grin flicking through Josh's scowl. The Cheyenne then barked out the stock Indian request; that the meeting take place *within* the fort.

Josh, as the sole member of the General's scout force who fully understood the complexities of the Cheyenne tongue, the most difficult of the Plains Indian languages, was waved forward by Custer. Translating the brave's demand, Josh's momentary uplift of feeling was brought hard down by the commanding officer's peremptory refusal.

"Tell the heathen rascal we'll do no such thing. Tell him we'll meet right here or not at all. If he comes in peace, that is one thing. But if there is the least demonstration advise him we are armed and ready."

The big scout nodded abruptly, turned to the waiting brave and shrugged apologetically. "Yellow Hair says he is sorry. He cannot see his brothers in the fort. He

46

says it is better right here where all may sit like men in the open and unafraid. *Nahoxtahan!* Tell that to Mox-taveto."

The Cheyenne warrior's face darkened. Josh listened intently to his angry objections, then repeated them to Custer. "This boy ain't happy, General. He says Black Kettle doesn't like to meet at night. It makes him suspicious. He says that always before they've met in the fort. He doesn't want to tell Black Kettle these things. Says better you should wait till morning and talk in the fort."

The scout paused, dropping his voice. "I reckon maybe he's right, General. You know what I've told you about these Plains redskins not liking to do business after sundown. The dark is bad medicine for a Cheyenne."

Custer's spaced-tooth grin momentarily straightened the droop of his mustache, then was gone.

"Never mind your cultural lectures on the mores and manias of the noble red man, Joshua. I'm quite as well acquainted with them as you are. Please repeat my conditions, sir."

"Beg pardon, General. You meanin' to say you're cornerin' them in the dark, a-purpose? Makin' them goosy, deliberate?"

This time the mustache didn't lift, but the voice did. "Oh, come now, Joshua. You're getting soft in your old age. Get on with it, man. Of course I've planned it this way!"

Josh knew that voice when it began to get high, and that wild light that began to get into those pale eyes when the General was strung-up. Benteen had been right. For some reason, Custer was mortal hot to talk to the Cheyenne. There was sure as hell something cooking in his tricky mind beyond just baiting old Black Kettle.

When he had given the Indian Custer's second refusal, the brave wheeled his pony without a word, and raced for his own lines now drawn up on the far side of the river.

Custer took advantage of the interval to rearrange Thompson's troopers.

"Column ho, by the flank, right! By the flank, left!"

The order, gauntlet-flung to Thompson, was passed on by that officer. The men reined their mounts smartly into a halfmoon line flanking Custer and his little knot of officers and scouts.

Josh caught the look Benteen shot him and scowled his wordless agreement.

Everything was right on schedule. The Boy General was getting high-mighty and huffy before one word had been said. The other officers, too, Major Joel Elliott, Custer's second-in-command, Captain Miles Keogh and young Lieutenant Tom Custer, looked to be as bit-champing and shoulder-chipped as the General.

"Carbines at the ready, Thompson." The terse order fell on the heels of the first. "I don't like the looks of that mob over there. I'll not be intimidated within sight of my own command post."

As the youthful captain repeated the order, and while the short Spencers were still being snaked from their saddle boots and cross-barred athwart the horses' withers, Josh was at Custer's side.

"Say, General, them naked guns ain't goin' to promote no spirit of sweetness and light, are they?"

"I trust not, Joshua." The peg-toothed grimace was more smirk than smile now. "That brash rascal is here to put on a show of force, precisely as I anticipated. He knows he can't talk real peace to me again. He's simply trying to bluff me into it this time. Can't you see that, sir?"

"Can't say as I can, General." The shrug was non-committal. "The boys at the store tell me they think the old buzzard really means to tame down happen you give him the chance. They figure he's got some kind of a deal to offer for ridin' Injun-herd on the real bad ones."

"Oh, nonsense, Joshua. Don't try to sell me those Dog Soldiers again. You and the rest of the scouts have got Mad Wolf on the brain. We know who's behind all this trouble and it's not Charlie Bent and the Dog Soldiers, by Heaven!"

"Listen, General," Josh's plea was dead straight, "give them a chance this time. They've got wind of all them troops Sheridan's gatherin' over to Fort Hays. They may be simple but they ain't stupid. I know them Cheyenne, General. I can smell a bad Injun far as the wind can carry his stink. I think this Black Kettle's all right."

"Yes, you've always thought so," the officer's voice was rising again, "but let me remind you, sir, that I *haven't!*"

"All the same, General," his voice dropped even

49

lower, "I've got a hunch this is your last shot. I reckon I'd give them their chance happen I was you."

"They've had their chance, by Heaven," snapped Custer, that bad, quick light Josh had learned to distrust lancing his pale eyes. "They'll not get another from me, nor from Sheridan."

"Why talk to them, then?"

Josh's cool question, though it trod the touchy borders of insubordination as easily as if he were querying a squad corporal about the way to the latrine, brought, surprisingly, nothing but a quick return of the wide-toothed grin.

"You'll see, Joshua, you'll see! Don't bother me now. And don't worry. I've got them this time and I don't mean to let them up!"

The tall scout frowned, not missing the peculiar excitement. He knew his man well enough to realize Custer was fairly bursting with some new yellow-hair brainstorm, and that further questioning was as out-of-order as a skunk at a school picnic. He had no time, in any event, to push the issue.

Across the river, the Cheyenne were on the move!

The savage caravan, snaking out of the desolate sandhills beyond the Arkansas and splashing on into the shallow stream to bear down on Custer's nervous huddle of troopers, was an awesome sight.

First rode one hundred garishly painted Dog Soldiers, the military tribal police of the broad-faced southern nomads and the roughest cut in the whole card pack of South Plains hostiles, including their blood cousins the Kiowa and Comanche.

50

Josh's first thought upon identifying the vanguard as a Dog Soldier unit was for Mad Wolf. But search as he might, nowhere could he single out the familiar axe-blade face of his self-appointed exterminator. Quite clearly and for reasons not calculated to quiet the white stomach, Axhonehe had chosen to absent himself from this tribal peace program.

Behind the leaderless Dog Soldiers rode the solidly packed, color-splashed mass of the regular Cheyenne warriors numbering, to Josh's rough count, no less than five hundred vermilion-smeared braves. To their rear straggled a mixed horde of travois and pack ponies bearing the motley complement of deadpan squaws, big-eyed children and yellow-toothed oldsters of Black Kettle's tribal village.

The minute he made out the squaws and pony-age youngsters, he kneed Wasiya to Custer's side.

"Better have them troopers boot them carbines, General. This ain't no war party. Last thing an Injun will do is bring his women and young ones on a paint spree."

Custer nodded but made no move to implement the suggestion. "You'll never learn, Joshua. There's no end to their trickery. You cannot trust an Indian, sir."

"I don't trust them, I *know* them."

The flat emphasis froze Custer's small mouth, brought the ever-ready temper breaking through its thin crust of control.

"Are you saying I don't, sir? Look at them come, man! Don't be a fool."

Josh, his eyes never off the approaching flower of the Cheyenne Nation, swallowed his answer and set his

51

long jaw. It had, indeed, become a moment to try the tension on the trap springs of any man's nerves.

As the Dog Soldiers splashed out of the Arkansas to come thundering down on the thin line of troops, the black-feathered pack of them howling fit to lift the neck hairs clean off a man's nape, Josh, as he so touchingly put it to Apache Bill, who had joined him at Custer's side, "didn't know whether to spit or holler uncle."

What made it so tough was that horseback Indians always came down on a camp that way whether they meant to be friendly or to cut your guts out, leaving it to you to decide if they aimed to kiss you or kill you. The big scout, flicking his glance down the line of troopers and seeing the tight-faced youngsters raise their Spencers to sweep the front of the advancing red wave, did his deciding hard and sharp. Having done so, he threw rank, face, form and military foofooraw squarely out the prairie window. He paid Custer the sole courtesy of holding his advice down so that the officer, alone, could hear it.

"By God, General, you tell them boys to boot them carbines. Them bucks ain't goin' to ride into us, but by damn happen one of your youngsters shakes off a shot, we're all of us deader than a bull-tromped wolf!"

Custer whirled on him, sunbleached mustache lifting to the angry mouth corners. Josh beat him to the outburst, buttering his suggestion with the little half-salute he saved for such occasions.

"Damn it, General, you do it now. I ain't never steered you wrong."

There were perhaps three people alive who could

buck George Custer and get away with it. The first two were Mrs. Custer and Phil Sheridan. Custer indicated the third with his angry order to young Thompson. "Boot your carbines, Captain. On the double now."

With the repeat of the order and its fumbling compliance by the apprehensive troopers, the hostile rush had closed to a short hundred yards, its crazy pace unabated.

It was now Josh's turn to put the cinch to his shrinking stomach.

With the yelling Dog Soldiers fifty yards out, he began to figure he'd missed his call, and tensed to swing his own Henry repeater onto the leading chief. At thirty yards he was no longer figuring, he was dead certain he'd missed. Then in the last second the ten years he'd spent fighting the full cousins of these people paid off.

Forty feet from the mount-rearing line of Thompson's Troop, thirty from Custer and himself, the careening charge came to a halt.

All human sound ceased. As Josh sat watching, he was conscious only of the snaffling and shifting of the Indian ponies and of the clinking of the arms and harness of their riders. Without awaiting Custer's direction, he raised both hands, palms out, toward the Indians. It was the universal, prairie handsign of peace. Behind it he sent his deep voice, rapidly intoning the heavy Cheyenne gutturals.

"*Vahe, nomoto, nomoto,* you are welcome among us." He slashed his right hand down and across his left forearm in the handsign taken from the Cheyenne custom of cutting off the left arm of their enemies.

"Yellow Hair says this to you. You are welcome in this camp. Our people are at peace with yours. *Heovemeaz,* Yellow Hair, has said it."

The Dog Soldiers made no sign they had heard the overture, but the bulk of the regular warriors had now come up to crowd the rear of their line and among them a ripple of friendly *"hau, hau's!"* was heard.

Josh waved gracefully, ignoring the Dog Soldiers to address his remarks to Black Kettle's followers. *"He-hau, he-hau,* who is chief among you? Which of you is Moxtaveto?"

The big scout had never seen the notorious hostile. Knew him only by reputation as the head chief of the Cheyenne village slaughtered in peaceful camp at Sand Creek four years earlier by the crackpot Colonel Chivington and his Colorado Militia. He knew, by this same token that here was one Indian who had every right on God's green prairie to despise the white brother.

He was, accordingly, scarcely prepared for the answer to his question.

A wrinkled chief clad in the simplest of white elk-skins and armed only with a three-foot ceremonial pipe, urged his potbellied mount forward.

"Hau, I am chief, here. I am Black Kettle."

The deep voice was soft as new snow, the placid face behind it calm as a mountain lake at sunset. Josh's upset was obvious.

"You are Moxtaveto, father?"

"Aye, and you, my son?"

"You know me, father—"

For the first time in his life, he felt ill at ease before

an Indian. The simple dignity of the old man was over-powering. It made a man feel all wrong inside and made him hate to put his name into the harsh Sioux words that were infamous among these people. He scowled, angrily fighting his weakness. Yet still he heard the halt in his voice.

"—I am Ota Kte."

He had known the old man knew him, just as the bulk of his dead-still followers must have known him. Nevertheless, he was jolted by the ugly murmur among the Dog Soldiers at the sound of his hated name.

"*Hau,* I know you, my son." The surface of the old man's face didn't alter a wrinkle. "Your heart is bad for my people."

"Only for those whose hearts are bad for my people. You know that, Moxtaveto."

"Your heart is bad. You have killed too many."

The white scout shrugged and turned to Custer as the latter, realizing the talk was running overlong, bluntly interrupted.

"Tell him the Dog Soldiers must return beyond the river. They have no business here and I shall not talk to him so long as they remain."

Josh repeated the order to Black Kettle and the old-chief at once issued the required command. With the Dog Soldiers jogging sullenly toward the Arkansas, Custer abruptly stated his second condition.

"Tell him to bring his subchiefs only. Have them come to the tent over there. All the others will remain where they are."

His peremptory gesture swung Josh's eyes toward the

fort. The scout was surprised to see the big Sibley which had been erected just beyond the stockade, and to note the rising glow of the fire being built before it.

Well, that was Custer. Not the bucko, the Boy General, to squat in the dark and wrangle with a batch of heathens. Hell no, not him. Bring the rascals in front of an issue tent. Throw a big fire on them. Rank the troopers up solid, all around. Set the stage, proper. Make the red sons know they were talking to the United States Army, Lieutenant Colonel George Armstrong Custer commanding!

Starting to give the order to the waiting Cheyenne, he found Custer suddenly at his side, voice held down to play under the ear range of Major Elliott, Benteen and the others.

"And, Joshua. Tell him he must bring Monaseetah. Do you hear, sir?"

"I got you, General."

His next query, offhand idle, produced an odd vehemence in Custer.

"Who's Monaseetah? He's a new one on me."

"Black Kettle's interpreter. Just do as I say, Joshua. I've had enough of your infernal questions, man. Jump to it now!" Impatiently, he wheeled his horse, shouted to Thompson, and with Benteen and his staff galloped off through the growing darkness.

Black Kettle understood considerable English. Having easily followed the first part of the conversation, he had turned away to assemble his subchiefs. The remaining Cheyennes were beginning to dismount and set up camp as Josh came up to him with the remainder of the order.

"All right, father, let's go. Yellow Hair wants you to bring your interpreter, too."

"How is that, my son?" The puzzlement in the old chief's voice was genuine, causing the scout's eyes to narrow quickly.

"Monaseetah was the name he gave me—"

The dusk was deep now, but a man couldn't miss the dark flash which for the first time broke the wrinkles of the Indian leader's face. *"Havsevestoz, nivehohavo—"*

The Cheyenne phrase narrowed the scout's gaze yet further.

"Why do you say that, father? Why do you say it's a bad thing and you don't like it?"

In answer Black Kettle called into the darkness. "Emoonesta, come to my side!"

Josh translated the name as he watched one of the Cheyenne swing aboard a small paint mare and move away from the main camp. *Emoonesta,* Bright Hair. That was a pretty tame name for a Cheyenne Cut-Arm. A man couldn't see much to that, save how the General had messed it up. As a matter of fact, a man couldn't see much to the whole business. Couldn't see what the tarnal sin was needed with another inter-preter with him, Josh Kelso, fronting the council fire. Couldn't see—

His difficulty in "seeing" vanished almost before he got well started grumbling about it. His lean jaw sud-denly slacked open and his eyes widened.

The settling dark opened to admit the approach of the paint pony and its slender rider. The hush of the

Arkansas evening fell apart to the powdery caress of a low voice.

"I am here, father. Let us go."

Josh didn't hear the old chief's answer, nor his invitation to him to join them in riding to Yellow Hair's fire. He just sat and watched them pass in the purple dusk, his whole body, from elkhide footskins to shoulder-long hair, tight-strung as a war bow with the spine-jarring evidence of his startled eyes.

And when the prairie blackness had closed behind them and his unbelieving mind had fought itself to a standstill for a thought or a single iota of an idea on how to say it, there was still no way to beat Benteen's straight-out, eye-wide honesty.

That girl *was* the most *fantastically beautiful* woman that ever drove a mortal man's heart square through the roof of his dumb-open mouth!

6. The Sacred Pipe

THE COUNCIL GOT under way at 8.00 P.M. The full shade of the prairie night had drawn itself across the western horizon and outlined the leaping flare of Custer's bonfire and the close-packed half circle of savage red figures seated crosslegged before it.

Custer himself, with Josh and Benteen, was seated in the opening of the Sibley, Custer and Benteen in campchairs, Josh squatting on the ground to the latter's left. In the tent, three staff noncoms sat by the light of a hurricane lantern, rough paper and turkey quills in hand, waiting to transcribe for a hero-worshiping posterity the pathetic minutes of the last formal peace talk of a great Indian Nation. What they would write would be the literal wording of a palpably honorable hearing. What they would sign would be the dishonorable death warrant of a proud and ancient people.

At the moment, however, none of its principals, save perhaps Benteen with his painful knowledge of his superior's true character and his full access to the latter's prior exchange of plans with Sheridan and Sherman, had the least suspicion of Custer's motives in accepting the final meeting with Black Kettle's Southern Cheyenne!

Least aware of all of the possible presence of War Department intrigue and overly ambitious field-commander infamy was Joshua Kelso, Custer's Indian-hunting, court-favorite scout. Indeed, infamy, intrigue and overweening ambition were the furthest subjects from his mind.

For after ten years of safely dodging every lethal shaft winged his way by a succession of slant-eyed red women, Josh had been shot, dead center, by a pagan Cheyenne Cupid.

He was not only arrow-struck through the middle of his heart, but the shaft had wedged its barbs so solidly in his broad back it would quite likely kill him to cut it out.

Fortunately, or unfortunately, he was as unaware of this disaster as he was of the one about to be fashioned over Custer's council fire. For the moment, he only knew that his stomach was wrapped around an eight-pound rock, that his back and belly muscles were so tight he could scarcely breathe, and that his heart pounded like he was backpacking a bull elk, broadside, up the front of Pikes Peak.

He shifted uncomfortably, gulped in another mouthful of Arkansas night air, scowled at Custer and Benteen. Hang it all, why couldn't they get on with it? Custer just sat there grinning and folding his arms like a heathen Chinee, trying to force the Cheyenne to lose face by making the first talk.

And why couldn't he, Josh, learn not to mix civilized sowbelly and trade whiskey after living all winter on fresh cow and mountain water? His belly felt like it was full of placer gravel. By Cripes, a mountain son had ought to know better than to—

Yeah, that was right; he *had* ought to know better. To know better than to sit there horsing himself. Than to sit there breathing deep and holding his belly and blaming Custer or Benteen or Bob Wright's bad-fried fatback.

Where the hell was that God-beautiful Indian girl!

He'd seen her start for the tent. He hadn't been more than a hundred yards behind her and old Black Kettle on the way over and yet he hadn't seen simple sign of her since riding in to side Custer and Benteen by the fire.

God Amighty, but she was a looker. She had to be, to put rocks in the belly of a son who hadn't exactly set any records for backing away from free and fancy females. By God, she must be out there, somewheres. The infernal fire carried out about two or three rows of bucks, then a man couldn't see anything but prairie dark and—

His irate inner wanderings were cut off. Black Kettle

arose, stepped slowly forward, a smoldering ceremonial pipe cradled in his arms. The Fort Dodge Council was in session.

The white scout watched, fascinated. He had sat to more than a few informal, horseback palavers between the Indians and the Army. But this was his first full-dress meeting. It presented a disturbing picture, which burned itself deep into his mind and created the first foothold for a thought which had been working at him ever since meeting the Cheyenne patriarch earlier in the evening. What were his *real* feelings toward these strange red nomads? Were they warmer than he believed? Did he rightly know *what* they were?

He shook off the shadow of the thought. He shed it with an angry start like a man would shuck a blanket that he'd pulled up in the dark and found crawling with gray-back lice. His jaw was in its old set as he waited for Black Kettle to conclude the pipe ceremonial.

The compelling figure of the aged Cheyenne held his audience in silence. He stood for perhaps ten seconds, the copper parchment of his face upturned to the stillness of the Arkansas stars. Then he drew upon his pipe, blowing the smoke first east, then west, north and south, intoning between puffs the sacred peace prayer of the Cheyenne Nation. After that, he stepped forward quickly, placed the pipe on the ground between himself and Custer, and squatted crosslegged to face the army commander.

As the full light of the fire fell on the pipe, Josh's eyes widened. His words, sidemouthed to Benteen, were tense.

"The pipe! That's *the* pipe, Captain. Their Holy Medicine Pipe!"

Black Kettle now began to toll off the sonorous periods of his last plea for peace along the Arkansas, but Benteen, sensing the excitement in the scout's whisper, asked sharply:

"What do you mean, Kelso?"

"When he came into Fort Hays to talk peace this summer, did he use that pipe?"

"I don't think so. Why?"

"By God, Captain, when they trot out *that* pipe, they ain't horsin'."

Benteen did not follow his excitement and let him know it with the quickness of his response..

"*That* pipe, *this* pipe, what's the difference? They always lie."

Josh's eyes caught the officer's. His voice was short and bitter with worn-thin patience.

"Not over that pipe they don't, mister! It's their sacred medicine. Each Nation's got one; Sioux, Arapaho, Cheyenne, all of them. *Captain, that old man means to make peace this time!*"

"Better tell the Colonel." Benteen was at last disturbed by the scout's intensity. "I don't believe he's noticed it."

"Hoss feathers. He knows that pipe. He had his hands on it at Medicine Lodge Creek. By damn, Captain, I don't cotton to the smell of all this!"

His complaint was cut short by Custer's sudden gesture, summoning him to his side. Pointing to Black Kettle, the General demanded: "Where's the girl,

Joshua? Plague it, man, I told you to have him bring her!"

"I told him, General."

"Well, tell him again, right now, sir!"

Josh shrugged. Turning to Black Kettle, he gave the order. The old chief nodded to one of his braves, who departed into the darkness to return shortly with the girl. As she moved into the fire's full light and took her place at Black Kettle's side, Josh's eagerness for his second sight of her was brought up sharply by his simultaneous marking of Custer's obvious agitation.

The General was leaning forward tensely in his chair. His slender hands clutched the oak arms. His pale eyes, diamond-bright, followed the girl like a man bewitched. Noting the fact, the big scout scowled darkly.

With the scowl, however, he noted a second fact and took what small comfort he could from it. The little officer wasn't alone in his spellbound regard of the Indian girl. Every eye in Thompson's troop and in his own staff glittered just as hard and bright as the General's.

And not without cause. A man had to admit that, jealous or not.

Monaseetah was as slight and slender as a willow wand and she moved with the grace of a mountain reed in a spring breeze. She was clad in the single-piece doe-skin camp dress of the unmarried Cheyenne woman, her small knees, curving calves and slim ankles, as well as her rounded arms and hollowed shoulders, copper-naked in the shifting firelight. A man would just have time to get that body-glance of her, before his eyes fixed on her face and nothing else.

Unlike most Cheyenne women, her face was oval and delicate. It was as perfect and unreal as an Egyptian temple carving. Her cheekbones were high and slanting; her eyes narrow, oblique and fire-black; her nose, straight-bridged and short. Her mouth was square and full, and the underlip pouted in a moist, curving way that made a man want to smash it and get his teeth into it and grind the warm life out of it.

Josh was fighting for his breath when Black Kettle resumed his peace talk, breaking the spell the girl had put upon him and the officer corps of Custer's Seventh, and returning the council to order. With the old chief's remarks concluded, he waited for the girl to come forward with her translation.

To his surprise, Custer broke his stare from Monaseetah and snapped at him. "Well, what are you waiting for, sir? What did he say? Same old drivel?"

Josh eyed him, for the first time wondering what kind of an interpreter the girl was. He shrugged finally, putting the thought of the girl aside. After all, damn it, she was only an Indian!

Curtly, he repeated the sense of Black Kettle's statement.

"He says this time there's got to be peace. He's seen the soldiers at Fort Hayes. The Agents have told him why they're there. He says there must be no winter war. I allow he means it, General. That's the Big Pipe he's put on the ground. You know what that means."

"I know what it's supposed to mean. Is that all he said?"

"That's all. General, I think he means it this time. I allow you'd—"

"Thank you, sir. I'll do the thinking. Tell him exactly what I say, Joshua, and see that you don't change any of it."

The scout listened to the instructions, then turned to Black Kettle.

"Father, I believe you. I see The Pipe. I know it is holy. But Yellow Hair will not see it. He says he won't look at it any more. He says you are guilty. That you did those killings on the Saline River. And those on the Solomon."

"That's not a true thing, Ota Kte. You know who did those killings. You know who does all the killings. Tell him who it is."

Josh nodded solemnly. "I have told him, father. Many times. He will not believe it. He thinks you use the Dog Soldiers to excuse your own young men. He won't listen any more. He says the Agents have told him your Indians did it. Wynkoop says Satanta did it. Leavenworth says Black Kettle did it. I'm sorry, father."

Custer, drumming the arms of his campchair, interrupted demandingly. "What's he saying, Joshua? Come along, man, we haven't all night here."

"He says he didn't have nothin' to do with them Saline and Solomon killin's. Says the Dog Soldiers done it."

"Nonsense, sir! Tell him I'm tired of that lie. Tell him—"

"Beg pardon, General," the words stated the apology but the dark eyes denied it, "but I reckon it ain't no lie.

What killin's the Dog Soldiers don't do, you can lay to Satanta's Kiowas. Black Kettle's a pretty good Injun, as Injuns go. I allow Mad Wolf's your boy, all right."

"Tell him," reiterated Custer, bluntly ignoring the scout's suggestion and rising dramatically to boom out the offer in his best Surrender-at-Appomattox style, "that I assert, and all candid persons familiar with the subject will sustain the assertion, that of all classes of our population the Army entertains the greatest dread of an Indian war and is willing to make the greatest sacrifices to avoid it."

The big scout frowned, his mind twisting to the task of cramming the highflown peace-feeler into simple Cheyenne, his heart glad, all the same, that Custer was accepting the old chief's proposal.

Right now, with the old man bidding and the Boy General buying, he could see his cow ranch in the Nation floating off down the North Canadian. Somehow he didn't give a damn, was actually relieved and maybe even a little tickled about it. He showed it, too, with the little grin he gave Black Kettle.

"Father, uncover your ears. I have a good thing to tell you. Yellow Hair says you lie about the Dog Soldiers, and he doesn't want to hear that lie again. But he wants peace, father. He says the white soldiers want to avoid war with the red brother. He says he is ready to do anything to bring peace along the Arkansas. It is up to you."

Black Kettle slowly raised the fingertips of his left hand to his forehead, sweeping them in turn toward Custer. "Tell Yellow Hair that Black Kettle hears his words and his heart is full. Tell him my people go home now. Tell him there will be peace and that we are going home."

The Cheyenne leader paused, nodded thoughtfully to Kelso. "I do not understand you, Ota Kte. You kill my people, yet I heard you speak to Yellow Hair and I heard him reply to you. Your heart was better than his."

Josh felt the strange thrill of the words but his eyes and thoughts were no longer on the problems of Black Kettle or any part of the Cheyenne Nation save that slender portion thereof so maddeningly wrapped in clinging doeskins. The girl, in turn, was all slant, black eyes for him. As their eyes met, her full lips curved into a haunting trace of a smile.

"I don't understand myself, father. Not any more—" The delayed words went to Black Kettle but the dark eyes remained with the Indian girl until the old chief broke the spell by moving forward to retrieve the pipe.

Replacing the sacred relic carefully in its foxskin cover, Black Kettle turned to apprise his subchiefs of the mission's success.

"Yellow Hair says the soldiers want peace too. There will be no war this winter. And no more war after that. The Pipe is blessed. We can go now."

The subchiefs were already swinging aboard their ponies when Custer strode forward.

"Hold on, hold on! Tell him to wait a minute, Joshua.

Josh was a little slow in complying with the directive and Custer, noting the cause of the delay, barked angrily. "By Heaven, sir, mind your business! I'm not paying you to ogle Indian wenches. I don't countenance that in this command and you know it. Do you understand, sir?"

Josh, too far down the travois-track of infatuation to feel the lash of lesser emotions, grinned. "Yes sir, what'll you have, General?"

Still irritated, Custer rapped it to him.

"I want to know where these Indians are going to winter. Ask them where their camp will be. *Exactly.* Do you hear? I want to know the river and the specific part of it they'll be on. Carefully now, you understand? I don't want to alarm them."

The big scout's grin faded. The General appeared a shade too heated up. A sight too tensed for a man that just wanted to know were his red friends were going to spend their Christmas holidays. But then, hell. Likely, it wasn't the General that was too heated up. Likely it was him. What with the glare of the fire and those long, smoky looks the girl was giving him—

He put the thought aside, turned again to Black Kettle.

"Yellow Hair wants to know where his brothers will camp. Where they will be when the snow comes. So that he may know they are well and safe."

"On the Ouachita," replied the old Cheyenne unhesitatingly. "South a short day's pony ride from the first fork. It will not be hard to find. That's the first fork of the Canadian now, Ota Kte. The one the soldiers call the Wolf. In the Antelope Hills down there."

Josh touched his left fingertips to his forehead. "Yellow Hair thanks his brother. *Nataemhon,* good hunting father."

"Nataemhon," grunted Black Kettle and swung up on his pony to join Monaseetah, mounted and waiting. "Ride in peace, Ota Kte. We will meet again."

"Aye, father, we will. And you, girl," the tall scout's eyes abandoned Black Kettle, sought out Monaseetah, "*we* will meet again!"

"*He-hau, veho-hetan!* Yes, white man," the girl's words, softer than the smile behind them, carried clearly through the darkness, "we *will* meet again. *I swear it—*"

Before he could answer, the prairie blackness closed behind the departing Cheyenne. He was still staring after them when Benteen touched his elbow.

"Colonel Custer wants to know where that camp will be. What did the old devil say?"

He noticed that the commander was busy in the tent, sheafing through the staff noncoms' transcriptions, his quill scratching furiously as he added the high color of the Custer touch to the official recordings. "On the Washita," he grunted to Benteen. "Fifty miles south of Wolf Creek. The Antelope Hills country."

"Well, that ought to be close enough even for Custer. The poor devils!"

The way he said it stepped squarely on the bait-pan of Josh's still-puzzled mind. The jaws of his lingering doubt sprang ringing about. He twisted around, his Sioux-dark scowl hard as the core of a rifle barrel.

"How was that, Captain Benteen?"

"Just like I said," he let his lips shrink, the taste of the words too bitter even for a Regular Army mouth, " 'the poor devils.' The Seventh is moving out in forty-eight

69

hours—for Camp Supply."

"Camp Supply?" rasped Josh.

"Indian Territory," echoed Benteen acidly.

"And from Camp Supply?" he continued hard-eyed.

"To the Washita, 'fifty miles south of Wolf Creek. The Antelope Hills country.'"

There was no mistaking the deliberate mimicry of his own translation of Black Kettle's freely given directions. No misreading the naked disgust of the irony. Nor the brutal reason therefor.

Custer had set a white *wichmunke* for Moxtaveto, the Black Kettle of the Southern Cheyennes.

And the child-simple old warrior had walked straight into it.

7. *The Devil's Brand*

WITHIN MINUTES after the Cheyenne rode away from the council fire, Custer struck his tent and pulled out. In the flicker of the dying coals the two scouts smoked and talked quietly.

"Ten gets you twenty, Josh," nodded Apache Bill, "that this here palaver never gets writ into the Official Records."

"How so, Bill? Them sergeants was scribbling hard enough."

"Makes no difference. If I've sat to one with the General, I've sat to a dozen talks like this here one tonight. None of them got writ into the records that I know of. Sheridan will get a letter and maybeso Sherman. That'll be as far as she goes."[1]

70

"Could be, savin' for one to Mrs. Custer too. She'll get a ten-pager out'n this, you can lay."

"Yep, I allow. It beats all how crazy he is about that woman. I never seen a married man so constant. Reckon a man has to give him that much anyhow."

The remark led squarely into the worried hand Josh had been attempting to reshuffle in his mind for the past hour. "Bill," he drawled, trying his best to make it sound careless, "how *about* the General and this here Injun gal?"

"Oh, I dunno." The other scout made it careless without trying. "Course he did have her right along with him in the field this summer. Near onto six weeks, as I recollect. But he got shut of her in one hell of a tall hurry, you can bet!"

"How so?"

"Heard Mrs. Custer was comin' on from the east. Mister, you never seen a son shuck a squaw so sudden in your life."

"You sayin' he was squawin' with her?" The labored carelessness was long gone. "By damn, I don't believe it. Not of the General, I don't."

"I ain't askin' you to." The older man made cautious note of his young comrade's jawthrust. "And I ain't sayin' he was, neither. Hell, boy, nobody that really knowed him would. But, plague it, Josh, you know them senior officers. They're worse than a bunch of biddy hens catchin' their cockbird courtin' a duck. I reckon that outside of Captain Benteen and his own brother, young Tom, there ain't a commission in his command that wouldn't kick dirt on him happen they

71

wasn't scared to death he'd catch them scratchin' it up. Course you can't entirely blame them."

"What do you mean?"

"This here tomfool 'interpreter' business."

"I'm waitin'."

"You needn't be. That gal don't neither speak nor understand a cussed word of English."

Josh drew three times on his pipe and let the smoke come slowly through his teeth.

"You still think there's nothin' to it, Bill? No matter he had her with him so long last summer?"

"I said so. I reckon I ought to know, too, happen anybody does. I was with him and her twenty-four hours a day—and forty-eight on Sundays."

"But—"

"But, hell, Josh! Lookit the gal, that's all! Wouldn't you like to have her around? Just to look at? *Wouldn't* you? By God, wouldn't I? Wouldn't any man that was a man? Hell, you seen them officers givin' her the hard eye just now. Why, she rightly pulls the breath square out'n you. I can't help that she does, you can't help that she does. And sure as hell, Custer can't help it no more than you and me can. Why, boy, she can't even help it herself. She's just that kind of a woman, Josh!"

"Yeah, I reckon—" The agreement was unwilling and still a little uncertain.

There was no answering uncertainty in Apache Bill's heated ultimatum.

"You reckon right. Damn it all, boy, you know how he is about Mrs. Custer! A man couldn't love a woman no more than the General does her. He'd likely die

72

sooner than he'd do her any dirt. He can't help seein'
what's in that Injun gal no more than the rest of us. And
he'd want to see all of it he could, too, same as us. But
comes to touchin' any of it, I say he ain't! I don't want
to talk no more about it, you hear me, boy?"

"I hear you, old hoss," the young scout's relief was as
evident as the grin which came with it, "and I'll
remember it."

"See you do," grunted Bill. "You told me yourself
that he's got a hard eye for a proud hoss or a prime
woman. In this case I reckon he don't see no more in
the one than he would in the other. You can remember
that, too, when the time comes."

"I will," nodded Josh soberly. He stared into the fire
a moment longer, before continuing thoughtfully.

"Bill, you was sayin' that the General's boys are just
as set again him as they was last summer. I thought he'd
cleaned all that up when he got his commission back."

"Hoss feathers," grumped the older scout. "That's
nothin' but Custer-talk. There ain't a more unpopular
field officer in the whole lousy army, and he knows it.
Happen he didn't have Sherman and Sheridan frontin'
for him, he couldn't get the command of a latrine detail,
let alone a big outfit like the Seventh. Hell, they over-
slaughed five officers on his own staff to put him on top
this here dungheap at Dodge."

"Yeah, I know. How in tarnation does he do it, Bill?"

The grizzled scout shrugged. "Only him and God
knows, Josh, and neither of them's tellin'. He's already
been through a court-martial and two General Reports
that would have busted a four-star general to a buck

private. You recollect the ones I mean. Them two affairs down in Texas where they called him up for rough-handlin' his men and abusin' his command?"

"Yeah, I believe I heard. Seems like he can lead a sanitary detail through a ten-foot trench of bull chips and come out smellin' like a rambler rose."

"He can. I allow he's the luckiest one army buzzard that ever broke a good officer for cussin' on Sunday, or ordered a batch of homesick recruits shot as deserters for runnin' away from dog-rotten food and billets a sick rat couldn't sleep proper in."

Josh nodded thoughtfully. "Maybe you're right, Bill. I reckon he ain't got a real friend in the world that ranks less than a general officer."

"Savin' yourself, he ain't." Apache Bill's headchuck was half agreement, half challenge. Josh picked up both the look and the averment and handed them back abruptly.

"How about you, Bill? And California? And the others?"

The older scout shook his head. His answer was as genuinely puzzled as the frown which went with it.

"By God, I dunno, Josh. Somehow, a man will leave fat cow and prime fixin's to foller him on moldy biscuit and blowflied fatback. I done it, you done it, we all done it. But how come the tarnal hell we done it? That's what's got me chasin' my tail. By Cripes, I jest can't figger it, Josh."

Josh took his time, his answer coming in that low, slow way a western man will take when all the bluffs are in and the last raise called.

"I allow I *can,* Bill. Custer ain't like other men. He ain't the same breed. He don't think he is, and he ain't. There's men that allows no man's as bright as them. It ain't that it's so, mind you, but just that they *think* it is. And for them, that makes it so.

"They can answer any question. They can tot up any sum. They can rassle any bear and pin any bull. There ain't nothin' can beat them and no way they can lose. Not in their own minds, there ain't.

"Custer's that way, Bill. It ain't bred in a man, neither. Take his brother, Tom. Tom is out'n the same mother and he's by the same daddy, but he ain't the same man. He ain't no more like the General than you nor me. Tom's human and you and me are human.

"The General ain't, Bill.

"I allow it's some kind of almighty lightning strikes a man to make him like Custer. It don't strike often and it don't never strike in the same place twice. When it strikes a man it sets up a fire in him that'll burn him plumb to death before he's done. And it'll burn plenty of them that's standin' too close to him too. But all the same, when the Big Dark comes and such as you and me ain't no more than them dead coals there, the General will still be burnin' bright enough to see from here to Kingdom Come."

The young scout paused, seeking words.

"He's got the devil's brand on him, Bill, and you and me and all the others of us that's wild inside will foller him till hell freezes over!"

Bill, his simple mind stumbling along in bewilderment behind this outpouring from a man he'd never before heard string more than twenty words together, was still several strides off the pace when Josh, a little embarrassed, knocked out his pipe and rose with awkward haste to stride away into the cover of the prairie night.

It was a little after 9.00 P.M. when Captain Frederick Benteen looked up from his desk and cursed irritably.

"Damn it all, Kelso, I do wish you'd learn to knock!"

"Sorry, Captain. A man gets out of the habit in the mountains. There ain't no doors in a cowskin tent."

"Well, all right man, what's on your mind? As if I couldn't see it as clearly as you're standing there. Custer and those double-cross orders, eh?"

Taking his cue from the officer's brevity, he made it short. "Captain, I want to see them orders. I know it ain't regulation but you and me are more or less in the same mudhole. Leastways we are happen them orders is writ the way you said."

"They are, Kelso. What's the matter with my word for it?"

"It ain't your word, Captain Benteen." It was perhaps the third time the officer had heard him use the full address. He knew at once that the scout was deadly serious. "It's just that I can't believe the General would hoodwink them poor devils that way."

The officer looked at him. When his answer came, his voice was harried and nerve-thin.

"Now listen, Kelso, I can't do any more for you in this matter. I've already told you enough to get myself broken. Perhaps as you say we're in this thing together,

76

but the thing you have to remember is that first, last and always I'm Colonel Custer's executive. As such, there are limits to any association you and I may have, and this is one of them. If you want to see those orders, you'll have to get them from Custer. I'm sorry. And for God's sake man, don't mention me in connection with them!"

Benteen was on his feet, the brief interview clearly at an end. "I'll give you some advice, however. I wouldn't bother him now if I were you. He was in here not twenty minutes ago filing his reports on tonight's affair. He mentioned you. Something about did I think, or had I noticed, you going soft on the Indians all of a sudden."

"The gal, eh?"

"Possibly. As a matter of fact, probably. In any event I wouldn't push him on those orders. Not tonight, you understand?"

Josh stepped back, eyeing him steadily.

"I aim to see them orders, one way or another," was all he said before turning away.

8. Sheridan's Orders

MOVING UP THE PATH to Custer's quarters for the second time that day, Josh's mind was in more of a tangle than ever. Damn it all. It was one thing to take a free shot at a running buck. But to put out a bait-set for him and then drill him when he came up to sniff at it was something else again. Something a mountain hunter's belly didn't sit well to. Not, anyway, as long as there was the chance of a doe coming along to that bait-set with the buck, and not if that doe was a black-eyed Cheyenne beauty named Bright Hair!

The thought of the girl and of the stab of her sudden, sweet smile brought him to a stop. A man needn't have watched the Army fight Indians as long as he had, to know the way they went about it. And to know that when the Seventh's band started blowing "Garry Owen," the General's own regimental song, and the first companies set their horses bombarding down the village streets it was every Indian for himself and the Spencer carbines take the hindmost—which in nine cases out of ten were the squaws and toddle-age kids.

Standing there on Custer's stoop at Fort Dodge, he could see the beautiful body of the Indian girl flying off that little paint mare to the smack of the .54-caliber slug in her soft belly, as clearly as he could the bright splash of lamplight coming from the Colonel's window.

Shaking his head, he reached for the door. Remembering Benteen's acid complaint, he held up and knocked loudly.

"Come in, Joshua. I've been expecting you—"

The surprise served only to lift the angle of Josh's hackles.

Damn him, anyway. A man hadn't even had the chance to open his mouth and there he was already cutting the ground out from under you! He kneed the door open, strode in and stood truculently before Custer.

To add to his surprise, he found the commander in definitely level spirits.

"Well, Joshua, out with it. What's eating you, sir? I've been watching you. You can't get around me with your surly mountain ways, man. Something's had your wind up all evening. The girl, I shouldn't wonder. Am I right, sir?"

The way he said it, clear-eyed and quick, with the old peg-toothed smile backing it all the way, wet a man's powder before he could strike his flint. It made you wonder how you could ever have suspicioned he would have anything to do with Monaseetah, much less with plotting a cold-blooded trap for Black Kettle.

"Well yeah, I reckon, General. Her and the old man. Mostly him right now. Way things was goin' out there tonight, I reckoned you was workin' to peace-talk the old devil square into a set trap."

"What makes you think I wasn't, sir?"

The smile was gone. Seeing it go, Josh set himself for a blasting. He got instead a friendly hand on the shoulder.

"Joshua, you and I are going to come to an understanding. I was just talking to Benteen about you and I'm worried."

There it was again. His mind was shiftier than a once-trapped dog wolf's. He had already smelled out that you were going to brace him about his having told Benteen you were going soft on the redskins. Not only had he smelled out your brace but he was beating you to it by admitting it before you could jump him about it.

Josh sought awkwardly for his answer. "I allow you needn't be," he said, at last.

Having said it, he wanted to kick himself. Now, why had he said it, goddammit? He'd come in here to raise a stink and he was still aiming to raise it. Yet there he was standing there and assuring the General he wasn't!

"All the same, Joshua, I am." Custer said it softly, like a man that meant it. "I am, and I want you to speak freely. Ask your questions right out, sir. You'll get your answers the same way. You know that."

Now the big scout's jaw came forward. His dark eyes grew still.

"All right, General, I've got a couple. First off, what orders have we got comin' up immediate? I mean relatin' to them Cheyenne we just talked to."

Custer's intense expression didn't alter as he strode to his desk and seated himself. Pulling out an order file, he motioned to Josh. As the latter moved to the desk and sat down, he took up the first paper.

"This is the last General Policy Directive from Sherman. It is under date of October fifteenth, the present year. It reads in pertinent part, as follows:

. . . as for extermination it is for the Indians themselves to determine. We don't want to exterminate them or even to fight them. The present war was begun and carried on by the Indians in spite of our entreaties and in spite of our warnings, and the only question is, whether we shall allow the progress of our western settlements to be checked, and leave the Indians free to pursue their bloody career, or accept their war and fight them. We accept the war.

I shall do nothing and say nothing to restrain our troops from doing what they deem proper on the spot, and will allow no general charges of cruelty and inhumanity to tie their hands, but will use all the powers confided in me to the end that these Indians, the enemies of our race and of our civilization, shall not again be able to begin and carry on their barbarous warfare on any kind of pretext they may choose to allege . . .

"Now then," he tossed the paper aside, "that's number one. Any questions?"

"That apply generally," Josh grunted, "or just to the Cheyennes?"

"The Cheyennes, specifically. The Kiowas and Comanches south of the Arkansas are in the department of Colonel Hazen at Fort Cobb."

Josh shook his head, still trying to untangle the double-talk in Sherman's statement. "We don't want to fight them," and then, "We accept the war." "It is for the Indians themselves to determine," and then, "I shall use all the powers confided in me to the end that these Indians . . . shall not again be able to begin and carry on their barbarous warfare."

Read it anyway he wanted, a man could spell it out clearly enough. All the hostiles south of the Arkansas were going to be cut out of the fight by a trumped-up peace quarantine. Then Sherman's boy, Yellow Hair, was going to move in and murder every arms-age Cheyenne north of that stream. The only question remaining was, when was he going to make that move?

"Uh huh," he said at length, his noncommittal grunt not matched by the directness of his query, "now how about them orders?"

Again Custer held his silence. For his answer he

fished a second document from the file and tossed it to the scout.

"That's Sheridan's of the fifteenth, immediately subsequent to Sherman's announcement of the same date." He paused. "It's the order," here a little return flash of the smile, "which certain desk-dreamers in the Indian Bureau are pleased to refer to as 'the notorious General Order of October fifteenth.' Read it, please, Joshua."

The scout began frowning his way through the opening body of the order, concise and official looking over Little Phil's sprawling signature. Suddenly his eyes skipped to the last lines of the brutal document.

> . . . you are thereby ordered to proceed south in the direction of the Antelope Hills, thence toward the Washita River, the supposed winter seat of the hostile tribes; *to destroy their villages and ponies; to kill or hang all warriors and bring back all women and children* . . .

"And that, Joshua," the little commander's eyes caught Kelso's as they swung up from the order, "is number two. Any more questions, sir?"

"I reckon not." Josh was on his feet. "You knowed you was going to hit them when you let them come in to talk peace. Even if they brung the Sacred Pipe, your orders was writ when you talked to them." He paused, eying the famous officer, letting his final charge come quietly.

"And it so happens I know, General, them orders wasn't writ by Sherman or Sheridan. *They was writ by you!*"

"Those orders, sir," Custer was standing now, too, his pale eyes narrowed, "were written by Black Kettle, the day and hour of August seventh when he began to kill on the Saline and Solomon Rivers!"

"I know better, General," was all Josh said, as he turned away.

"Where do you think you're going, sir?" The officer's too-quiet question came as the big scout moved for the door.

It was in Josh's mind not to tell him, but in the end he could no more lie to Custer than he could to himself.

"After the girl, General. I ain't goin' to let your boys blow her guts out when they jump that village."

"Joshua—!"

It was a command. He heard it and understood it, and deliberately ignored it. His big hand reached for the latch.

"I'm sorry, General. You played an Injun trick on me, gettin' me to ask her people where their winter camp would be. Now I'm playin' one on you. I'm quittin' you flat."

"If you walk out that door, Joshua, you will regret it to the last day of your life." Custer was coming around the desk, the usual quick-rising anger in his voice strangely missing.

"You do not understand this situation. Neither you nor any of your mountain kind can ever understand it. I know you. You have, all of you, no matter that you profess it otherwise, a secret and abiding admiration for the Indian. You no less than the others, Joshua, despite your reputation."

He stopped in front of the towering scout, long curls back-flung as his intent gaze sought the face above him. "You are all halfbreeds in a sense, your feelings for these people entirely ambivalent. You profess to fight them. But you fight them like a scattered legion of mountain-demented Don Quixote's. You keep looking for something decent, noble and chivalrous in them, which is not there to find, even as you jab halfheartedly at their buffalo-hide windmills."

Custer stepped back and drew himself up.

"I do not ask you to understand that, Joshua. I only ask that you take my word for the fact that I do."

Josh hesitated. For a moment something in what the little officer had said had come will-o'-the-wisp close to clearing the confusion which had been his since the Cheyenne council. But even as he hesitated, the haunting face of Monaseetah was before him and he could only shrug, hard-faced.

"Could be, General. All the same, I'm goin'."

"Joshua—I ask you not to do it. I need you here—"

There was that in the voice which he'd never heard there; a dead earnestness, a sudden unabashed disregard of rank and relative position, a naked admission of long-hidden loneliness.

A man found it hard to believe but he couldn't miss it. Custer was asking him to stay, not as a paid scout or hired Indian hunter, but as the one thing he needed above all else. The one thing his headlong career had never given him time to make, nor his overpowering ambition to earn.

A simple friend.

Confusion growing with each silent second, Josh hesitated again.

"By God, General, I can't help it. I got to go to that gal. I'd sooner eat boiled buffalo dirt than run out on you, but I can't help it. I got to do it!"

Custer's attitude shifted suddenly. He had won and he knew it. He lost no time in abandoning the uneasy ground of his impetuous revelation and retiring to his prepared position of the Colonel commanding.

"You've got to do no such thing, man. There is no question of harm to the women and children of that camp. You read those orders, sir. They are explicit: 'to bring back all women and children.' That means to bring them back *alive,* sir. You will get your girl, Joshua. You have my word on it."

"I can't get it out of my mind about me askin' them where the village would be, after promisin' peace. That ain't the way I fight Injuns, General."

Custer was beside him then, small hand finding the broad shoulder once more, the old smile flashing its wide-toothed wizardry.

"You've let the girl unsettle you, Joshua. Remember those orders you just read, man. They locate the village as clearly as did old Black Kettle himself. Your question to him was nothing more than a confirmation of something we already knew. No odium can attach to you from it and it can have no possible bearing on an outcome which was in any event inevitable. Our course was determined weeks ago by the Indians themselves. It is contained and irrevocably stated in Sherman's own word—extermination. There is nothing you nor any man alive can do to alter that course. You must see that by now, sir."

He was trapped. There was no way out for him now, And if there was, it wasn't through that door. His hand fell slowly from the latch.

There was no gainsaying the General's claim that he knew beforehand where the camp would be. Nor the dead certainty of Sherman's directive, nor Sheridan's General Order. When it was put to a man that way, he had to admit it. He had to admit, too, the truth of Custer's shot about the girl. There was no question she had him unsettled and going soft on her relatives.

Head down, sunbrown hands clenched, the big scout surrendered.

"I'll stay, General—"

He heard the dull acceptance in his voice and knew that once more the Boy General had him mired in the bull wallow of a bad decision. He knew, too, that he had to let him know it.

"But I got to say one thing." As Custer waited, pale-eyed, his deep voice dropped, the accusation in it flatly quiet. "I used to think that killin' Injuns was *my* business. Right now, I reckon it's yours!"

Custer stood motionless while the heavy seconds stalked the eye-locked silence. Finally he moved, strode wordlessly to the desk, removed a second file and took from it a succession of reports.

Without further notice of Josh, he began to read:

"August 7th, instant, Saline River: 300 Cheyenne moving along a 20-mile path, killed 15

86

settlers and carried off 5 women . . .

"August 11th, instant, Solomon River: same war party, crossing from the Saline, killed 6 settlers, scalped another alive . . .

"August 18th, instant, small Cheyenne band raiding along the Pawnee Fork, dismembered a settler alive, in front of his wife, later killed, and his two children, subsequently carried off and to date unreported . . .

"8th September, instant, Cimarron Crossing: war party identified as Sand Creek Cheyenne entered a wagon park to trade. Seized 17 white teamsters whom they subsequently burned amid the contents of their train . . .

"9th September, instant, Fort Wallace: wood hauling detail attacked. Six U. S. contractors killed, scalped and mutilated . . ."

The officer's voice moved ahead, ignoring Josh's hand-waved remonstrance; the precision of his diction never varied, his eyes flicked from manuscript to listener as he discarded each report in turn.

"1st October, instant, Spanish Forks: large band tentatively identified as mixed Arapahoe and Sand Creek Cheyenne killed 4 men and outraged 3 women, the last of whom was violated by 13

87

Indians then scalped in front of her 4 small children, the children then murdered one at a time. Investigating detail found axe still in woman's skull. Certain identification of weapon as Southern Cheyenne . . .

"3rd October, instant, Fort Dodge: 12-month report children carried off, this district: 14 known to have frozen to death while captive in hostile camps. Two camps identified, High Bear's and Roman Horse's, both Cheyenne . . .

"6th October, instant, Fort Lyon: party of 60 Cheyenne raiding along the North Canadian surprised 5 haycutting contractors. All mutilated. No survivors."

Custer paused, then leaned forward over the desk.
"There is one more of these little items, sir. One with which, lest memory fails me, you enjoyed some small personal connection!" The bitterness of the cynicism was heavily troweled-on, the harsh acid of its spreading forbade interruption.
"It is here, sir, in my hand." He waved the crumpled sheath of reports. "But I shall not trouble to read it for you. It is recent enough, you will permit me the liberty to assume, for even your abbreviated remembrances. Allow me, sir, to *recite it* for you, from memory—*and to the comma!*

"14th November, instant, Fort Coon, Kansas Territory: Relief squadron from Fort Dodge arriving on above date under Lt. Wm. Cook, found Sergeant L. C. Woods and ten troopers of his outpost detail under hostile attack. The Indians, positively identified by the survivors as Arkansas Cheyenne, withdrew in the face of the relief's advance . . . six men wounded, four dead. The latter group, a wood detail from Fort Dodge under 1st Sergeant Ben F. Henderson. They were found scalped and mutilated two miles east of the guard outpost on Big Coon Creek. Sergeant Henderson was unrecognizable."

Custer stood up, watching Josh for a full five seconds. At last, he nodded.

"Yes, *Kelso!*" It was the first and last time he ever used the name. "You 'reckon' correctly."

The following words fell so softly Josh's keen ear barely caught them. They came backed, nonetheless, with a sudden flaring of the pale eyes which seared them into his memory.

"Right now, killing Indians *is* my business!"

9. *Black Kettle's Tipi*

JOSH TOSSED RESTLESSLY. For a fall night getting on into winter it was uncommon hot. The cussed hay appeared bent on jabbing a man every time he turned. On top of that the drumming and chanting from the Cheyenne camp beyond the stockade was keeping Wasiya gingered up.

After an hour he gave up and admitted it wasn't the

gelding stomping around that was keeping him awake. It was the girl. He cursed silently, remembering his pledge to Custer.

Followed another ten minutes of bed-punching, and that was it.

When a man was used to sneaking around situations where any noise lustier than a mouse sneeze could mean his hair, it wouldn't be any trick to slide in and out of this camp. What Custer didn't know wouldn't hurt him. Besides, happen a man had in mind to see that Indian girl again he'd best be about it. The Cheyenne camp would be clean gone come daylight.

Fort Dodge was built in a halfmoon, the two points based on the Arkansas. Back from the river a ways was a twenty-foot bluff where the main barracks of the enlisted men were dug in and sod-roofed over. Once down that bluff and past the sod shanties Josh had only to hit for the river, drift south a spell and then cut back in across the open prairie.

Ten minutes later, he was skirting the Arkansas willows.

Minutes after that he was shadowing in on the Cheyenne camp. The only trouble he'd encountered had been with a bunch of night-grazing cavalry mounts being held outside the fort under herd guard. He'd had to pass so close to the horses he'd been able to identify them when one of the troopers struck flint to his midnight pipe—Captain William Thompson's troop of the Seventh.

Ahead of him now, he had the Cheyenne pony herd. It was placed as always by these red nomads between themselves and the potential enemy: in this case and in spite of all the palaver and pipe-smoking, Yellow Hair and his Cheyenne-chasing Seventh Cavalry.

Josh nodded grimly as he noted the old chief's caution. Then wondered whether it was really caution or something else. Something else spelled a lot more like suspicion. Or maybe downright information.

The pony herd was nothing. He had been too long in the South Park country to smell like a white man. His buckskins were deep-cured with the woodsmoke of ten years of tipi fires. He floated past the Cheyenne remuda without lifting a solitary roman nose from the rich graze of the Arkansas uplands.

Then his troubles began.

The camp was a big one. It spread over a quarter of a mile of open plain. There was nothing to draw a bead on save the big cowskin cone of Black Kettle's lodge. Outside of that, there wasn't a tipi in the whole layout, so a man's approach was about as private as a sow grizzly crossing a snowslide.

Right now a man began to wonder what he was doing out there. Sure, he could call out and make an open walk-in. That way he'd be safe enough as far as the Indians were concerned. But just let him show himself in front of the whole tribe and the General was certain to hear of it. Next, he could belly around the camp hoping to spot the girl and signal her out, risking in the process getting gutshot by some spooky horse guard. Or lastly he could smarten up and light a shuck right back where he'd come from, forgetting the whole thing.

But as long as he was hell-bent on seeing the girl—

Setting his jaw, he dropped to his knees and began snaking toward the silhouette of Black Kettle's lodge. He was careful to keep it squarely between himself and the light of the dance fires.

At the rear of the lodge he thought once more about how badly he wanted to see Monaseetah. The guttural barking of dancing braves, not forty feet from him, stiffened the hairs on his neck. Gritting his teeth, he lifted the rear covers and went under.

He was luckier than any white man who would deliberately belly-sneak in on five hundred celebrating Cheyenne had any right to be.

"*Niva tato?* Who is that?"

A deep voice muttered the challenge from behind the glow of a pipe not six feet from his nose.

"*Nanehov, nihoe,* it is I, father!" Recognizing the voice, he let his breath go gratefully. "Your friend, Ota Kte."

"Ota Kte!"

Josh's eyes adjusted to the darkness of the tipi and he could see Black Kettle now. He could see, too, the steady muzzle of Black Kettle's carbine.

"Aye, father. Gently there, with the Holy Iron! I have come to seek your help, Old One. As a son to a father."

The old Cheyenne nodded, motioning him forward.

"You are very foolish to come into this camp in such a way. I could have shot you. The pony guards could have shot you. Yellow Hair would have called it murder."

Josh squatted crosslegged on the buffalo robe, facing the old man. He returned the nod soberly. "You could, and he would," he agreed succinctly. "But I could not let Yellow Hair know that I came here. He has my word that I would not do it."

"Your word is no better than that, Ota Kte?"

"What do you think, father?"

"It is the girl then." The old man's statement fell softly, startling Josh with its certain insight.

"Now why do you say that, father?" he countered awkwardly.

"*Haheneeno.*" The Cheyenne leader shrugged. "A man knows these things. When a young brave is not at war there are two things he will risk his scalp or his honor for. Food in his belly. A woman in his blankets."

"I must talk to the girl, father. You understand these things and I am glad. When I saw her today my heart was big and my eyes full of joy."

"Hah!" The snort was eloquent. "You mean your eyes were big! I didn't notice the heart. It's all the same when you're young though."

"You will bring her then? Here to the tipi? I ask it, father. My fingers are touching the brow."

"Only a moment, yes. The squaws will be returning from the fires soon. It is late and we travel early."

He waited in the half-gloom of the lodge. Seconds seemed to grow into hours before the old man's form again blotted the entrance flaps. Behind him was the girl. At the sight of her Josh felt the thick blood hammer in his wrists and temples.

"*Vahe Veho!*" Her low voice went through him,

leaving him suddenly weak. "You are welcome, White Man. You make my eyes glad again."

He struggled for an answer. Before he could find words, Black Kettle's warning mutter was falling.

"Talk quickly now. You have only a moment. The dance is ending. I will be outside. Remember, my heart is good for you. When you hear the grass hawk whistle, you will know the squaws come."

With the admonition he was gone, leaving only the darkness of the tipi between Josh and the Indian girl. She moved toward him, and he arose to meet her. She spoke first.

"We have no time, *Veho*. Listen to me. I know that what is in my heart is also in yours. When you look at me I do not think of Ota Kte, the killer of my people. I think only of the White Man I see. Such a *Veho* as I have never seen before—"

"You listen to me, girl!" His interruption stumbled uncertainly; his mind whirled at the implications of her words. "We can't talk of these things now. Not in this place. I came here that you might tell me how I can find you when your people leave this camp. You told me at Yellow Hair's fire that we would meet again. I came here that you might tell me when that will be. And where, Bright Hair."

"I have not forgotten, *Veho*. Had you not come, I would have sent for you."

With the thrill of this new promise, the girl hurried on.

"I will wait for you the second sun from tonight, when that sun is sinking. There is a place on the South

94

Road beyond the Arkansas. A spot near the river where the spring flows. It is heavy with willows and cottonwoods there. Do you mark that spot, *Veho?*"

"Middle Spring," he said tensely. "On the Cimarron. Past the Dry Crossing, past the Jornada. Is that the place, girl?"

"That is it, *Veho*. Monaseetah will be there. We will talk and you can show me with your hands what I have already seen in your eyes!"

The way she said it, the words low and fierce, brought Josh to his feet. In two strides he was across the darkened lodge. He seized the roundness of her arms, high up, and his thumbs tensed to the swell of her breasts. His wide lips smashed downward upon the demand of her parted mouth. His hard body cradled the eager, forward thrust of her soft one—

The long-drawn quaver of the nighthawk's whistle broke the brutal kiss in mid-demand. The girl backed away from him and ducked, shadow-swift, through the tipi flaps. And he stood there with two last-minute memories: the perfume of her body against his buckskins, the salt and the blood of her torn mouth against his lips.

For a moment he remained motionless. Then he dropped and rolled under the rear skins of the lodge. He came erect outside, listening intently. Within, deep grunts announced the arrival of Moxtaveto's squaws.

For the first time in twelve hours, he allowed himself the luxury of a grin. He was still enjoying it when he turned and slid away toward the protecting shadow of the pony herd.

If it was a laugh Josh Kelso meant to have there back of Black Kettle's lodge, it was as well it was a silent one.

For with a Cheyenne, as with any Indian, the last smile went to the one who took the scalp. And Emoonesta, the Bright-Haired One, was a Cheyenne.

She was still smiling softly, long after the peaceful pony herd had closed behind the form of Ota Kte, Indian Killer.

10. Captain Thompson's Horses

SHORTLY AFTER MIDNIGHT Josh, starting upwind around Captain Thompson's grazing horse herd, ran into the trouble he had spent the past hour begging for.

His first warning was a tremble of the ground under his feet. He knew the sign. In the next second he dove headlong for the only cover, a six-foot gullywash in the prairie level.

His instinctive thought was that the Cheyenne horse herd had winded him and begun to run. But by the time he got his eyes back above the lip of the gully, he knew better. They were Cheyenne ponies all right and they were running. But they weren't stampeding. Astride each crouched a slit-eyed savage.

Much has been written, and will be, about the war-whooping, bloodcurdling cries of an Indian assault. About the heathen war screaming and caterwauling of the red warrior as he rides down upon his enemy. But any High Plains scout worth his salt could tell the writers something about that.

Any time the hostiles meant real business and were not just whooping it up for the benefit of some delegation from the Indian Bureau, they rode with no more noise than the churn of unshod pony hoofs and the grunts of cayuse ribs being caved in by barrel-swung rifle butts.

It was the classic pattern of the High Plains raider on profit bent. The profit these particular raiders were bent on taking was the choice cavalry herd of Captain William Thompson's G Troop. They were going to take it too. A man could see that plain as prairie moonlight. osh saw something else as well, before ducking his head and letting them thunder past. He saw three chiefs riding neck-and-neck in the van of the hostile swoop: a lean, hawk-headed devil in the middle, a towering blob flanking him on the right and a skull-adorned buzzard hugging his left.

Aii-eee, brother! Those were the Dog Soldiers out there. A man better remember it and keep his head hard down.

There was nothing wrong with Josh's memory. And he could tuck his neck tighter than a sleeping sagehen, happen the cover was scant and the sign read Cheyenne. By the time he dared take a second look over the edge of the gully, the Dog Soldiers had driven the cavalry horses past the fort and were hazing them for the river. He watched them long enough for the thrash of the stampede to hit the water, telling him the raiders were driving wide around Black Kettle's camp. With that, he was up and running.

Damn their lousy hides! There was a typical Indian

97

trick for you. A white man would never get on to the ways of their crazy minds. Let five hundred of them ride in and make a decent peace and fifty of them would ride out and start a war. Let a troop of cavalry make a successful palaver and the hotheads of the tribe would immediately figure the way to get back at the white soldier-brother would be to run off the selfsame horses he had sat on at the council.

Damn the red idiots again. If there ever had been a chance Custer would get cooled down by old Black Kettle's peace talk, that chance was now as gone as Captain Thompson's horses.

Cuss them as he would, though, a man needn't pretend they were as dumb as they acted. Mad Wolf had failed to come into that council for a good reason. And such of his boys as had come into it had come knowing they would be booted out by Custer. Black Kettle wanted peace and he thought he had made it. Mad Wolf had thought the same thing. But the Dog Soldier chief wanted war, not peace. And, come blue norther or slush-thaw chinook, he was going to have it!

Particularly when getting it was no more trouble than running off a prime horse herd within sight and rifle shot of the biggest Pony Soldier camp west of Fort Riley.

He redoubled his silent curses as he called out his identity to the main gate sentries and loped past them toward Custer's quarters.

The lousy, no-good, settlement-raiding red sons. They'd fixed it now so's old Moxtaveto would get the full credit for the horse herd run-off and guaranteed that war would come to the Washita right on Sheridan's dirty schedule. They'd spoiled any last chance he or anybody else might have to talk Custer out of a winter campaign. They'd ruined any outside shot whatever of a regular spring and summer chase whereby a man could figure to earn the pay he needed for starting that North Canadian cowspread. They'd fixed it, too, so he'd likely never again lay eyes on that beautiful Indian girl.

Goddam that mangy Mad Wolf clean to hell, and all his murdering Dog Soldiers with him. If it was the last Indian Josh Kelso ever killed, he was going to put *that one* under for keeps!

Knowing none of the troopers guarding the cavalry herd had beaten him into the fort, he was surprised to see the lamplight in Custer's office as hard at work as it had been three hours earlier. The surprise didn't slow his knock, nor the boot of his moccasin-toe against the door planks.

He came into the commander's office narrowing his eyes to the brightness of the lamp. As quickly as his eyes narrowed, they widened again.

"Gabe, for Cripes sake! If it ain't the old he-coon hisself!"

With the shout, he was belaboring the old mountain man. Jim Bridger, protecting himself as best he could, backed off complainingly.

"Blast yer hide, ye slabfoot mountain ox! Whut ye aimin' to do, tromp a man to death? Lay off now, you hear me, dang ye? I didn't sashay all the way out here to git put under by no White Comanche!"

Custer sat back, giving master and apprentice time to get over, mountain-man style, the fact they hadn't seen one another since the older scout had given up fighting Blackfeet and Mormons in the days of his beloved Fort Bridger. When the assorted greetings and Green River insults had quieted down, he lost no time in updating Kelso on what had brought his famous tutor back to the frontier.

Aged and infirm, the old Indian fighter had made the long overland trip from his Missouri homestead to urge Custer to abandon his plans for a winter campaign. Bridger felt the cavalry could not survive in the field the rigors of the High Plains blizzards. He had come in by army ambulance from Fort Larned within the past hour. His pleas, passionately made, had already been denied.

Josh remained quiet until Custer had gotten that far. Then, before Bridger might again take up the argument, he brought the meeting to present order.

"Well, Gabe, I allow this here winter campaign was my own little brain shower, but that ain't neither here nor there right now. What's here, is the General all gingered up to fight Black Kettle. What's there," the young scout pointed the prairie beyond the south stockade, "is Mad Wolf a'runnin' off every last head of Captain Thompson's hosses."

"What the devil are you saying, man?" Custer was on his feet, thin face livid.

"I already said it, General. The Dog Soldiers just run off G Troop's hosses."

"By the Lord, sir, I don't believe it!" The officer's face clouded, his voice dropping. "Who told you, Joshua?"

"I never take nobody's word for nothin'. I reckon you know that."

"You've been outside, sir?"

"Somewhat."

"With the Cheyennes?"

"More or less." The shrug was noncommittal. "You want to hear about my life with the Injuns, General, or what happened to Thompson's hosses?"

"By thunder, sir, I had your word. I want to know what you were doing outside the stockade!"

The second shrug compounded the indifference of the first. "I didn't cotton to the way Mad Wolf hid out on the council today, nor the looks on such of his boys as he sent in, when you sent them packin'. I figured old Axhonehe was up to somethin'. Figurin' same, I took myself a *pasear* over the wall just now and cussed near got myself run down. They come by me hand-close on the first pass. I seen them, you can lay."

"You're sure?"

"I said I seen them. Mad Wolf, Big Body, Yellow Buffalo, the lot of them. I told you Black Kettle wasn't mixed in with this bunch."

Before Custer could vent the spleen this defiant claim deserved, or the silent Bridger get started to questioning it, the door crashed open to admit the bug-eyed front runner of Thompson's troopers.

"Beg pardon, Colonel Custer, sir, but them lousy Cheyenne just run off our horses!"

"What horses, Corporal?"

Custer's query was as matter-of-fact as though he were questioning the trooper on the condition of his carbine. Again, Josh wondered at his capacity for control in front of troops. He could rave and rant like a rotten-spoiled kid so long as nobody military was within earshot. But just let the lowest buck private on the post step into range and he was all at once Lieutenant Colonel G. A. Custer, Commanding, and don't let anybody forget it!

"Captain Thompson's, sir." The trooper's reply came over Kelso's thoughts. "Every last head of G Troop, as we had 'em on graze just south of the fort."

"Did you see any of the Indians, Corporal? That is, to identify them with any certainty?" Custer was eying Josh, not the flustered soldier.

"Yes sir, they was the Cheyennes. Rode down into us right from their camp yonder."

"Did you recognize any individual? Any of the Indians who were at the council this evening?" The questions came deliberately. "Was there moonlight enough to see reliably by?"

"Yes sir, there was, and yes sir, I did. I seen old Black Kettle hisself, a'ridin' right up in front and a'leadin' the whole shebang!"

"That's a damn lie, soldier!" Josh was towering over the trooper, dark eyes blazing. Custer's voice cut in between them.

"That will do, Joshua. I'll not have you bullyragging the men. I want this boy's story and I'm quite competent to get it without your help."

"This 'boy,'" the scout nodded acidly, "better get his

102

own story—and get it straight! I don't aim to stand by and listen to no more rot from a green-bellied cavalry boot. Not when it comes to Injuns, by God. I seen them Cheyenne, General. They was Dog Soldiers!"

The trooper, sensing his commander's sympathy, fought back defiantly.

"They was from the camp, Colonel, sir. We seen 'em comin'. And I seen that there Black Kettle too, clear as day!"

"I've had it, General. You can—" He was starting for the door, starting to say that Custer could draw his pay, when he had to step back to avoid being run over by the rush through the open doorway of the corporal's fellow herd guards.

"Beggin' your pardon, Colonel, sir," the spokesman for the three took up the corporal's claim, "but we seen them Cheyenne comin' from that camp and we seen Black Kettle too. And Smitty here, he seen somethin' else!"

"All right, Smith, what did you see? Out with it, man."

"Yes sir, well sir, I was the last one away, bein' on the far side of the herd when they struck us. As I legged it in, I looked back toward the Injun camp and they was pullin' out, sir. Headin' smack for the Arkansas, fast as they could mount up and make off!"

"Good! Good!" Custer's pale eyes were snapping as he wheeled on Josh. "You hear that, Joshua? What do you say now, sir?

The big scout, still seething, was nevertheless glad he hadn't gotten to ask for his pay. He had had time in the ten-second interval to think once more of Monaseetah, and to realize his best chance of ever seeing the Cheyenne girl again was in sticking, burr-tight, to Custer and the Seventh Cavalry. Regardless, he was bound to speak his professional piece.

"I say, figure it this way. Happen you was the old man, what would you do as soon as your own hoss guards run in and told you the Dog Soldiers had just lifted some of Yellah Hair's hosses? He knows you, General, remember that. And he knows what damned liars your men are. He figured it just as sure as he was standin' here listenin' to us, that you'd blame him for the run-off. So he just up and got shut of you as far and fast as he could. Naturally."

"All right, Joshua—"

That "Joshua" didn't fool a man for a minute. Custer was hopping mad and holding down only because troops were present. A man knew that, and he didn't need the little rooster's next words to prove it.

"You may go, sir. I shall want you back here at four A.M., and I suggest you bring some better manners and a quiet mouth when you come. That will be all, sir."

Josh turned without a word, paused only to shake hands with the embarrassed Bridger.

"Sorry, Gabe. Didn't aim to drag you into any family ruckus thisaway. See you tomorrow, old salt."

"Sure as shootin', boy. You grab yourself some sleep now, hear? You're edgy, Josh."

"Yeah, I reckon." He managed a shade of the old grin. "*Nataemhon,* old hoss."

"Good huntin', boy—" The aging scout echoed the

104

old Cheyenne phrase as he moved to follow his tall protégé to the door.

Josh moved out and away from the lamplight. He paused, as he did, to look back quickly. The forlorn picture of the old mountain man, rheumy-eyed and gaunt his goiter-misshapen throat bulging past the frayed collars of his settlement shirt, his trembling hand lifted to wave uncertainly from the yellow frame of the doorway, brought a sick, slow tug to his heart.

Somehow, he knew the old man was saying goodbye. He hesitated, accordingly, while the lamplight still picked out his own youth-lean form. Flicking the fingertips of his left hand to his forehead he spread them swiftly with the point of his long arm, in parting salute to the lonely figure in the doorway.

He waited only long enough to see by the return sign that the old man understood, then turned away, softfooted, to vanish in the outer darkness of the parade yard.

It was the last time he ever saw Jim Bridger.

11. *Young Tom Custer*

THE THIN GRAY of the four o'clock, false dawn put the hunch of its chill in the saddled back of Wasiya where the gelding stood in front of Custer's office. Presently the Sioux pony lifted his nose, cocked an ear to the flood of light released by the opening door, and whickered softly to the familiar, gaunt figure of his approaching rider.

He was rewarded, shortly, by a kick in the ribs and

some suitably terse directions.

"Hump it, hoss." Josh's weight settled in the saddle. The tone of his grunt let the gelding know he was in for a rough day. "We got a damn diaper detail to wetnurse. Howsomever," the voice lifted to the chronic, quick grin, "happen we're pure lucky we won't lose no more than a night's sleep out of it."

Following his rider's knee-guide, Wasiya swung out of the street and headed for the main gate. He broke into a lope as he caught and passed the little column of mounted troopers already moving out of the fort. Josh reined him in alongside the youthful officer heading the column.

"Mornin', Tom. The General tells me he's lettin' you get your feet wet today."

"Yeah, Josh," Tom Custer grinned the reply with a proper return of the scout's sloppy salute, "and sending you along to see that I don't get them damp above the knee, eh?"

He nodded, receipting the boy's rich grin with one of his own dry specimens.

Tom was as different from the General as they came. He was a head taller, six heads handsomer and anyway three heads more human. He was friendly as a spaniel and not too much smarter. If the boy had a brain he'd never gotten the chance to prove it, the way the General mother-henned him. Besides, the kid was that convinced his older brother was the greatest cavalryman since Jeb Stuart that he made his own life a looking glass for the General's, reflecting every claim, idea, order or afterthought the former might

106

see fit to hold or hand out.

Withal, though, he was normal as rain in April. And just weak enough in his worship of his brother, to leave off of it short of wearing it thin. Tom would take a stogie quick as the next and his addiction to the occasional cup was as well known as his famous brother's hatred of the habit. A man wouldn't want to say young Tom was a drunk but he could allow the boy had a fair start to getting as sopped as the rest of the Seventh's staff, than which no officer corps on the frontier had a worse or wetter record.

"Yeah," he broke the pause to agree with the youngster's probe, "I reckon that's so. But you needn't get huffed about it. Happen I hadn't convinced the General there wasn't no more than thirty head of hostiles in the bunch what run off Thompson's hosses, you wouldn't have got the detail, boy."

"Come along now, Josh!" The infectious grin was spreading again. "You're not hinting you deliberately mislead the General so that I'd get the chance to chase these redskins?"

"Somewhat. Course there *was* only thirty of them actually run off the hosses. But I happen to know there's another two hundred and seventy of them where that thirty come from. I allowed if the General knowed it was that big a bunch he'd have wanted to go after them hisself."

"I don't follow you, Josh." The boy's smile faltered with the words. "Are you saying you went out of your way to keep the General from going after these Cheyenne?"

"I am."

"I don't believe I like the sound of that, Joshua." The smile was gone.

"Like it or lump it, boy, but get it straight. I'd rather chase three thousand ordinary Injuns than three hundred Dog Soldiers. Had the General come along I couldn't have held him off of them. With you I figure I can. And boy, when we get out yonder and the tracks start gettin' prime hot, you remember that. So long as you and your eighty lads don't want to wind up with your hair hangin' down a Cheyenne lodge smokehole, you hold up when Josh Kelso tells you to. You hear me now, Tom?"

The youngster shot an uneasy glance back toward his small column. It looked much smaller now that Fort Dodge was falling so rapidly to the rear. He turned with a sober nod to the waiting scout.

"Sure, I hear you, Josh. You don't have to worry, man. I've got my orders too, you know."

Josh was at once concerned, thinking Custer had slipped in some dangerous instructions in briefing the youngster before talking to him. Watching him carefully, he said, "What you mean by that, boy?"

" 'You are, sir,' " Tom Custer mimicked the Seventh's C.O. perfectly, " 'to do precisely what Joshua proposes in any given situation. And you are not, sir, to use your own judgment in any case. Is that clear, sir?' "

Josh picked up the concluding grin and tossed it back.

"We'll get along, boy." His accompanying thumb-jerk went quickly over his shoulder toward the following troopers. "Tell them to pick it up. We ain't got all week."

The youthful officer's "forward ho!" rang out immediately. The column responded by moving from a trot to a lope as it swung left to cross and move away from the Arkansas, bearing almost due east into the trackless grass of the open prairie.

It had been 4.30 A.M. when Josh had turned the column away from Fort Dodge and across the Arkansas. Ten hours later they had seen no more sign of Captain Thompson's stolen horse herd than the wide track of its passing which now, as at the crossing, stretched clearly away eastward.

Frowning, he pulled Wasiya up and grunted to young Custer to wave the halt to the following column. Pointing to the high swell of prairie confronting them a half-mile ahead, he spoke quickly.

"Well, Tom, what you want to do? Past yonder rise you get into a bad batch of sandhills. We ain't even seen herd dust yet and I don't cotton to the looks of things."

"Hell, Josh," the youngster didn't share his brother's restraint of vocabulary, "we're not well started yet. Besides, the lack of dust doesn't mean anything, does it? We've been on buffalo grass all along. That keeps the dust down, doesn't it?"

"It does," nodded the scout. "It keeps it down so you don't know whether they're ten miles or two hundred yards ahead of you. Gettin' into them hills like we will be now, you can't see far enough ahead to even take a guess, neither."

"I'll take one. My guess is that we're still way behind them, Josh. Let's move along. We've got lots of time.

Remember, we don't have to get back to the fort."

He was remembering just that, and scowling as he remembered it. Custer's orders had been to trail the raiders as long as possible, then, failing a contact, to swing south and west to join his Camp Supply column in the field. This last was exactly what he wanted to avoid. No army scout, least of all Josh Kelso, admired spending a night in the open with a green lieutenant and eighty raw recruits. Not, at least, when that open was inhabited by three hundred Cheyenne horse raiders.

Still, a man knew young Tom was right. They did have lots of time and no good reason for turning back.

"All right boy, let's do it this way. You and me takes twenty troopers and tops out on yonder swell. The rest waits here. That's a bad country past that ridge. I got me an idea we'll be glad we didn't poke our whole nose past it."

Tom Custer agreed at once, leaving the main column with Lieutenant Edward Law and moving for the high ground ahead after arranging with Law to move up on signal should they find something.

Two minutes later he and Josh were atop the ridge and had indeed "found something."

As the latter had predicted the ground sloped sharply past the crest of the rise. Beyond the slope lay a level saucer of grass. Beyond that began the precipitous channels of the Kansas sandhills. But what widened the eyes of the young officer was not the slope, nor the saucer, nor the sandhills.

It was Captain Thompson's horse herd standing peacefully in the middle of the open grass below, unattended save by half a dozen sleepy Cheyenne guards.

"By God, we've got them, Josh!" He was turning to wave the "forward ho" when his companion seized his unflung arm.

"Not quite, youngster. Wait up now."

The disgruntled officer wheeled on him but was given no chance to get started.

"Look, Tom boy, use your head. You see how close them hosses is bein' held to them sandhills?"

"Certainly. What of it?"

"Them hills could hide the whole Cheyenne Nation, let alone three hundred hoss raiders. Check them hair-braids and three feathers on them guard bucks. Them's Dog Soldiers, son!"

"A trap, eh Josh?" The boy smiled a little weakly, realizing the situation belatedly. "Using our own horses as bait—"

"Yeah, Tom. But I allow this is one trap that's set just right to get back-sprung!"

Catching the rare excitement in his scout's voice the young officer questioned him quickly. He got his answers in the same vein.

"Signal Law to come up and lay low just this side of the ridge. After that me and you and our twenty boys will ride on down like we didn't smell nothin'. When they jump us we cut and run back for the ridge, leadin' them up and over and smack into eighty cavalry carbines. You got that boy?"

Custer got it. The preparations were carried out. A noncom was sent racing back to instruct Law's troops who were now moving forward. The rest of the troopers on the ridge nervously kneed their mounts down the slope after their commander and his hard-faced scout.

When they were three hundred yards from the herd the sleepy horse guards came awake. Turning, they fled for the sandhills as thought there weren't another Indian to aid the horse guards in Kansas Territory. Then, when they were fifty yards into the hills, they came racing back out of them as though they had miraculously found every hostile south of the Arkansas. Which indeed it appeared they had.

Mad Wolf's three hundred ambushed Dog Soldiers came belching out of the hidden gullies with such a rush they very nearly swallowed up Josh's counterbait before the scout could get the startled troopers turned around.

Once the race stretched out, however, the big cavalry horses opened up the distance between themselves and the scrawny mounts of the Dog Soldiers to a hundred yards. This space was widened to nearly two hundred by the time the slope was surmounted and the counter-bait party had wheeled its mounts into position with the waiting line of Law's men.

The rest was easy the way such things went.

There never was the Indian, Dog Soldier or other-wise, who would linger around to argue about odds of less than three to one on well-mounted and well-led white soldiers. Josh had figured on that.

The hostile horde came pouring over the crest of the ridge in typical Indian order, the fastest ponies and boldest riders well in advance. These startled vanguards threw their ponies on their haunches the minute they saw the waiting cavalry line. Their following companions piled over the ridge and into them at full speed.

At the moment of maximum snarl-up, Josh nodded to Tom Custer and shouldered his Henry carbine. The steady bark of the repeater was seconded by the timed volleys of the eighty Spencers behind it.

Josh counted twelve ponies down in the first volley. By the time the second was ripping into the retreating hostile rear, no less than twenty Cheyenne ponies were struggling on the ground. But with the usual Indian alacrity and of course the superb Cheyenne horsemanship, the disorganized Dog Soldiers managed to scoop up most of their wounded as they fled the ridge in the face of the immediate charge led by Tom Custer.

One brave, alone, lingered too long in attempting to aid a wounded fellow, letting Wasiya bring Josh down on top of him.

The scout drove the giant Sioux gelding into the scrubby Cheyenne pony, knocking the little animal sprawling. Before the warrior could recover Josh had him in a South Park bearhug with his skinning knife planted above his right kidney.

"Don't move, cousin. I'm not going to kill you."

The guttural Cheyenne assurance was superfluous. The terrified brave had already assumed from the identity of his captor that his time was overshort, and was beseeching Maheo, the Cheyenne Almighty, to witness that he died without fear and in pursuance of his sacred duty of killing Pony Soldiers.

By the time Custer returned from his short pursuit of the Dog Soldiers, driving the recovered horse herd ahead of him, Josh and his skinning knife had struck up a speaking acquaintance with the Cheyenne buck.

An acquaintance not painful to the red man alone.

Adding it all up now, as he hung back to outride the column's rear against any surprise return of the routed Dog Soldiers, the white scout wrinkled the unburned bridge of his nose with considerable anguish. He grimaced savagely as he scowled his unspoken curses through the rising dust of the recaptured cavalry herd. No matter how a man turned it, it came out the same.

Somebody had tipped off Mad Wolf about him having been in the Cheyenne camp the night before!

And had done it fast enough for the Dog Soldier to bring his boys down onto that herd of Thompson's before he got back to the fort. It didn't seem possible they could have moved that fast but it had to be that way.

The captured Dog Soldier had made that clear when he'd said that Mad Wolf had ordered the raid by telling them Ota Kte was passing close to the herd and would thus be named to scout for whatever soldier party set out after the raiders. It was hard to swallow but judging from what the brave said, the whole thing had been set up and run off on the outside chance of drawing him away from the fort with a small pursuit party.

That much of it didn't bother him. He'd known all along the Dog Soldier chief was after him, and that he was idiot enough to try anything to get him. But the one thing which jolted a man was that *somebody* had told Mad Wolf that he'd been in, and just left the Cheyenne camp.

That somebody had to be a Cheyenne.

There were only two Cut-Arms in that camp who'd known he was in it. Black Kettle for one. Monaseetah for the other.

From there a man could twist it some more, and all he wanted. It still came out one answer.

There was no sound reason on God's green prairie why the old Cheyenne chief would put the Dog Soldiers onto him and that horse herd. It would be the last thing the old man would want, to get Custer riled in any way. Especially in any way that would associate him with the Dog Soldiers.

A man could set his jaw all he wanted to, and scowl his damndest through that horse-herd dust. And cuss in Cheyenne, Sioux, Comanche or Arapaho. There was one Indian, and one alone, who could have set Mad Wolf onto him in such a hurry last night.

Her name wasn't Black Kettle.

12. Middle Cimarron Springs

ON JOSH'S RECOMMENDATION Lieutenant Custer abandoned his plan to head west in attempting to intercept his older brother's column on its line of march over the Jornada or Dry Crossing between the Arkansas and the Cimarron. The scout warned that young Custer's own column, without water for the horses since leaving the Arkansas the morning of the 14th, would have to strike a stream by noon of the 15th or be in serious trouble.

He chose, therefore, Josh's suggestion of the longer

course of following down the Lower Crossing of the Jornada to strike the Cimarron and move up that stream's channel to join the General's column at its first night-camp out of Dodge—the Lower Spring of the Cimarron.

The column, moving at a forced walk-trot, the best gait possible in consideration of the large herd of loose stock being driven with it, cut into the Lower Crossing road about 6.00 A.M. It turned south along the ruts of the abandoned wagon route, forcing the pace for another three hours. There was no sign of following hostiles.

Ten o'clock brought them to the Cimarron and the unpleasant fact of having Josh's prediction it would be dry at this season borne out. The last of the water in the men's canteens was employed in washing the clotting dust from the horses' nostrils and in squeezing a few precious drops into each mount's swollen mouth.

They pressed on at once, a four-hour, horse-killing ride bringing them in distant sight and water-smell of Lower Spring about 2.00 P.M. They were camped, and the last head of stock watered-out and on graze by three o'clock.

Tom Custer, soldier enough to know when he had missed a bad blunder by a few hours, and man enough to admit it, called Josh aside and expressed his gratitude. The taciturn scout quickly shrugged the compliment aside, but not that quickly his keen mind didn't think about how differently the other brother would have handled the same situation.

In his entire association with the older Custer he

couldn't remember having once been thanked for a good job well done. Plenty of praise and promise beforehand, always. But let the affair be well or brilliantly brought off, no matter there might be reward and to spare in it for all concerned, the General always managed to somehow wind up with his own thumb in the middle of the plum.

Shortly before dusk, the senior Custer's column moved in along the main road of the Middle Crossing. Josh was amazed at its size—twelve full companies of the Seventh, together with an ammunition and supply train of over forty wagons. Among the officers he recognized Majors Joel Elliott, Gibbs and Tilford, Captains Benteen, Keogh, Hamilton and Yates, Lieutenants Moylan, Brewster, Longan and Cook. The selection let him know the Boy General had handpicked his companies with dangerous care. Outside of Benteen, Joe Tilford and Miles Keogh, with maybe Billy Cook among the juniors, the officers of the Camp Supply column were all pretty much cut to Custer's own slapdash pattern. Particularly was this true of Joel Elliott, the Colonel's second-in-command.

He knew the senior major nearly as well as he did his commander. Elliott was not alone Custer's second-in-command but was as well, to the scout's rueful knowledge, his chief's camp-favorite and boon buffalo-hunting companion. A man could guide out many a long column of Indian chasers without being backed by a better combination of bad-reckless commanders. True enough, there wasn't a brace of field officers on the frontier to match them for guts and go-ahead. But when a man could read military brands as certainly as Josh could, he had to know that Major Joel Elliott was as flank-marked for trouble as ever his long-haired commander.

Custer's present spirits reflected his scout's uneasy presentiments. His main column had seen no hostile sign and although its scouts, California Joe, Apache Bill, Ben Clark, Jimmy Morrison and the Mexican, "Romeo," insisted the lack of sign was "bad doin's," Yellow Hair was in his usual Indian fettle. Which would be to say, in Josh's short way, "he was ridin' high, smilin' wide, and seein' bad."

Tom Custer's report did nothing to diminish the Little General's optimism and before the cook fires had made a decent bed of coals a man could choke himself on the smoke of overconfidence fogging that Lower Spring camp.

Despite his professional misgivings, Josh was pleased enough to find his primary employer so well taken with himself. And with the auspicious outlet of his campaign to put himself and his Seventh Cavalry back on the military maps. And back, too, on the front pages of the eastern newspapers which so assiduously printed those maps when the "fiendish" quarry was dark red of skin and the "heroic" huntsman bright yellow of hair.

A man needed to catch Custer just right happen he aimed to get any special favors. The General was one who liked to keep his scouts in close where he could accompany them and better their advice with his own. Josh Kelso had no intention of being "in close" to either the column or its commander, come sundown of the following day. Whether a man really thought that plush-bodied Indian girl had double-crossed him or not, he couldn't get the powder burn of that kiss off his lips.

Come the hell or high water of Custer's disapproval or otherwise, he was going to be in that cottonwood grove at Middle Spring of the Cimarron "when the sun was low" tomorrow afternoon.

He'd get his answer out of the girl as to how Mad Wolf had found out about his visit to Black Kettle's lodge. But before he got that out of her there was something else he aimed to get. Something the thought of which put the blood thick and dark in his face.

If he never got another thing in his life, he was going to get the rest of that kiss. He was going to get it or die trying.

He was suddenly conscious of nothing but the remembered press of the Indian girl's body in the darkness of Moxtaveto's tipi. Impatiently, he sought out Custer's orderly.

The young trooper soon returned with the word that the Colonel had dined, dismissed his staff and would indeed be most pleased to see his favorite scout and fellow buffalo hunter.

Once with the ebullient officer, he eased into what he'd come for as gracefully as he could, being first forced to sit still to the rambling narrative of the buffalo seen on the way down, in particular one herd of bulls spotted in an enclosed valley just south of the Arkansas.

"By Heaven, Joshua, I had the glasses on them twenty minutes. Counted no less than fifty record heads, sir. There's plenty of grass and water in that draw and they're unquestionably there for the winter. We shall have a time of it, sir, believe me, once we've gotten this cursed Cheyenne camp cleaned out."

"Yes sir," he made deliberate use of the rare respect, "I imagine we will, sure enough. Right now, though, General, I've got somethin' else in my craw. Can't seem to get it down, neither. I'm hopin' you can help me, as usual."

"Why certainly, Joshua. You know I follow your recommendations wherever possible. What's on your mind, sir?"

"Me and the boys have been talkin'. Joe and the rest of them agrees with me that things is too quiet. But they also agrees with you that it's best for the bulk of us to stay right with you so's you can keep your personal eye on the looks of things as we move along."

He placed his little load of bushwa very carefully in the vulnerable lap of Custer's vanity. He was relieved to note the commander fold his slender hands over the neat pile with obvious relish.

"That's quite right, sir. Now come along, Joshua, what's working in that Cheyenne mind of yours?"

"I want to go on ahead, General. Tonight, I reckon. Aimin' to scout your track between here and Middle Spring. I got it in mind them Dog Soldiers me and Tom brushed with ain't so bad hurt they wouldn't think of swingin' wide and tryin' somethin' fancy at the spring."

"Good idea, Joshua." Custer surrendered to the scout's back-scratching. "Matter of fact, I was going to suggest just that. Old Hard Rope and my Osage scouts joined us yesterday so I can spare you overnight. See you're back with the column by tomorrow noon, however. And don't spend any of *my* time looking for your Cheyenne light-of-love. I'm paying you to pursue Indians, to be sure, but not amorously, sir!"

He put his peg-toothed grin behind the sly remark as Josh, rising to go, returned it with a sober nod.

"Why, I ain't thought of her since last we talked, General," he lied, straight-faced. "Leastways, not so's you could notice it."

"That's a confounded falsehood, sir. On both counts. No man could help thinking of that girl, least of all a mountain elk like you. And you needn't think I haven't noticed you doing so, sir!"

The grin was still behind the good-natured innuendo and Josh, clearly relieved, took it at face value.

The General might be a lot of things but there wasn't a small bone in his body. Nor, when it came to white man's morals, a bad one. A man knew now, if he hadn't all along, that there'd never been anything body-wise between Custer and Monaseetah. A man of his make-up might make light of many an ordinary confidence but he would never joke with another man about a woman both might have known. Apache Bill had been right. The time had come and he was remembering what the older scout had said. The General admired that Indian girl as he would a proud-fine piece of horseflesh—just that straight-out, clean-minded way, and not one damn way more.

"I allow you shot me center both rounds, General. You ain't lost your aimin' eye, by Cripes."

Turning to go, he returned Custer's friendly wave.

"See you downtrail, tomorrow, happen Mad Wolf don't see me first."

He rode only far enough out of the cavalry camp to be well clear of it for an early start in the morning. A man wanted his eyes and ears sharp for tomorrow's ride. The best way he knew to whet both was with about eight hours' good sleep. Unsaddling the gelding, he picketed him close in to the river. In a matter of seconds he was deep into the trained-soldier-sleep of the professional frontiersman. He came awake around 4:00 A.M., saddled up and moved out.

He saw nothing in that morning's wary ride, stopped to water and graze Wasiya about ten o'clock, mounted up and moved on.

It had turned off blazing hot for a November day, the way it will freakishly do in the Cimarron country, and between him and Middle Spring now, the river cover was so thin it wouldn't decently shade a short lizard. By the time he sighted the cottonwoods and willows of the spring he was sweat-hot and ready for water.

Scouting the perimeter of the grove, he rode in to find Middle Spring as inviting as ever. The gushing spring and eighty-foot pool of river water footing it could not have been better designed to strike a desert-wilted mountain man as prime fixings.

He was purposely an hour early for his "appointment" with the Cheyenne lady, aiming thus to avoid any outright traps she might have set up for him. It was clear from his preliminary scout that no such plan was in operation. The grove had been too still and peaceful to rate a second look. After enough years at it, a man developed a feel for things like that stretch of brush. The hell with it. Right now everything was sitting pretty at Middle Spring of the Cimarron, and he could tend to himself for a change.

Following a long drink from the spring, he dragged Wasiya's saddle over to a handy sunny clearing, loaded his pipe and stretched out on the short curl of the buffalo grass.

Ah, that was more like it, mister! Nothing like a stone bowl of shagcut and a twenty-minute catnap to lift a man's troubles.

Or, better yet, his scalp. . . .

13. The Holy Iron

THE FIRST HINT he had that all was not well along the Cimarron was when a chance, sleepy-eyed glance showed him Wasiya flaring his curious nostrils towards the far edge of the clearing. Six foot two of nerve-strung white scout came rolling to his feet.

It had to be Indians coming, even though he'd padded a circle around that grove as cautious as an old dog lying down in tall-grass snake country. So what the hell did a man do now? Sprint for his gun? Stand there with his arms folded, hoping they'd take him for the second coming of Anpetuwi, the Sun God? Or go diving into the nearby brush where he could get ten seconds to think?

It wasn't much of a choice. Josh dove.

123

The shade in the brush clump was as cool as the laugh which came with it.

He whirled, plastering his back to the nearest sapling, sunblinded eyes squinting to adjust the shadows. The laugh came again and with it, this time, some words in a guttural tongue he had cut his second teeth on.

If he had thought Monaseetah looked good in the prairie dark of Black Kettle's tipi or in the uncertain flicker of Custer's council fire, he had a second think coming in the cool daylight of Middle Spring grove.

She was a little thing, less than armpit high to Kelso, very light copper in color, with level eyes and that rare, mahogany-bright hair you sometimes saw in the Southern Cheyenne. Her features were as regular as a high-bred white woman's and her figure, hardly damaged by the cling of the thin elkskins, was like none you'd ever seen on a white woman, high- or low-bred. A man needn't have crawled through as many tipi flaps as he had to know those rising breasts and shifting hips under that tanned elk were as bouncy-firm and juicy as a winter apple.

"Vahe, Veho!" She repeated the snowflash of her smile, bringing his wandering gaze back to her face. "Welcome to my tipi, White Man."

Josh began to demonstrate his skull was stuffed with something sterner than the pap he'd been using for brains the past half-hour. He watched her closely, answering in Cheyenne.

"It's easy to talk pretty words. I want to know what is in your heart. Why have you come here? What do you want of Ota Kte?"

"I did not come to talk pretty," said the girl, "but only to look pretty." She stared at him full-eyed, the dazzle of her smile doing nothing to give the lie to her answer.

"Aye," he nodded, tough intentions melting under the heat of her regard, "it's a true thing. Your tongue is straight. You are very beautiful."

It was her turn to hesitate. *"He-hau,"* she smiled, demurely, "the *Veho* is pretty too. *Hoko hotao!"*

He thought this last remark over, the translation leaving him at once man-proud. To be standing in front of a beautiful young girl, no matter she was only a red Indian, and to have her running her eyes up from your toes to your scalplock and not missing anything in between, either, was addling enough. Add to that that she looked you square in the eye and told you you were a "real bull buffalo," and any man was heading himself into a stampede.

Sternly fighting down his thoughts, he put his unwilling mind once more to his present position.

"Listen, girl, I'm in a bad country here. There is much danger for me." He watched her again, hard-eyed. "Where are the Dog Soldiers, Bright Hair?"

"There is no danger for you, *Veho.*"

"You lie," he said flatly. "And keep this in your mind. If your tongue is not straight, the snout of this Holy Iron is." He patted the Henry barrel. "Where are the Dog Soldiers?"

"My tongue is straight, *Veho.* There is no danger. The Dog Soldiers are two suns east, driving the horses they stole from the soldier camp."

The fact she knew about the horse herd run-off

quickened his suspicions. *"Ame vita!"* he snapped. "That's a pile of pure fat!"

"No Ota Kte, no!" The smiles were gone. "My tongue is straight!"

"Remember, Bright Hair, the Holy Iron is watching you."

"Let him watch something else." The girl's plea came with the supple gesture, pushing the rifle bore away from her stomach. "His eye in my navel makes me nervous!"

Josh nodded, the shade of a smile chasing the frown lines for an instant. After all, maybe it made sense. She could know about the horse herd run-off. Indian news had a way of traveling faster than any white man could ride. And apparently she didn't know the herd had been recovered. That stood in her favor.

"All right, girl. Let's talk about something else. Like you and me, perhaps—"

With the words he moved toward her, his ears suddenly closed to all danger, his eyes seeing nothing but the full-bodied look of her standing there staring at him.

She stepped back, the smile playing again, her mood shifting as quickly as a prairie breeze.

"Do you swim, *Veho?* As good as a Cheyenne?"

The impish suggestion stopped the scout, catching him without an answer, making him stammer.

"I don't know. How good can a Cheyenne swim?"

"This good, *Veho!*"

Her answer was muffled by the upsweep of the elk-skin dress as it went off over her head to be carelessly flung on the grass. He gasped as the red blaze of the late

126

sun struck the girl's body.

From the high-pointing breasts to the slim insteps of the dainty feet, she stood stark, pagan naked.

He was kicking off his own moccasins then, shucking his leggins, skinning out of his shirt and diving cleanly after her into the river pool of the Cimarron. But it was no contest.

His natural elements more closely associated with the proximity of his britches to a horse's back, or his moccasins to the feel of prairie grass, Josh was not at home in the water. After a minute he gave up his losing pursuit of the Indian girl and hauled out on a midstream sandspit to watch her gleaming body knife around the shelv ing bank of the spit.

By damn, here was a woman. The man on the sandspit was beginning to know that.

Ride, shoot, build a fire. Just let a man name it, she could do it. No doubt she could bead a moccasin, gut game, mend a buckskin shirt, tan a robe, pound pemmican and boil dog too. But what the hell? Was that against her? Was it, happen a man was thinking of setting up a cow ranch right in her backyard? And thinking, too, maybe, of asking her in as a fifty-fifty partner?

Josh found himself thinking it wasn't. Doubtless all along God had cut him to size for an Indian girl. He just hadn't been brainy enough to see it. Likely they would make it down the trail pretty fair, him and Monaseetah.

Presently, the girl had had enough of the water.

Flushed and smiling she came to him, sitting cross-legged in front of him with the request he try his clumsy

127

hands at a task they must, as any proper Cheyenne husband's, become accustomed to: the care of his woman's hair.

Her simple request, along with its innocent implication of her future being accepted as that of his woman, brought a loneliness and longing into him he had never known. Such as the poignant feeling was however, he did not let it interfere with the business to hand, that of the braids.

When he had gotten them undone with a deftness which well might have led the Indian girl to wonder how much practice he had had, she shook her head to fluff the hair, speeding the process with quick, flinging motions of her hands. In a matter of seconds the bright mane shone like burnished metal against the tiger glow of her skin.

Now, when Josh would throw his lean arm behind her neck and bury his teeth playfully in the hollow of her shoulder, she wriggled free, jumping to her feet, glancing apprehensively at the angle of the sun and counseling a prompt return to shore.

He arose, taking her offered hand. Her voice came softly.

"Carry me, Ota Kte. I do not wish to wet my hair again."

Nothing loath, he picked her up, not just exactly thinking about the softness of her buttocks on his forearm, nor the firm thrust of her bare breasts against his chest, but just the same knowing he had something bet ter than just any bag of bones and hank of hair in his arms.

She for sure knew it too.

That crossing was so shallow she could have forded it on her hands and knees without wetting a braidtip!

Ashore, he put her gently down on the short pile of the buffalo grass and remained standing over her a moment, his hand still holding hers. She looked up at him, squeezing his hand, with the curving smile. He returned the little pressure, still standing awkwardly, suddenly now, and for the first time, feeling unsure of himself. Feeling shy. And clumsy. Schoolboyish, almost. And certainly, beyond any invitation of the wicked smile and gleaming body of her, very much in love.

Suddenly then, she sensed his hesitation, and guessed, instinctively, its shift of meaning. Without realizing that it had done so, she let the impulse of this swift knowledge remove the bold sensuousness from her smile, re place its wanton lure with a softer curve. A curve of quick, responsive tenderness. A curve, almost, though fleeting and quickly hidden, of haunting sadness.

It will be no different, the world over. It never has been. A maid may seek a man with every provocation of moistly beckoning lips and bold, demanding weave of wanton, soft-fleshed body. And a man may answer to that seeking with the drive of his passions hammering harshly and brutally within him. But only up to the old, old point. The oft-told, time-tried, unfailing moment. The inevitable instant. The particular, unpredictable, capricious minute of passion's progress where love, actual, awkward, of-the-spirit and wondrous "first love," steps unbidden to the fore.

It is in that little fragment of remarkable time that lust becomes worship, passion gives way to adoration, and a kiss becomes a pledge, not a demand.

Josh Kelso was knowing that moment, and knowing it with a poignant, all-pervading sense of bewilderment and heart's confusion which his simple mountain man's tongue could not, in a million years of untangling itself, have intelligently stated.

And Monaseetah was, in her own turn, feeling the first uneasy approach of a real love. Not so deeply as Josh. And not yet so completely and confusingly.

She came to her feet, the tenderness of her smile growing. She moved into him, standing on tiptoe to reach his lean cheek, kissed him lightly and quickly, and as quickly moved away. By unspoken, thoughtless consent, she retrieved her elkskin camp dress, and he his buckskin leggins.

Returning to the sand, she drew him down beside her. They talked slowly at first, and with that halting deference which comes in the wake of desire turned aside for spiritual exploration.

Even now, Monaseetah said little, but the talk, once unleashed, tumbled out of Josh like a mountain stream in full spring thaw. It was the talk of a lonely man, long without anyone who would listen, or who would care to listen. It was soon enough done with his dark and solitary past, and coming swiftly now to the Indian girl and to his suddenly born dreams for their future together. But as he would speak, at last, of his love for her, Monaseetah pressed her slim fingers to his lips, bidding him nay with the troubled shake of her small head. Her soft arms were around his neck then and he was holding her, and feeling the burn and quick run of the tears against his naked shoulder.

He stroked her hair, soothing her with tender, deep-voiced Cheyenne love-words, cradling her in his arms like a child, repeating again, and then again, his no longer awkward promises of their life to come. When she had at last stilled her sobs and lay in easy-breathing quiet within his arms, the shade of the cottonwoods had crept forward to hide their trysting place, and the sun was only an orange-pink ball tipping the western horizon.

14. Ota Kte's Trap

THEY RESTED, fully dressed now and side by side. The girl's coppery hair was outflung on the scout's buckskinned shoulder. The remaining heat of the earth came up through the muscles of their bodies, flushing them with the slow waves of long relief. Josh idly fingered the beaded waist of Monaseetah's camp frock, then let his big hand seek and find the warm pressure of her slim bronze one. He continued to stare, long and thoughtfully into the gathering gloom of Middle Spring grove.

Presently he spoke, voice soft with the hour's memory.

"I am far from my camp, Bright Hair, and the day is going. I must travel soon."

"Aye," the girl whispered, her bright smile fading

with strange swiftness, "the moon will be fat tonight. The trail will be good. I am grateful to you, Ota Kte, but you must hurry now. *While there is yet time!*"

Josh, his head full of the coming moonrise and the just-past sunset, missed the peculiar emphasis. His mind was confused now and his heart hopelessly confounded. His tongue remained obstinately mute. He thought a moment, trying to form his words so she wouldn't get any too-fast ideas on what he meant.

A man always felt different afterwards. Like maybe he'd said too much already. You had to watch these Indian women. Like you had to watch a lost dog. One pat on the head too many, and they were apt to follow a man plumb home. He wasn't in any position to be followed right now. Maybe not even of a mind to be followed, now or anytime. Damn it all, a man didn't know. He just didn't know—

"I'll remember you," he said at last and lamely, knowing that wasn't what he'd meant to say at all.

"To remember is nothing," she said quickly, downcast eyes sweeping up his buckskins to hold on the tanned granite of his face. "To forget, though, that is something."

"I won't forget you either, girl—"

He clamped the words off, not meaning to have let them out. Damn it, why couldn't a man just let it go? Just get up and out of there like he had with others like her? Or were they like her, by damn? Maybe that was the rub of it. Maybe a man had best quit horsing himself. Had best admit this little Cheyenne squaw had winged him with an arrow he'd never break off.

"Veho," her voice blocked the growing trail of his confusion, "when I came to this grove my heart was not as it now is. I had not looked upon you with my true eyes. I had not had your great hands upon me, nor your true love-words in my ear—"

Something in the way she said it took the softness of the ground from under him.

"What are you trying to say, girl? I don't like the sound of your voice now. Something is wrong."

"May Maheo forgive me," the girl muttered, "Moxtaveto and my people never will!"

"What do you mean?" He caught the sudden glance she eye-tailed around the edge of the clearing behind them. The hackles of fear rose in him now, straight as the hair on a strange dog's back.

"Lie down, Ota Kte, here by me!" She dropped back onto the grass, her whisper coming to him fiercely.

"Damn it, gal—"

"You fool, Ota Kte! Do as I say. Down here by my side, quickly!"

He dropped then and he dropped fast, his lean belly shrinking at the crowding tumble of her words.

"I have lied to you, Ota Kte, but listen that you may know my tongue was straight at last. I love you, *Veho.* As Maheo is my witness, I love you now! But it is too late. I have plotted to trap you here—"

"I knew it! By God, I knew it!" He heard his own thick whisper, shifted instantly from the hissed English to the growl of the Cheyenne. "You and what other one? Quickly now, girl!"

"Axhonehe, my promised one."

133

Mad Wolf! This beautiful girl and that filthy murderer promised to one another? Working together all along to trap him in cold blood?

"Moxtaveto knew nothing of it, I swear." Her whisper raced savagely ahead. "Oh, hear me now, Ota Kte, my true love. I would die to save you now. You who have honored me with your heart. You who have asked me to be your woman. To share your fire. To—"

"*Hekotosz!* You stinking red vixen!" The vicious curse came, breath-low. "Where are they?"

"Do not move to arise, Ota Kte!" The soft warning came with the smiling lips which reached for his neck. "They are behind you. They are just coming up through the grove. They will wait for you to see them before they move upon you. If you will play at the love-motions—pretend we are in a lovemaking—they may hesitate yet a moment more!"

Appreciative as he was of his unseen enemy's predicted forbearance, Josh had no intention of taking advantage of Mad Wolf's generosity. While awkwardly trying to comply with the girl's order to make strategic love to her, he shot an eye-tail glance over her shoulder.

Aii-eee, brother! Monaseetah's tongue was straight now!

Guiding their gaunted ponies toward the clearing's edge, and being hawk-shadow-still about it, were a baker's dozen of Cheyenne Dog Soldiers. God Amighty, here was a salty enough set of chaperons for any chief's daughter! A man could see the first twelve of the approaching hostiles qualified as such, without hardly he had to look at them. The thirteenth, without he had to look at him at all.

It was Mad Wolf!

Well, there was one way to go. A man could roll away from his make-believe embrace with the girl, taking up his rifle on the roll. Then he could snapshoot Axhonehe in the belly. That way, no matter the rest of them rode him under and got him down the next minute, he'd at least have paid off his pledge to get the murdering red son. And he'd have left Monaseetah a suitable wedding present to boot.

Half a second before he made his move, he checked himself. By God, yonder came a longshot chance! Knock-kneed, maybe, and cowhocked for sure. Arrow-scarred and splayfooted, too, and mud-yellow and raunchy as a Kansas City alleycat. But by God, a chance!

Muzzling the tender browze of the riverside grass, wandering his carefree way out of the encircling timber and along the bank of the Cimarron directly toward the waiting scout, came Wasiya.

The Dog Soldiers paid scant heed to the big pony. The dramatics of the situation were too diverting.

Vahe, Veho! By the Gods this little she-fox, this Bright Hair, this tiny squaw-to-be of Axhonehe's was a clever one. What a wonderful way to *wickmunke* a pale-faced sneak. *He-hau, he-hau!* This was one time Plenty Kills was going to give a scalp instead of taking one.

Aye, by Maheo, but hold the guns now. Don't use the Holy Irons, just the arrows. Feather him just a little, not too much. Keep the shafts low and into the legs only. Just get him down. Remember, Axhonehe has said he wants this one alive!

While the grinning Dog Soldiers hesitated, Josh didn't. His lightning roll and bent-double race for Wasiya caught them off guard. There was no time to nock an arrow, let alone draw one. The belated rage of their war cries blended with the echo of Josh's Sioux shout at the gelding. Their scrubby ponies churned the dry dirt of the clearing in the eagerness of their start after the fleeing Winter Giant.

But no sowbellied Cheyenne scrub was going to catch that big Hunkpapa pony in the first forty jumps, nor its the next eighty. Wasiya had Josh out of arrow range before the Dog Soldiers' ponies got their scrawny haunches well under them for the first leap.

Ahead of the scout, across the river, lay a hundred miles of wide open, waterless short grass. To his right up the river lay a rocky cut up-country bad for running and leading no place but right where the Cheyenne would love to have him go.

His best chance was along his own back-trail. He took it without undue debate. Swinging the gelding hard left, he sent him belly-skimming down the open bank of the Cimarron.

He didn't trouble looking back to glory over his tactical brilliance. Rifle slugs were now whistling close enough to give a man pleurisy just by the draft they set up, and if that wasn't hot pony breath blowing on his backside it would do till some came along. Mad Wolf's warriors had their ponies that close to Wasiya's rump they could have spit spang over his crupper happen the wind had been right.

In response to his rider's inspired Sioux yelling Wasiya flattened out, gradually opening the twilight between himself and the Cheyenne mounts.

Josh grinned. To be certain sure, he was a long spell from home. But the deer-fast yellow gelding had him well on the way. Failing any one of thirteen chances they'd yet get winged by a stray ounce of Indian lead, him and Wasiya had it made.

Turning to throw a final shout of derision at the pursuing Dog Soldiers, he felt the sudden, jarring wrench in the powerful withers and heard Wasiya's desperate neigh. He knew one of the reaching forefeet had found and driven through the thin crust of a prairie dog hole, and tried, too late, to throw himself clear of the falling gelding. The blinding shock of the ground came into the side of his twisting head.

After that, he knew only a long cool blackness in which there was no slightest sound, no least hint of further feeling or body motion. . . .

15. Dead Mule Mesa

WHEN HE REGAINED consciousness there was enough of the early moonlight to let him see he was still in Middle Spring grove. And to let him see a few other things.

Not ten feet from him stood Wasiya, apparently none the worse for his fall. It was the way with those cussed gopher-hole stumbles. Either a horse broke his leg or his damned neck, or he didn't get a scratch. Yonder

137

there, past the spring, Mad Wolf and his Dog Soldiers were girthing-up their mounts. Squatting guard over Yellow Hair's late favorite scout was Etapeta, Big Body, the bore of his Sharps' breechloader wandering the region of Josh's temple. Nowhere in the whole of the moonbright clearing was the least sign of Monaseetah.

Beyond these facts, he had only time to ascertain that his head felt as cracked as a yard-egg, and that he was bound hand and foot. Then Big Body was hoisting him up and dumping him across Wasiya's withers.

To this insult was added the injury of lashing his hands to his feet under the gelding's sweaty paunch, to keep him, in Big Body's touchingly solicitous words, "from falling off and hurting himself."

The head-hanging, spine-jolting start from the grove was now made. Mad Wolf and Big Body led the little column with the latter towing the unwilling Wasiya. Josh's return to consciousness lasted for perhaps half a mile before the blessed darkness once more reached up and folded him in.

When he came around for the second time it was early daylight, the Dog Soldiers having made their night camp and being now in the process of departing it. Recognizing the familiar snaggle of cottonwoods protruding through the riverbank's blistered gums, Josh was surprised to realize they were no more than ten miles past Middle Spring grove. Apparently, for a reason not clear at the moment, the Cheyenne raiders had moved on only far enough to avoid Custer's immediate advance.

Before his aching head could make anything of this the column was on the move once more. Its start brought the second surprise of the morning when Mad Wolf ordered Wasiya led up alongside his own gaudy piebald stud. There he directed Big Body to untie the scout that he might join them and "ride like a brother."

As an afterthought it was decided to bind his feet beneath the big gelding's belly, but to all outward appearances he was now a member of the expedition in good standing. Here, again, the reason for the move escaped him. But not for long. Twenty miles down the trail it became as clear as South Park sunshine.

So that was the way the march strung out: Mad Wolf with Josh and Big Body making the dust for the rest of them to eat; Black Dog, a subchief who with twenty new braves had drifted into the camp sometime during the night, along with the scowling Yellow Buffalo and the original dozen Cheyenne bucks bringing up the rear.

Josh, his head clearing and his strength returning, kept his eyes on the surrounding country and the way of the trail through it, his mind turning ceaselessly on the problem of escape. So far they were following the main track of the Camp Supply road up which Custer and his main column must soon come. Well and good. When and if a man could make his break he'd have no trouble hooking up with the troops. But Amighty God, what a country to make a break in!

The naked plains waved away in endless bulges fit to make a man seasick with their monotony. Off west the vague mountains shimmered in the uncertain sunglare. As far as a man could see or hear, it was a vast, dead, empty land, the only noises those of its present human and four-legged trespassers.

Hour after wordless hour the hostile column bore southwestward. Noon halt came and passed. Still the savage caravan jogged steadily on, the restless, constant swing of Mad Wolf's eyes telling Josh the Dog Soldier chief was looking for something.

It was perhaps 2.00 P.M. when he found it.

Suddenly the hostile leader jerked his pony's head around, spinning the wiry beast to a stop. Josh's eyes were only a flick behind the chief's in spying the cause of the halt. The six black dots floating in the sunbake ahead steadied down and stopped swimming, then came sharply into focus.

Men. Mounted men. Four of them Indians and mule-mounted. The other two, white men and horse-mounted.

Across the prairie now, he saw the six dots pull into one. He knew from that, and was glad that his white brothers and their red companions had spotted the Cheyenne. If it was going to be a fight it would least-ways be one, and not a dry-gulch slaughter.

And a fight it was, or in any event Mad Wolf made it look like one.

"Let's go, cousin." Big Body's purring voice reminded him with a shove of the Sharps' muzzle. "I don't want to miss this. I want to see it. And Axhonehe wants it to see you!"

The scout missed neither the leer nor the words it underlined. He had no time, nonetheless, to ponder their meaning.

From the way the four mules of the trapped men lay, their heads outflung at grotesque angles, he knew their riders had forted up by cutting the throats of the animals. The surviving two horses were down with the men behind the dead mules.

"Hold yer fire now, Bill. Easy, old salt. Leave the Osages shoot fust."

The white voice carried clearly past the sandhill behind which the Dog Soldiers had taken cover. Josh's recognition of it was no quicker than Mad Wolf's.

"Yellow Hair's scout, Yellow Hair's Big Scout!"

The Cheyenne chief's snarl and the gloat of triumph in it was instantly seconded by Yellow Buffalo's nod, as the voice of the second white man was heard answering the first.

"I gotchy, Joe. Hold yer boys down, Hard Rope. Wait till the black-feather jaspers get in good and close now."

"*He-hau!* You hear that other one there?" Yellow Buffalo's grin spread itself another six teeth. "Him Yellow Hair scout, too. Him damn Apache Bill, you hear?"

The scout's belly pulled in. Yonder past the hill were California Joe and Apache Bill. With old Hard Rope and three of his Osage scouts. Out looking for him, Josh Kelso. Just exactly as Mad Wolf had figured them to be.

Too late, he saw the full depth of the Dog Soldier's cunning. It wasn't just as simple as trapping him in that grove back yonder. That was only part of it. If Mad Wolf had used Monaseetah to bait him, he was now using him to bait his fellow scouts. To draw them out and away from Custer's column. To cut them off, trap

141

them, kill them. To put out Yellow Hair's eyes and stop his ears before ever the Camp Supply column got halfway to the Washita!

But if Josh thought he had guessed the entire scope of Mad Wolf's crazy planning, he had a second guess coming.

Dismounting, each of the Dog Soldiers now took a short horsehair rope from behind his saddle, braiding it hurriedly into the tangled mane of his nervous mount. These ropes, about six feet long and looped on the free end, were new to him. He watched their adjustment with professional interest.

With the ropes in place, Mad Wolf instructed Big Body to expose himself on the hilltop with the hapless Kelso. He added that should Ota Kte feel called upon to so much as open his mouth or lift a hand in reply to his fellow scouts' recognition he was to be shot through the kidneys.

With that, Mad Wolf got down to business. He paused only long enough to make sure his guest fully appreciated the situation.

He-hau, was it clear now? They were going to kill all those scouts over there except one of the Osages. He would be left to carry the news to Yellow Hair that Plenty Kills was riding like a brother, and of his own free will, with the South Arkansas Dog Soldiers.

"Vahe, Veho!" He concluded the address with a friendly wave. "Welcome to our lodges, White Brother!"

With that and with nothing else save their rusty trade muskets, looped horsehair ropes and thirty-one bellies full of rash, red guts, the Dog Soldiers followed their slit-eyed chief down upon the waiting army scouts.

Josh had only time to hear Apache Bill's shout of recognition as the latter saw him top the hill with Big Body. Helpless to return the call, he could only improve this moment by adding to his Indian education the adept use of the Dog Soldier "war rope."

Coming in rifle range of Custer's scouts each of the hostile riders kicked one foot through the looped end of his horsehair thong, hooked the heel of his other foot across his mount's whipping spine and threw his body behind that of his pony. The maneuver left the desperate army scouts nothing to shoot at but crazily galloping horseflesh.

And horseflesh does not go down so easily.

The trapped scouts' six shots disappeared into the closing savages without visible result. The garishly painted ponies thundered straight in. Thirty yards from the slaughtered mules it looked as though Maheo, God himself, could not have stopped the Dog Soldier ponies.

But Maheo doesn't smell like a dead mule.

Where the Cheyenne Almighty might have found himself hamstrung, a few quarts of mules' blood moved with startling effect. Twenty yards from the dead animals the leading ponies broke and split around the mule fort, the hated smell of the mule blood sending them into a frenzy of bucking and pitching.

Mad Wolf was bright enough to feel the jab of the lancehaft of hard luck when it had been shoved into him and broken off. Before the army scouts could get in their second shots he drove his scattered warriors back under the cover of Kelso's hill. They had indeed shot down both of the white men's horses, but it was not enough. The state of affairs clearly called for a council of war.

Black Dog, a medicine man of reputation, urged an immediate return to the attack, quoting a vision he had ust received from the holy navel of Maheo. Mad Wolf, a saner military mind and an agnostic of long standing, briefly instructed him to take his vision and replace it in God's bellybutton.

Oxahos! Dry pony dung! It was no time for prophecies.

Still, because of the fanatical Dog Soldier hatred of all whites and because of the latent prestige in lifting the hair of California Joe, Yellow Hair's official Chief of Scouts, Mad Wolf yielded to the insistence of his followers, agreeing to wait until darkness might make a sneak-in possible.

Yellow Buffalo at once protested that nighttime knew no color, that it would hide a white man as well as it would a red. "We wait, they get away," he complained bitterly, again using the broken English of which he was so proud. "Goddam now, you see!"

But the other braves had had enough of the white scouts' daylight marksmanship. *Oxahos!* They were just lucky somebody hadn't been killed as it was. Four ponies had been hit and Gray Bird's mare would never travel again. Hawk Man had a bullet crease across his skull you could see the bone through and Little Elk was sitting there with a hole in his rumpcheek big enough to stick your thumb in. *Nohetto!* Enough was enough.

The decision to wait for a cover of darkness stood.

Through the intolerable hours of sunblaze and fly-biting, the Dog Soldiers squatted on their side of the hill, the trapped scouts suffered on theirs. There was no shade in either camp, and no water. When night came at last, the hostile chief and his fellows moved around the hill and carefully toward the now invisible mule fort.

Halfway there, they crouched in the darkness, gathering themselves for the charge, sharp ears tuned to the location of the dead mules. It was well to take a last-minute pause, making sure their approach was so far undetected. Those cursed white scouts out there were not the ones you came up on with impunity—even in the dark!

Josh, his ears tuned as strainingly as the Cheyennes', at once wondered if the silence out by the dead-mule fort wasn't unnaturally heavy.

Apparently it was. Yellow Buffalo came to his feet.

"*Eoxeoz,* it stinks. Too quiet out there. Him damn Apache Bill gone. Him only wait for darkness too. Him smart. Yellow Buffalo told you. You go, we see." His angry growl, going to Mad Wolf, was answered in kind.

"*He-hau,* I think Heovhotoa says a true thing. Let's go and see."

And go and see they promptly did, Josh and Big Body along with them. California Joe and Apache Bill, along with Hard Rope and the Osages, were clean gone. And gone, clean. They had taken nothing with them save their guns. The Dog Soldiers had waited five minutes too long. Yellow Buffalo stood vindicated. The night, indeed, knew no color.

Pursuit short of daylight was questionable and Mad Wolf would have none of it in any event.

"There is no time," he grunted in response to Black Dog's demand that at least some of them follow the escaped scouts. "Yellow Hair is too close and the plan is even better this way. Yellow Hair might not have believed the Osage that Plenty Kills rides with us like a brother, but his ears will be open to the white scouts. Mad Wolf goes now."

Shortly, their ponies sagging under the added carry of the scouts' fine saddles and rich food packs, the impatient band was pounding for the main Dog Soldier camp at Willow Bar twenty miles up the Cimarron.

Mad Wolf, with Josh and Big Body back in their places at his side, held a hard pace; 10.00 P.M. and the full light of the rising moon found them topping out on the broad granite swell overlooking Willow Bar. The Dog Soldier chief had ample cause for his grunt of satisfaction. It had been a fine day. *Nataemhon,* good hunting indeed. The very best in a long time.

16. *Axhonehe's Hospitality*

IT WAS A BIG CAMP, the shadowy flood of the moonlight letting Josh count no less than two hundred and fifty lodges strung like dirty, cowskin pearls along the silvered rope of the Cimarron.

The hair-raising buffalo wolf howls by which, after the time honored custom of the Cut-Arm People, Mad Wolf announced his arrival on the long granite ridge overlooking Willow Bar had the big camp crawling with three-feather Cheyenne bucks in less time than it took the returning Dog Soldiers to slide their weary mounts from the ridge to the level of the river.

Even as the scout was making terse mental note of the comparative scarcity of squaws and young children among the gathering hundreds of Axhonehe's followers, Mad Wolf was speaking.

The ensuing remarkable account of the dead-mule fiasco struck Josh as a work of pure Indian genius. His deep voice barking angrily the lean chief strutted for his faithful, the weird shift of the victory fires serving to limn the drama of his exultant posings in a manner which had even the white scout's hardened jaw dropping.

". . . *Eahata!* Listen to this! With my trap I caught Yellow Hair's scouts in the open, even as I planned. Killing them would have been like stoning rabbits. But the cursed blood of their mules made our ponies wild. Faster than Maheo's lightning then, a new plan came to Mad Wolf. Let them all go. Let them all tell Yellow Hair they had seen Ota Kte among us. Riding right with us. Watching us attack his white brothers. Not answering a word when they called out to him.

"In this way will begin our vengeance on Plenty Kills, making all his white brothers remember him as a traitor to his own people. And in *this* way will it end—"

The dark-skinned chief paused, eyes sweeping the spell-bound ranks of his followers.

"I have given my sacred pledge to kill Ota Kte for

147

you. I will do it, my brothers. I will *burn* him.

"When I am the true chief of all the Cheyennes, I will do this. When Moxtaveto is destroyed by Yellow Hair and when we have killed all the Pony Soldiers, then I will burn Ota Kte.

"And so we shall have our war. We shall have it until the last white man is driven from our lands. Mad Wolf has spoken. May Maheo bear me witness. *Remember my words* . . ."

As Axhonehe concluded his snarling diatribe, Josh grimaced bitterly.

Remember his words? How in God's name could a white man ever forget them?

There it was now, his whole rotten-bellied scheme. Right out in the open at last. Let Custer knock off Moxtaveto and his peaceful Cheyennes. Let Axhonehe and the Dog Soldiers seize power over what was left, guaranteeing to keep the war going so long as there was no bad-medicine buck to follow the Dog Soldier flag.

Never mind, now, the fact he meant to put Josh Kelso under along with old Black Kettle.

Never mind his Indian-crazy plan to make Custer think his pet scout had turned Cheyenne.

Now more than ever, the big thing was to break loose and get to the General. Happen a man could get away, knowing what he now knew—could get to Custer before it was too late to stop his slaughter of Black Kettle's guiltless tribesmen—could convince the General as he now felt he could that the Dog Soldiers were the whole culprit—could bring the full force of the Seventh Cavalry down on these murdering outlaws instead of on Black Kettle's good Indians—could somehow—

The big scout's racing thoughts were broken off bluntly.

Having built his bonfire, Mad Wolf was giving over its blazing stage to Black Dog and his howling braves. He himself was retiring in slit-eyed triumph to the sanctuary of his lodge, there to seek food and such other comforts as his present three wives might see fit to provide for the next tribal chief of the Southern Cheyenne Nation.

In this latter pursuit he insisted on the unhappy company of his "guest."

Preceded by Yellow Buffalo and dogged by his constant shadow, the hulking Big Body, the puzzled scout followed Mad Wolf into his tipi. Big Body remained outside to, in his own loosely grinned words, "Look at the moon a while yet—"

Ducking through the entrance flap, Josh gasped. The kingly aura of Mad Wolf's lodge was overpoweringly beyond description.

About all a man could do was say that if you took a dozen green buffalo hides, buried them in sick-pony dung till spring, dug them up and sewed them into a twelve-foot cone, then let four or five unwashed savages live and cook and breed and belch and break wind inside for six months, you might begin to get a whiff of the idea of Axhonehe's home.

If the Dog Soldier chief's abode was a cesspool of stinks, his habits and morals fitted the incredible smell ounce for foul ounce. He and his chief hireling, Yellow Buffalo, sat to the iron pot of boiled dog contributing a running fire of double-ended flatulence as their main social effort, letting the solicitous squaws tend the selection of a flow of choice dog cuts for their mighty menfolk.

Josh, never having acquired the taste for fricassee of man's best friend enjoyed by the majority of white mountain men, tactfully refused the readily identifiable puppy's head offered him on the point of a Green River knife by one of Mad Wolf's squaws. Instead, he sat back in the shadows of the sideskins, chewing a shag of dried buffalo beef and letting his weary mind hammer at the dimming hopes of his sole remaining aim—escape to Custer.

An interminable half-hour later, Mad Wolf stood up to announce that all would forthwith retire.

"I am sleepy," he grunted. "We will all of us sleep now."

With the words and with that peculiarly Indian quirk of courtesy which demands equal treatment for the doomed captive of unquestioned bravery in war, he waved graciously toward Josh, indicating to him the third squaw, a rotten-toothed harridan who was clearly verminous if not downright venereal.

"You sleep with Little Fawn, Ota Kte. She is good. Old. Knows everything."

The grinning squaw started toward him as he found his feet.

"No! Ota Kte says No!" he blurted awkwardly, seeing Mad Wolf's face go blacker than a strangled Ute's with the blunt refusal.

"*Oxahos!* Pony dung! Ota Kte dares to say No to my

woman?" The Dog Soldier chief was on his feet, staring challengingly across the cooking pot. "How does he say it then? How does he mean it?" The delicate balance of the question teetered on his slow reach for his handsomely engraved rifle.

"Aii-eee!" disclaimed Josh hastily. "The woman is all you say. More, much more. Fragrant as first mare's milk. A real fawn. But curse the luck, it is a devil's fate. I cannot sleep with any woman just now!"

He shrugged, feigning an embarrassment that was false only in its claimed origin.

"I am sick, *here.*" With the eloquent gesture, he pointed the source of his hurriedly invented contagion.

"Mavetoxz!" exclaimed Mad Wolf, patently pleased with the depth and sensitivity of his social perception. "As you say, it is a devil's fate. You will excuse us then?"

Josh's agitated agreement ended the whole matter. Mad Wolf grunted a sober acknowledgement of his white guest's thoughtfulness and summarily dismissed the no longer required Little Fawn. With the squaw's departure, he and the impatient Yellow Buffalo at once joined ardent forces and turned their delayed attentions to the remaining squaws. This action shortly put the nervous white scout as far from the four red minds as the distant craters of the moon.

Josh's hopes, burning almost out but a moment before, flared quickly. By Cripes, maybe this was it! Maybe, hell. It *was* it. A man could sense that now. This was the time, the place, the prayed-for moment.

The excitement of it put every last nerve in his body

on vibrating edge. His slant glance whipped toward the slightly parted tipi flaps. One look was enough. The way was clear in that direction!

Easing along the sideskins as slowly as a sun shadow at high noon, the big scout inched toward the entrance. Belly-flat and breath-held, he made the last three feet unnoticed, thankfully poked his pale face into the clean, free air beyond the flaps.

To the east the stars were fading in the milky haze of pre-dawn. The light was not yet strong enough to carry a man's eyes much past the end of his anxious nose. But there was enough of it to show him that short as the remaining darkness might be, he was going to spend it right where he was.

Just beyond the parted flaps, his gross body hunched against the morning chill, squatted the lump-still Etapeta.

"*Pave vona,* good morning, cousin," grinned Big Body. And viciously drove the iron-heeled butt of his buffalo rifle full into the white scout's peering face.

17. March of the Dog Soldiers

"NASEHAOHO!"

Big Body illustrated the order to arise with a shove of his Sharps' barrel. Josh, mind groping once more toward consciousness, stumbled uncertainly to his feet.

As the full light of the morning sun struck his eyes, he raised his hand to shade them. The slight touch of the hand brushing the battered face brought a wince of quick pain and a sudden flash of returning memory.

Behind him the sideskins of Mad Wolf's lodge were being rolled off the rib poles by two of the chief's squaws, the third stacking them into the travois behind a droop-headed pack pony. All over camp the process was being repeated. The Dog Soldier camp was on the move again.

Down on the bank of the Cimarron, athwart the willow-bristling sandbar which gave the place its trail name, Mad Wolf was haranguing a gathering of the braves.

Evidently the dark-skinned chief and the main village were going to part company. Mad Wolf and a party of picked braves were to continue under forced march up the Cimarron and across to the Canadian for the Washita, and the village was to move by regular stages for the same objective. The primary object of Axhonehe's detour was to combine business with pleasure by horse-raiding along the lower Santa Fe Trail. Fresh mounts were badly needed for the coming clash with Custer and the raiding band might, with luck, encounter an out-of-season herd being driven up from Mexico.

No sooner had the Dog Soldier chief announced how it would be than he began telling off those who would accompany him. As each name was called, the brave would step forward, strike his breast proudly with the flat of his right hand and growl deeply. "I hear my name. *Vahe,* let's go to fight!"

When Mad Wolf had called his last man, the remainder put up a rolling mutter. *Eoxeoz!* No good. It stank. When a Plains Indian had earned himself coup ratings of half a dozen eagle feathers he clearly didn't care for being left behind among the old men and boys. Their leader put down this grumbling quickly enough.

"*Hekotosz!* Be quiet, all of you! There will be fighting enough for all when we join our Arapaho brothers in that *wickmunke* for Yellow Hair. Do you hear me now?"

It was the first time Josh had heard that the Dog Soldiers had a definite trap worked out for Custer, let alone the fact the Arapaho were in it with them.

"*Hau! Hau!* We hear you. We all hear Axhonehe!" The warriors' deep answers rode in over his thoughts.

Mad Wolf turned and stalked haughtily toward his war pony. Josh nodded and wheeled to follow him. Here was something a man in his moccasins could afford to remember. Happen there was any outside chance still left of his getting away, he would do well to smell out the details of that trap before leaving. That kind of information would go a long way toward convincing the General his boy Joshua hadn't wasted his time among his self-appointed "Cheyenne brothers." And happen Joe and Bill had pushed it to him about seeing him with the Dog Soldiers, the General was apt to take just about all the convincing a man could conveniently hand him.

Swinging up on Wasiya to follow the horse-raiders out of camp, the big scout nodded once more. The track was getting hot and the time, short. And Custer was halfway to Camp Supply!

Mad Wolf made his noon halt at Battle Ground Bend of the Cimarron.

The hostiles took no food on their noon halts, only

stopping because a horse is no Dog Soldier and needs to breathe once in a while. Twenty minutes and they were on their way again, holding the ponies to a jingling walk against the unseasonable blast of the dropping sun. Two hours and ten miles later they hit Upper Cimarron Springs, the last wagoncamp on the Camp Supply road.

With darkness and the ponies rested, the red horsemen took the trail again. They still followed the regular military route, going the five miles up the Cimarron to Cold Spring and leaving the river there to head southwest into the second desert crossing and the thirty dry miles to the North Fork of the Rabbit Ear River. When they forded the North Fork at midnight Josh would have sworn half the mounts in the caravan were three hobbles from going down. Yet with barely a ten-minute pause to blow and water they hit the trail again, holding a rolling canter until dawn and four-thirty found them another twenty miles south and just entering into the main track of the Santa Fe wagon route.

Here the first real hills encountered since leaving the Cimarron thrust their brown backs up out of the naked desert. Striking a winding stream within the first range, the Dog Soldiers swung down off their staggering mounts and called a halt. Every warrior in the group, save one, was asleep in five minutes.

For all his weariness, Josh fought against joining them. But presently, seeing that Etapeta remained as awake and watchful as himself, he shrugged and gave in. The hell with it. He wasn't going to try any more early-morning sneaks on that big buzzard. About one more working-over with that Sharps' butt and a man wouldn't know himself in the mirror. He was asleep almost before the thought faded.

Two hours later, with the seven o'clock sun bouncing off the tops of the Rabbit Ear Mounds, the trail name of the hills in which they had made their dawn halt, the Dog Soldiers were off again. And an hour after that, they found what they had apparently been looking for—their field commissary!

Josh allowed that Cibolero buffalo camp was something. Swarming with coffee-colored women and soot-eyed youngsters, squealing Mexican curs and wandering, gaunt-flanked oxen, the whole disorderly sprawl seemed strung together with endless ropes of drying buffalo beef.

From what Big Body had grudgingly to say while he and his captive charge joined their comrades in stuffing themselves with Cibolero beef and bread, these happy nomads were the Mexican version of the white market hunter. Their full lives were spent roaming the Canadian River uplands in their wood-wheeled oxcarts, killing and jerking buffalo beef for the trade in Santa Fe and Taos. They were the friends, perforce, of the red and white wanderer alike, this popularity bought and paid for by their willing offer of fresh bread and meat. The bread was brown as beanmeal, hard as bedrock, tasteless as trail dust. But it was bread, and to white travelers weeks without anything but fatback and cornmeal it was hardly less welcome than to the gluttonous Cheyenne.

As a Texas border boy Josh had of course heard of the fabled Ciboleros. Nevertheless, he sat quietly to Big Body's growling discourse on their manners and habits, hoping that by giving the subchief enough lingual rope he might get him to hang himself with some kind of *real* information.

When Mad Wolf's band had eaten to the point where a dozen of them had had to walk out of the feeding circle and vomit, the Dog Soldiers got up off their haunches and caught up their ponies. Bidding the Ciboleros a belching farewell, they pounded hell-bent for the next stop.

This proved to be at five that afternoon when Black Dog, riding back from scouting ahead, reported the end of their search. Six white men with a herd of five hundred horses were coming north along the Trail.

How were the horses? *Vahe!* Real good. Spanish, they looked to be. Coming up from Chihuahua for trading in the eastern settlement. *He-hau!* They were top horses, no doubt of that. Just the thing they were looking for to mount the jaws of their *wickmunke* for Yellow Hair. Just what they needed now that their own ponies were winter-thinning.

Josh's alert mind pounced on the remark. But his easy query, going at once to Big Body, was as casual as a man excusing himself to make water.

"If your friends could open a trap as easily as they do their big mouths, brother, old Yellow Hair would be a dead soldier right now—"

"He *is* a dead soldier, cousin!" The vacuous Big Body snatched greedily at the carelessly flung bait. "And the

157

mouths of our traps have big teeth. *Aii-eee,* cousin, and lots of them. Three thousand, maybe more. Do you hear?"

"Oh, sure, I hear your big mouth."

The studied insult brought the giant Dog Soldier's pony shouldering into Wasiya.

"Listen, *Veho,* you know that big bend of the Ouachita? And how Moxtaveto's camp sits on this side of it?"

"Of course," Josh lied evenly. "What fool wouldn't."

"Well, do you know what will be around that bend when Yellow Hair rides into Moxtaveto's tipis? Right around on the other side, hidden by that big hill where Yellow Hair will never think to expect it? Aha! You guessed it, cousin. The whole of Little Raven's Arapaho, better than *two thousand* of them. And all the Dog Soldier Lodge, too, even some Northerns who have come down to help out. You hear, cousin? More than one thousand of us, every one wearing the three black feathers."

The big brave paused triumphantly, his slab face leering into Josh's.

"Now how does that strike you, Ota Kte? Let's hear how big *your* mouth is now, cousin. I'm listening!"

Josh's reply was cut off by Mad Wolf's orders for the approaching horse herd. But even as he watched the Dog Soldiers ready their ambush his mind was detailing the full import of Big Body's revelations. The end-product of that detailing was blank-wall certain. If Custer wasn't warned in time, he was just what Etapeta had labeled him. *A dead soldier.*

Axhonehe's pack, ambushed in waiting, rushed the white caravan the instant it showed around the trail-bend. Five minutes after the shooting broke out the entire herd of five hundred horses had been swept away. Not a shot was fired by the white herders in defense of their property; a piece of discretion which beyond certain question accounted for the fact they reached Custer's column to report their loss.

The Dog Soldiers drove their stolen herd ten miles down the Santa Fe Trail, intercepting the North Fork of the Canadian River shortly before sundown. Here they halted, watered the ungainly herd and split up.

Mad Wolf, with Josh and Big Body and six chosen braves, picked fresh horses from the Spanish herd and pushed on at once. Their course, as nearly as the captive scout could determine from the set of the early stars, was almost due east, swinging south of the Canadian and straight out toward the waterless panhandle of his native borderland.

Noting the direction, the weary scout nodded grimly.

The time for questions was done. The red die was cast and the compass point of its casting could be told by the way the North Star was falling away behind a man's left shoulder. The way those ponies were pushing they would raise the headlands of the Dry Fork of the Washita with first light—the southern flank of the Antelope Hills by dusk—the Big Bend of the Main Washita by midnight. It was journey's end for Joshua Kelso.

Mad Wolf was going home.

18. Moxtaveto's Mettle

SOME TIME BEFORE midnight of the nineteenth, Mad Wolf's advance party struck the main Washita thirty miles west of that stream's entrance into the Antelope Hills.

Josh was, as always, amazed at the homing instincts of the nomad raiders. They had traveled thirty-six straight hours across a land as featureless as a brown-grass billiard table. Unguided save by a handful of prairie stars and the wide swing of the Arkansas sun, they had nonetheless come in off the trackless short grass within one mile of their first landmark and a half-hour of their final objective.

A short while later, moving eastward down the widening valley of the Washita, they struck the first group of lodges. There were no more than sixty of these, their distinctively symboled sideskins designating them as Cheyenne. Josh, on the point of dismissing them as the guard camp for the immense pony herd through which they had ridden the past ten minutes, took sudden note of the big black lodge centering the group. He'd seen that set of skins before, and not long before. It was Black Kettle's.

Mad Wolf halted his lathered command in front of the chief's abode, the yapping of the half-dozen camp curs worrying at the ponies' heels announcing his arrival. A handful of sleepy-eyed squaws answered the canine summons but there was no sign of the tribal headman.

Mad Wolf upended his carbine and levered four shots,

160

the Cheyenne Good-Medicine Number, over the ridge-poles of Moxtaveto's tipi. His boastful challenge rode in over the impromptu fusillade.

"Ho, you, Moxtaveto! Come out now. See what Axhonehe has brought you. The war is on, old man, and we have counted the first coup!"

For Mad Wolf, Josh reckoned the greeting was one of rare good humor. He awaited Black Kettle's response to it with considerable interest.

The response came neither in good humor, nor did it come from Black Kettle. It came instead from Antelope Woman, the old headman's elder squaw and one Cheyenne, quite clearly, who feared neither the devil nor his Dog Soldier advocate.

"May Maheo curse you, Axhonehe!" Her dour greeting preceded the emergence of her craggy features through the parting entrance flaps. "Take your stinking soldier dogs and be off! You know as well as you sit grinning there on that runted stallion that Moxtaveto is not in his lodge."

Mad Wolf refused to depart from either his good humor or his present position. Sensing something peculiar about any mood but his normal bad one, Josh watched the Dog Soldier closely.

"Come now, woman, don't tell us the mighty Moxtaveto is not at home? Don't tell us he isn't in the camp of his people when the enemy threatens!"

"He is where you sent him, you skinny whelp of misfortune. Out counseling the Kiowas and Comanches to return. Out bringing them back from where your scouts chased them with their big lies about Yellow Hair

161

coming to destroy us. Ride along, mad dog. You will
see their empty lodges down the river there. You will
see how well your lies have worked. Be gone. May
Maheo spit in your eye when your hour comes to face
him!"

With the curse the Indian woman wrenched the tipi
flaps closed and disappeared. For the first and only time
in Josh's memory, Mad Wolf laughed. With the laugh
he turned triumphantly to Big Body.

"You see, Etapeta? You see what a brain your chief
has, brother?"

"Aye, it worked." Big Body added his thick-lipped
grin to his leader's. "I never thought it would. Those
scouts you sent ahead to spread the fear were a good
idea."

"Ten Bears and Lone Wolf are afraid of war. I want
no Indians who are dreaming of peace in this camp
when Yellow Hair comes. Just old Moxtaveto, that's
all."

Josh whistled silently.

This damn Axhonehe was crazy like a coyote. Ten
Bears was the top-dog Comanche chief. Lone Wolf was
second only to Satanta among the Kiowas. To have
gotten them both out of the way to soften old Black
Kettle up for Custer was a stroke of pure-red military
genius.

"Now listen in there, old woman!" Mad Wolf's inter-
rupting shout was sent to the silent lodge. "When Moxtaveto comes in you tell him I have captured Ota Kte.
You hear that, woman? Old Plenty Kills himself! Tell
him I am going to burn him for our people. Like I

promised in my pledge to the Lodge. You hear me?"

There was no answer from the lodge and the Dog Soldier, his short string of humor exhausted, wheeled his pony.

"She heard me all right. Let's go. I'm thinking now it may be well to burn this white dog *before* the old man gets back."

"Aye, then the old devil can't stop us." Big Body's agreement was instant. "But all the same I'd rather work on him with this skull club. Of course I mean after you've taken his hair."

"Be still, you fool. Come on, let's go."

With the order Mad Wolf put heels to his mount, his braves racing to follow him. Big Body grinned and turned to Josh.

"Well, come along, cousin. When the next War Chief of the Cheyenne says something, it's best to listen." With the advice, he slashed Josh's mount across the rump with the butt-swung barrel of his rifle, jumping the nervous beast into a wild gallop.

"*Hii-yee-hahh!*" The red giant's thundering shout was abetted by the simultaneous discharge of his rifle toward the listening stars.

"Let's go, cousin. Let's go to war!"

The approach of Mad Wolf's returning raiders had the Cheyenne main camp in an uproar minutes after they rode in sight of Black Kettle's lodge. Josh was unceremoniously dumped into the noisome shelter of the tipi of Stone Calf, Black Kettle's deputy chief. There he was left to ruminate on the little pleasures inherent in an

163

army scout's life in Indian Territory.

Meanwhile, a booming council fire was lit just outside the tipi's parted flaps and the name chiefs of the sprawling camp got down to serious discussion. With no other heritage available Josh perforce fell disgruntled heir to the sum and substance of that discussion.

Its offhand bequeathal shortly lifted his ears very nearly clear of his aching head.

In ten minutes he had as unpretty a picture of Dog Soldier dirt as the intriguing hand of Mad Wolf could paint. Translating the grunts and handsigns of the consulting Indian a man got the unhappy impression that the string of his future was shorter than a bitten-off bear's tail. And that Colonel George Armstrong Custer's number wasn't anyplace but way up.

In the first place, with his trusting tribal chief well out of earshot, Stone Calf was wavering toward the cause of the Dog Soldiers. Josh had always figured Black Kettle's second-in-command for a bad Indian, a judgment now born precisely out. In the second place Little Raven, the number-one Arapaho, was clearly with the Dog Soldiers, confirming Big Body's earlier boast. In the third and unpleasantly final place, while there was still some little argument as to the wisdom of attempting to trap the justly feared Yellow Hair, there was none at all relating to the deserving justice of an immediate end to Ota Kte. His past crimes against the people were a total indictment. The slip-eyed jury presently hearing his poor case was bound to come in with Axhonehe's requested verdict: guilty of Indian murder in the first degree.

The sentence would be automatic—death at the burning pole.

There were some other minor informations disclosed to the sweating scout. Chief among these was one relating to a Cheyenne he had sudden cause to recall; Monaseetah, his one-time lady love.

The girl, whose absence he had not had time to remark, was away from the camp traveling with Black Kettle. Following her return and Mad Wolf's seizure of power, and of course the sometime-in-between burning of Plenty Kills, the nuptials of the Cheyenne princess and the Dog Soldier heir presumptive would be duly celebrated.

The idea proved at once attractive to the attending chiefs. It would weld the erstwhile peaceful faction of the tribe to the hostile element. It would strengthen the entire Nation for its coming Holy War with the Pony Soldiers.

For the hundredth time since his caputre, Josh tested his bonds. For the hundredth time he cursed them and subsided. When these South Plains butchers trussed up a bird they didn't short any corners. A man couldn't have gotten out of that spider net of braided horsehair picket ropes with one hand free and a four-foot cavalry saber in his hip pocket.

For perhaps the first time in his life he turned his reddened eyes skyward. He stared long and thoughtfully through the open smokehole of Stone Calf's lodge. Presently he had himself a few well-chosen, soundless words with the white man's Maheo. Nothing like the heat of a hostile council fire and the upcoming stench of singed scout-meat to make a settlement Christian out of a South Park heathen.

Happen God Almighty didn't soon call for a hand in the deal, Josh Kelso was cashed in.

The following morning, even while the red-painted, twelve-foot length of the cottonwood burning pole was being planted beside the Washita, Josh got a last-minute reprieve.

It came in the angry person of old Black Kettle jogging his lathered pony into the midst of the preparing festivities shortly after sunrise. The appearance of the aging chief created a furor well calculated to test the mettle of any savage commander.

The quiet-faced Cheyenne had no base iron in the veining of his character. He was old and the once total grip on the loyalties of his guileless followers was slipping with every mile Custer's column put beneath the advancing feet of the Seventh's horses. But he was still the headchief of all the Southern Cheyenne.

He now put the cold steel of that prestige squarely up to the infuriated Mad Wolf.

The Dog Soldier demonstrated his own dangerous alloy by cannily refusing the showdown. It was too soon. Everything was coming his way. There was a good seven suns yet before Yellow Hair could be expected to reach the Washita. The Pony Soldier chief had not yet reached Camp Supply. There was time, lots of it.

With a flowery covering speech about his sacred vow to kill Kelso, and about his thoughtlessness in not

166

awaiting Moxtaveto's blessing on its termination, Mad Wolf made his temporary peace.

As Josh wondered at this change in tactics, the reasons for it came riding up the Washita from the direction of the recently deserted Kiowa and Comanche lodges. The moment he recognized old Ten Bears and the furtive-eyed Lone Wolf he had his answer. The Kiowa and Comanche warrior strength was back in camp and with it the precarious balance of power had teetered back to the old Cheyenne.

Even so, with Indians, where a face has been lost, part of it at least must be restored.

Mad Wolf pressed his advantage to wring from a clearly unwilling Black Kettle his blessings on the mating of his beautiful niece and the plotting Dog Soldier.

Black Kettle wasn't through bargaining. In return for this concession he demanded and got the replacement of Stone Calf with Magpie, a lifelong friend, as deputy chief, and the immediate release to him of the captive scout Ota Kte.

There was a wave of angry growls at this latter insistence but the old chief made it stick, covering it by playing his trump card.

"Listen, my people—" the old Cheyenne's voice quieted the muttering ranks of his followers, "I have returned with hopeful news. Ten Bears says that at Fort Cobb there is a new Peace Mission. He says that Colonel Hazen, the soldier chief there, has orders to give sanctuary to all peaceful Indians, and much money to buy us food."

The silver-haired old man paused, weathered hands sweeping eloquent accent to his plea.

"Do not take the war trail, my people. Wait for me to return. I go now to treat with the soldier chief at Fort Cobb. He will let us come in. We will go there and be safe. Only those whose hearts are big for war will stay and seek out Yellow Hair.

"I will return and you will know whose tongue is straight. I ask you to wait for me."

Black Kettle's speech had a marked effect on the main body of the Cheyenne. The whole camp fell into an uneasy quiet to await his return from Fort Cobb.

The news of Colonel Hazen's orders to provide sanctuary against the approaching threat of Custer's campaign of extermination cut the ground from under the exhortations of the war leaders.

He-hau, it was no time for fighting. The ponies were already thin and the snows would come any day now. *Vahe,* let there be peace. Let Moxtaveto return from Fort Cobb and lead them into its protection. Hazen Chief had a good heart, everybody knew that. The words of the old chief were always best. Wait for Moxtaveto. *Nohetto,* let that be the end to it!

Thinking swiftly, Josh still couldn't untangle the hopeful surprise of the Hazen mission. He was as set back as any of the Cheyenne to hear of the unprecedented "sanctuary order." Not that it wasn't a hell of an idea. It for sure made good sense. In fact, so good a man could scarcely believe it. Not, at any rate, a man who knew the way the army operated and who with his own eyes had read Sheridan's orders to Custer not ten days gone. True, Hazen's district was a separate and distinct command from Sheridan's, but somehow a man couldn't bring himself to think even the Army could be that balled up on its own orders.

Something smelled wrong about the whole setup. Big, bad-medicine wrong.

All through the endless hours of the 21st, 22d and 23d, Josh paced the confines of Black Kettle's lodge awaiting the return of the chief's mission to Hazen.

He was no longer bound hand and foot, at least not by rawhide and horsehair. But Mad Wolf wasn't whelped yesterday, or the day before. He had Big Body and a guard-changing shift of Dog Soldiers strung so tightly around old Black Kettle's lodge that a grayback louse couldn't have crawled twenty yards from it without being stepped on and squashed by a patrolling Dog Soldier's footskin.

With dusk of the 23d, while he was squatting outside the lodge with Magpie for his evening's airing, he heard the wolfcall of the Cheyenne tribal signal echoing in over the darkened prairie from the east. Ten minutes later Black Kettle rode up to Magpie's supper fire, flanked by the tribal chiefs who had accompanied him. These were Stone Calf of the militant Cheyennes, Ten Bears of the Comanches, Lone Wolf of the Kiowas and Big Mouth of the hostile Arapahos.

But the composition of Moxtaveto's retinue was lost on Josh as his eyes alighted on the figure at the old chief's side.

He had not seen Monaseetah since Middle Spring

grove. But anger, treachery, hate and heartpain combined had not been able to keep the picture of her face from his mind. She had ridden with him every weary step of the way from that love-trap on the Cimarron. Now here she was again, as hauntingly beautiful as ever.

His eyes, however, sought the return of hers in vain. The Indian girl sat her calico mare staring blankly over his head, her gaze as straight and stony as any in the dark-faced company around her. By not so much as a long black lash flicker did she recognize the living presence of her betrayed white lover.

Turning bitterly from the girl to the faces of the peace mission, his jaw clamped.

If a man could read a face, he could read a red one as quickly as a white. On any face in that hard-eyed group, from the mahogany-dark frown of Little Raven to the pale, pockmarked scowl of Stone Calf, one word and one alone was written: *disaster.*

Seconds later the silent group, accompanied by the expressionless Monaseetah, had turned its ponies past Black Kettle's fire to file into the darkness toward the main Cheyenne camp and Josh, seated with Moxtaveto in the flap-closed interior of the old chief's lodge, was listening to the fateful terms of that disaster.

19. *The Burning Pole*

GNARLED HANDS moving swiftly, voice held low, Black Kettle tolled off the deathknell of his people.

"I am too old, my son. I have lived too long. I see the end of it all now. Hazen Chief cannot help us. Yellow Hair will come and Axhonehe will have his way."

"Are you sure, father?" Josh's questions fell tersely. "Is there no chance left? Are you certain Hazen Chief is powerless?"

"I told him I had tried to make peace with Yellow Hair but that my scouts had since brought me word that he was coming against me. I told him my camp was on the Ouachita, forty miles east of the Antelope Hills, and that Yellow Hair knew where it was. I told him I had only one hundred and eighty lodges and that I spoke only for my own people. Even so he would not hear me."

"What did he say? Perhaps there was a misunderstanding, father."

The old man shook his head.

"There was no misunderstanding, Ota Kte."

"What were his words, father? Exactly, I mean. Do you remember them? Perhaps there is yet time if you have mistaken his meaning. Perhaps I might go with you, to him. Or you with me, to Yellow Hair."

Again the aged chief shook his head.

"I remember his words. They will stay in my heart like a riverstone, never wearing away. The Cheyenne are lost, my son."

"Quickly, father. There is little time. His exact words now—"

Wearily the old man recited the military requiem of his tribe, the words Hazen's, the last and lost-hope inflections his own.

" 'I am sent here as a peace chief,' Hazen Chief told us. 'All here is to be peace, but north of the Arkansas is General Sheridan, the great war chief, and I do not control him, and he has all the soldiers who are fighting the Cheyennes and Arapahos. Therefore you must go back to your country, and if the soldiers come to fight, you must remember they are not from me, but from that great war chief, and it is with him you must make your peace. I cannot stop the war but will send your talk to the Great Father, and if he gives me orders to treat you like the friendly Indians I will send out to you to come in; but you must not come in unless I send for you, and you must keep well out beyond the friendly Kiowas and Comanches. I hope you understand how and why it is that I cannot make peace with you.' "

"Was that all, father?" He put the question softly, as Black Kettle's voice trailed off.

"No!" There was quick bitterness in the denial.

"When Hazen Chief had spoken, Lone Wolf and Big Mouth betrayed me. They told him my heart was good but that I could not speak for my young men, and that my young men were big for war. Then Stone Calf, that son of a sick she-dog, made their words sound true."

"You mean he talked war in front of the soldier chief? Deliberately, father?"

172

"Aye, deliberately, to show Hazen Chief that Lone Wolf and Big Mouth spoke the truth. He struck his chest there in front of the soldier chief, and he said he could see no point in a truce of a few moons only. Next spring, he boasted, the Sioux and Northern Cheyenne would come down and help us clean out the whole of the Arkansas. Hazen Chief fed us all and treated us like chiefs, but Stone Calf and the others, all save old Ten Bears who is my friend, they rode off muttering because he would not give us everything in the fort."

He paused, weathered hand shaking as it struck the flint to the blackened bowl of the stone pipe.

"It is the last smoke of Moxtaveto, headchief of all the Southern Cheyenne. Ten Bears has told me he must take his people to Fort Cobb. Lone Wolf will follow him, no matter his brave talk in front of the soldier chief. Even now the lodges will be coming down. The Kiowa and Comanche will depart, and Moxtaveto will wait for Yellow Hair alone."

Josh watched the smoke drift upward, let his words come soft and bitter.

"We are dead, father, you and I. I say goodbye now, and I touch the brow for the last time. My heart is good for you."

With the words, he lowered his head, touching the left fingertips quickly to his forehead. He was on his feet then, the softness long gone from the harsh bark of the Cheyenne syllables. His muscular aim reached for the chief's rifle.

"Give me that gun, old man! I am going now. It is

173

better to die than sit here waiting for Axhonehe. *Zeo notaseas!*"

Black Kettle seized the gun, sweeping it away.

"No, my son. You must trust me. Moxtaveto is dead but Ota Kte will live! I have arranged it."

"Give me that gun, father!" His voice turned ugly. "You cannot arrange anything. Your power is gone, here. You know that. You have said it yourself. Axhonehe will be down on this lodge within the next breath."

"Aye," the smile was strangely happy, "my power is gone and Axhonehe will be here even as you say. But in here, my son," he tapped his head significantly, "I am still chief over that Dog Soldier cur. You will see!"

"You're wrong, father—" Josh moved, wrenching the weapon away from him. "I'm not waiting to see. I'm going presently. *You* will see, old man. When Axhonehe appears in front of this tipi, he is a dead Dog Soldier. I have made a vow, *too, Moxtaveto!*"

The sudden snarling of the tribal drums barking the news of the returning peace mission's arrival in the main camp downstream rolled up the Washita to break the silence. Black Kettle shrugged eloquently.

"You can die by your own way, or live by mine. The decision is yours, Ota Kte. I am waiting, my son."

Josh was waiting too, his wavering mind spurred by the building tide of sound racing up the Washita.

Mad Wolf was on his way. Black Kettle's power was broken by the failure of his mission to Fort Cobb, and Axhonehe was coming to redeem his pledge to the Dog Soldier lodge. The compelling vision of the bright red burning pole flashed through the moment of his indecision. Swiftly he turned on the silent headchief.

"All right, father. I'm listening."

"Listen well, my son. Axhonehe is upon us!"

He had no real need of the admonition. The muttering rush of the old chief's following words, startling and hope-building as they were, scarcely had time to reach him before they were ridden under by the turf-showering halt of Mad Wolf's braves beyond the tipi flap.

Black Kettle was rising then, the muzzle of his returned rifle burying itself in the crawling region of Josh's kidneys. The sudden look of hate and contempt suffusing his patient face was as genuine as any South Plains thespian ever affected.

"Out the flap now, Ota Kte. Quickly before he has a chance to call out!"

"I am your prisoner, father." The bone-dry grimace managed a trace of the old grin. "Deliver me to your enemies like the weakhearted old traitor you are. *And may Maheo forever bless you!*"

Lying in the familiar blackness of Stone Calf's tipi, Josh reflected at uneasy leisure on the tallow-smooth working of the first part of Black Kettle's promise. Outside the lodge, the hostile yelp and yammer of the second preparation for the burning of Plenty Kills went forward apace.

The old chief, acting the loyal white-hating Cheyenne to the last proud feather in his seven-foot war bonnet, had succeeded in his wily gamble to beat Mad Wolf in the primary move. He had emerged from his tipi to surrender Josh to the Dog Soldiers at the end of a patently sincere rifle barrel. Outmaneuvered, Mad Wolf had angrily accepted the prisoner. He had then vented his spleen by throwing a cordon of tribal police around the big black lodge, leaving the old man a virtual prisoner in his own camp. Even at this late hour the Dog Soldier was taking no chances of a last-minute emotional appeal by Black Kettle to his changeable tribesmen. Nothing must now stand in the way of the much delayed burning of Ota Kte.

Knowing the customary hour for such festivities, Josh added the three hours which had passed since his "treacherous" delivery by Black Kettle to the time of that act's happening—around eight o'clock. *Aii-eee,* brother! Plenty bad arithmetic! Happen a man could still tot a simple Indian sum, that made it close to eleven now, and left him a thin-poor hour for the rest of the old chief's far-fetched pledge to come about.

The thought of that second part added another pint of perspiration to his already sopping backbone.

It was all well and good for Black Kettle to have told him, even though he'd refused to reveal his identity, that he still had one loyal friend among his fellow tribesmen. And that that friend would manage Ota Kte's escape sometime before midnight. The bad part was that a man didn't have to guess much as to who that mysterious "one loyal friend" was. And having guessed it, he had to admit that old Magpie, staunch friend or no, was a pretty rickety warhorse upon which to throw much of a hope-load.

Not that the old rascal might not try. But suspicious of

him as the Dog Soldiers would naturally be, Black Kettle's best friend had about as much chance of getting close to Stone Calf's tipi as a coyote to a mother-guarded buffalo calf.

Still he was all the chance a man had left and happen the old coot showed up, he wasn't going to let his senility stand in the way of his following him as far and fast as his creaky legs could lead.

Two things were in favor of a getaway.

Trussed up as tight as they had him and with the whole danceground swarming with drum-crazy Dog Soldiers, they'd put no actual guard in front of the tipi. Beyond that Stone Calf had thoughtfully pitched his skins to back up on a thick stand of river willows that reached clean to the water's edge.

His nerve-tuned reflexes jumped to the sound of the knifeblade slashing the rear of the lodge. Fascinated, he watched the slim blade lance through the taut cowskins. The next minute he was stifling a gasp of recognition.

That small head and slender arm following the knife through that opened tipi wall were a long way from senile or shaky!

Monaseetah came to him, shadow-swift, the soft crush of her lips on his warning back all questions. The knifeblade flashed faster than a man could follow it. He was free and following the Indian girl back out the slitted skins thirty seconds after her wordless appearance.

A three-minute sneak brought them to the banks of the Washita, Josh careful to see that his following moccasin prints stepped into and obliterated the girl's.

At the river there was no pause. Monaseetah slipped into the darkened flood and let the current carry her down and away from the flaring reflections of the dancefires. Behind her, the tall scout bumped the guiding drive of his legs against the shallow bottom, his dark head cutting the surface only inches behind the girl's.

Ten interminable minutes later their combined swimming and floating had carried them a quarter-mile downstream of the camp.

They came out of the water on a long stratum of slab rock leading to a growth of cottonwood saplings back from the river. On the naked rock their tracks dried and disappeared as they entered the screening brush. He recognized the high withered shadow of the gelding even as the girl's first words were coming to him.

"It is your Winter Giant, my love. Take him and ride. Do not stop to talk. Goodbye, Ota Kte. My heart rides with you—"

Her words were broken off by the hard smash of his kiss.

"God bless you, girl," he muttered. "You know where my heart rides."

"Aye, Ota Kte, always—"

She clung to him a moment then, her lashes wet not with river water alone. When she broke away, her voice had gone harsh. The Cheyenne gutturals hissed at him.

"Go now, *Veho!* Before I am missed!"

"Before *you* are missed, girl?"

"Yes. Don't argue, my love. I must be in the camp when they find you gone."

"I won't ride without you, Bright Hair." The refusal was flat, final.

"You will have to. If I am missed they will kill Mox-taveto. They will know he planned this if I am not there for them to see. There is no other way, Ota Kte."

He cursed viciously. She was right, of course. Happen those Dog Soldiers got it in their minds Black Kettle had arranged the slip-out, they'd kill the old chief, sure.

"Suppose you do get back? They'll find those cut ropes in the lodge—"

"They will find nothing!" With the denial, the girl reached in her dress, pulled out the slashed piece of the horsehair ropes. "You see, I have them here. I will bury them on the way back. They will never know how it was done. I saw you covering my tracks with yours back there."

Her old sunbright smile flashed suddenly, stabbing him like a knife in the heart.

"The escape of Ota Kte will still be a miracle when our children's children are telling the old tales!"

Like it or not, a man had to buy it. He had his chance to get back to Custer now, and he couldn't refuse it. Not after the girl had risked her life to give it to him. Besides, there were too many more lives beyond his and the Cheyenne girl's mixed up in the rest of that miracle of hers; the remaining slim bet that Wasiya could still get him clean away from the Washita.

He had to go, and to go fast. The last, best chance for all of them was in his getting to the General and stopping him short of Black Kettle's winter camp.

"I'll be back, girl," was all he said before swinging

179

aboard the restless gelding. *"Zeo notaseas!"*

"Zeo notaseas," she echoed softly. "I'll be waiting for you, Ota Kte—"

20. The Winter Giant

HE KEPT WASIYA down to a swinging walk the first two miles. They followed the south bank of the Washita, taking advantage of the outcrops of bare sandstone featuring that side of the river.

Across stream the prairie lay open and swampy, the soft turf of its bottomlands setting a perfect track-trap for the man who would be tomfool enough to ride a twelve-hundred-pound gelding across them. The late moon was climbing fast and within an hour the whole plains would be a blaze of near-white light. With that damned Blind Coyote and his guiding hand, Yellow Buffalo, up front of the Dog Soldier pursuit, a man couldn't be too cautious where he left his barefoot pony prints.

Wasiya was one horse in a score of hostile pony herds but the rib-gaunt old devil had been ridden down to his hocks in that crazy march from Middle Springs, and four days on winter grass hadn't gone halfway to putting the spring back in his pasterns.

Fifteen minutes downstream of Black Kettle's camp he brought the gelding up, slid off him and cocked a primely interested ear back toward the dancing war camp.

He was still close enough to catch the bounce of the dance fires off the night sky over the Big Bend. The wind lying where it did, light and warm from the South-

180

west, would let a man pick up any ear-sign of a ruckus in the hostile celebration. Ten seconds of listening brought him nothing but the swirl of the Washita and the dying rustle of the night breeze among the leaves of the riverbank cottonwoods.

Wagh! All was well in Mad Wolf's firelit front yard. The red sons hadn't yet spotted his getaway. By now the girl would be back in Moxtaveto's lodge.

Unknotting the muzzle-wrap Monaseetah had so properly installed on Wasiya to keep the gelding from whickering before he had his rider out of Cheyenne earshot, Josh took one last look and listen toward the Dog Soldier camp.

Half a held-breath later he was piling aboard the startled Wasiya and kicking him through the shallows of the Washita.

A deaf-mute with both ears plugged and buggy-blinders on couldn't have missed that commotion. There was enough unhappy Dog Soldier yapping going on in that camp to raise new hair on a scalped Sioux's head. The boys had come to Stone Calf's tipi to pick up their trussed white bird and had found him long flown.

Across the river lay the open prairie and a ninety-mile night ride to swing wide northeast then straight west to intercept Custer on his line of march from Camp Supply. It was 1.00 A.M. of the 25th and the General had been scheduled to leave that field base on the 24th. Knowing the General the way he did, a man could gamble that what the orders called for, Custer would come up with. It was 100-to-1 he'd left Camp Supply on the exact hour of his orders and was already in the field heading for the Washita.

That left a man in his footskins with three options.

He could make his wide swing to hook up with Custer, taking his chances Mad Wolf would figure him to do just that and would head the Dog Soldiers straight north to cut him off halfway around his big circle.

He could hold his own line due north from the Washita, not swinging back west to join the General at all, but just keeping on pounding Wasiya's rump until the gelding had him due east of Camp Supply. Then all he'd have to do was ease west and home-out, scalp-safe, on that powerful base.

He could take the simplest way of all. Just give the gelding his head straightaway down the southeast valley of the Washita and come out a short seventy miles later in the "peace sanctuary" of Colonel Hazen's commission at Fort Cobb.

He hesitated, the trail-taking howls of the Dog Soldiers nudging his natural regard for the shoulder-length Kelso locks.

He owed Custer next to nothing. The vain-crazy Indian killer had refused to open his ears to every warning he'd offered him. He had laughed or snapped off every level-headed suggestion put to him. He would by now have heard California Joe's report of seeing him with the Dog Soldiers on Dead Mule Mesa, and would more than ever suspect him of going soft on the Cheyenne. Like as not, he would turn him over to a guard detail and route him back for Camp Supply the minute he struck the column.

Still, a man had his loyalty to think of, and when the hostiles were howling a scant six miles off his backside and the burning pole was still waiting for him back along the Washita a man had sudden reason to remember which side he was on.

He had reason, also, to remember what he knew about the Arapaho-Dog Soldier trap waiting for Yellow Hair back there in the Big Bend. And about the fact the General thought he had no more than eight or nine hundred of old Black Kettle's "peaceful" Cheyenne on his hands once he got his troops to the Washita.

In the end a man had a last thought. It was a thought which set his jaw stiff as lake ice in January, and put his hand to jerking Wasiya's halter rope so hard around it nearly took the gelding's head off.

It was a thought which had to do, first off, with a Cheyenne face, yellow-toothed and grinning evilly with its Dog Soldier vow to put Ota Kte under and wed-up with Moxtaveto's niece. It was a thought which had to do, second off, with a remembrance of a wrinkled red hand touching a weathered brow in final respect and farewell to an enemy white man whose loyalty had in the last hour of trial surpassed that of any of his own tribesmen. And a thought which had to do, last off, with a memory neither in his mind nor in his eye, but in his heart.

The picture of Monaseetah smiling up at him in the hurried dark of the downstream cottonwood grove—the refeeling of the quick burn of her hungry mouth on his—the tearwet caress of her dropped lashes—the quiet promise of her parting promise, "I will wait for you, Ota Kte," brought the final curse.

"Hee-yahh, little hoss! Custer's ninety miles away and we got *a wickmunke* to report! And sure as hoss sweat stinks, old son, a howlin' 'Mad Dog' Soldier to shoot!"

The harsh words were seconded by the vicious drive of the moccasined heels into the gelding's flanks. Wasiya jumped into a hammering gallop. The drumfire of his unshod hooves faded quickly and was gone.

Once again the sum of one of Josh's Indian arithmetic problems added up.

As he drove Wasiya northeastward across the Washita uplands, the sounds of the Cheyenne pursuit dropped away behind. Within another five miles they were lost altogether and he pulled the lathered gelding down to a ground-eating shuffle trot, the natural trail gait of the plains-bred saddle pony.

But as Wasiya's gait slowed to a trot his rider's thoughts picked up to a gallop. Second guesses were coming fast and with them some hard facts which didn't add up as smoothly as the simple hunch that Mad Wolf couldn't hold his exact trail once he was well away from the Washita.

First, a man had to admit that his plan to outride the Dog Soldiers with a ninety-mile swing-around would no longer hold.

Next, he had to realize his only chance of coming up to the Camp Supply column in the field short of its Big Bend destination, was to cut due west right now.

But the country ahead for half a day's ride in any

direction was flatter than an old squaw's chest. With daylight, a mounted man would stand out on that short grass as black as a two-thousand-pound bull buffalo in the middle of a forty-foot wallow. And with Dog Soldier patrols crawling the country between him and Custer thick as sowbugs under a turned-over cowcake, a man wouldn't have a Chinaman's chance. He'd be spotted before the sun was two hours high and scalped before it was three.

Still a mountain jasper in his saddle had about as much choice as a Kansas darkie in a Kentucky Klan meeting.

The flint of the scout's grin struck its light briefly.

Such as the Arkansas Option was, a man reckoned he'd have to take it. And take it mortal fast. Happen he aimed to get to Custer he'd never make it riding the red fringe of Mad Wolf's north-flung gauntlet.

Once more Wasiya spun to the head-jerking demand of the halter rope. Spun hard left and jumped obediently to the hammer of the sweat-stained moccasins. Spun hard left and pointed the roman ugliness of his sooty nose as due west as the sink of a six o'clock sun.

An hour before dawn the southwesterly breeze faltered and died. The prairie became grass-rustle still. Wasiya swung his muzzle nervously, searched the dead air and whickered softly. Josh stirred in the saddle, adding his own uneasy grunt to the gelding's complaint.

When ten days of unfailing southwest wind, bearing up from the parch of south Texas and old Chihuahua the dry desert breath of the longest November hot spell he could remember, suddenly quit blowing, a man could begin to worry. He could in this infernal country. The wind never quit unless she was fixing to switch, and a man could sweat a little until she decided to let him know which way she meant to switch.

For the next hour and until the leaden daylight came filtering eastward across the empty reach of the plains, Josh sweated. But twenty minutes after the first sick light of the twenty-fifth began to grow, his perspiration was shut sharply off.

The unnatural hush and humidity of the past hour began to move. Slowly at first and not direct enough for a man to mark it. Then Josh, watching the unfailing barometer of the buffalo grass, saw the delicate nap of the prairie carpet wave and rustle away into the southwest. A moment later the first south-spreading ripple of the grasses was succeeded by a second, and a third. Less than a minute after the first warning wave, the full lengths of the brown grama stems were holding far over and steady due into the southwest.

With the flattening of the grass the temperature began to drop. In a matter of half a mile his shirt, damp-wet since leaving the Washita, was frozen to his broad back, the creak and pop of its adjustment to his hunching muscles putting more than the mere chill of its own discomfort into the tightening small of his spine. Another half-mile and the caked trail lather lacing Wasiya's steaming flanks was crusted solidly over by a quarter-inch rime of hoar-frost. And still the wind was no more than a mouse-rustle in the buffalo grass.

But it was that kind of mouse-rustle which put a High

Plainsman's prairie instincts straight on edge—along with the clamp of his hard-set teeth.

There weren't many things Josh Kelso figured to be afraid of. That creepy ghost-rustle through the panhandle short grass was one of them. When the grama started to stir where there was no wind; when it rustled and whispered and lisped at a man as though ten million tiny mousefeet were moving invisibly through it; when it lay all flat in one direction and that direction, pointed by the restless gibberish of its crowding stems, lay dead and due southwest; it was full time for a man to pucker his gut and admit he was plain, damn, scared stiff.

Again Wasiya whickered, the uneasy swing of his belling nostrils now steadied directly away from the south pointing press of the grass. Josh, his nervous gaze following the gelding's, cursed silently.

Well there it was, mister. Him and the gelding had had it. Mad Wolf, Custer, Monaseetah and all the rest of them could make it out among themselves. It was Josh Kelso and his horse against Waniyetula, the Blizzard God of the North Plains Sioux now. All bets were off and the Dog Soldiers were a deader issue than last year's Agency beef.

That greasy cloudbank crouching northeast up there past the Main Canadian wasn't any summer shower. The way it was bellying and mushrooming down across the prairie hush; the way it was shutting off the daylight quicker than a man could watch it go; the growing minor key hum of its god-awful power building in the dead air all around him; the pure, raw, snowstink of its winter-rotten breath, let a man know once and for all straight where he was riding.

And where he was riding was dead into the hollow gut of a Blue Texas Norther.

The smash of the snow's storm-howl roared and crashed against the staggering gelding, clogging his rolling eyes and clotting his close-pinned ears. Atop the failing pony, Josh fought the snow away from his own mouth and nose, gagging and cursing at the breath-killing strangle of it. His arms were like frozen clubs now and in the clamp of his long legs around the gelding's ribcage there was no longer any feeling below the knee. In the shelter of an eight-foot cutbank he halted the gelding and forced his numbing mind to the last decision.

For four hours they had fought the white hell of the Norther, the scout trying always to keep the full blast of the wind on his right shoulder, hoping thereby to hold a rough course westward.

But in the belly of a High Plains blizzard the compass point of the storm's fury swings crazily as a rudderless sea wreck. Four times alone in the past twenty minutes it had shifted the drive of its giant's fist, smashing him and the gelding now north, now east, now south, now west. And in the black bowel of a blue-ice Norther no way is north. None east. South, nor west. A man loses all sense of time and direction under the constant bloodcry and yammer of its incredible noise.

And shortly he loses his other senses. The eyes first,

from the stark blindness of straining through the serous drying blast of the ice slivers. The ears next, their drums ruptured by the incessant high-level scream of the hurricane wind. And lastly, the whole feeling in the body goes, the tortured flesh and bone no longer able to transmit the last warnings of the freezing skin.

As the scout huddled in the lea of the tiny cutbank, his final senses fought their ways into the frost waste of his slowing mind.

His hearing was gone and he had not been able to see the black flick of Wasiya's ears for the past hour. Trying now to move, thinking to dismount and give the gelding a last respite, he found he could not bring his off-leg over the ice glaze of the saddlehorn. He knew, the next instant, that God hadn't intended him to. Happen a man had made it down off that pony he'd have legged over his last saddle. He would never have remembered to try and mount back up and he would never have made it had he remembered.

It was the last hour he and big horse had ahead of them, and *he* was done. Blind, deaf, powerless to move, three quarters frozen, he'd made his dead-end human effort. It was up to the horse now.

Up to twelve hundred pounds of steel-tough, Sioux buckskin. Up to a mud-yellow bundle of bad nerves and bellows-sized lungs. Up to a high-withered North Plains horse who in the seven years since he'd quit sucking his wild dam's leathered udders, had never been ridden down to the baserock of his bottom. Up to a rattailed, burr-maned pony whose last ride would tell

189

a man how well his Sioux breeders had named him.

Wasiya . . . the Winter Giant . . . it was up to him.

Josh leaned clumsily forward. The effort cracked the set-ice gluing his buttocks to the frozen cantle of the saddle and broke the sleet glaze covering the blue of his barely moving lips.

"It's your head, little hoss. Fight it off, goddam you, fight it off—"

Wasiya rolled the whites of his wicked eyes and swung his muzzle toward the mutter of the cracked voice. Blowing the clotting snow from his sooty nostrils, he nuzzled briefly at the hanging arm of his rider. He shook himself like a great yellow cat as the grunting reassurance of his soft whicker went to the no longer listening scout.

Moving out from the shelter of the cutbank the big gelding swung sharply to his right. As he went, he heeded no shift of the hammering wind, heard no siren voice of the Blizzard God's angrily beckoning howls. Instead, he drove powerfully and arrow straight along the needlepoint of his instinct-chosen compass.

The yellow-gelding was neither deaf nor blind and his long-forgotten Sioux herdsman had named him well.

Wasiya, King of the Big North Snows. *Wasiya,* The Real Winter Giant. . . .

21. *Canadian Crossing*

THE FACE ABOVE HIM seemed floating in the empty air, now drawing closer until it almost touched him, now receding swiftly until it was lost in a distance as far and hazy as some outer star. Still he knew it. Recognized it as surely as he would his own. The bleached droop of the haystack mustaches, the compelling glare of the coyote-wild eyes, the petulant set of the small mouth. Diminishing or rushing up at him, whirling, fading, star dim or suddenly moonbright, there was no mistaking that face. It was Yellow Hair's.

The fire ran into his mouth, spread racing down his throat and balled up in his stomach to explode like a burst of grapeshot.

There were more faces above him now and with the fire one of them sprang into clear, hard focus, pushing the others back into the nebulous fringe of the outer group. Dr. Coates. Thin-jawed, fierce-eyed Major "Scalpel" Coates, Custer's buffalo-chasing Assistant Surgeon.

The fire ate down his throat again and now he felt the slop-over trickle of it running across his jaw and down his chest. And he smelled the raw, familiar, god-blessed stink of it. Whiskey, by Christ!

He sat bolt upright, his shoulder catching Coates and knocking him halfway across the tent. The next instant he was on his feet, tottering for the flap-laced entrance.

"Catch him, boys, he's going down!" Coates's sharp

191

order came as the big scout staggered. "All right, get that cot and that damned snow out of here. Bring me half a dozen blankets and a bucket of hot coffee. On the double now!"

Minutes later Josh was sitting up in the warm bundle of the blankets, gulping the steaming coffee and forcing the story of his capture and escape through the unwilling stiffness of his lips. When he had concluded, Custer merely nodded.

"You're lucky to be alive, Joshua. That muckle-dun Percheron of yours brought you in. The good Lord knows how. Probably found the river and followed it up to strike our camp."

"What river, General?" His question blurted awkwardly, the cracked, frost-burn blackness of his lips still refusing to function properly. "By God, not the Washita?"

"The Canadian, Joshua."

"The Canadian! Goddam it, then you're almost on top of them. Listen, General—"

"You listen, sir. Coates says you're not to talk any more. He's had you packed in snow for three hours and you can thank him you still have arms and legs. I think we owe him the courtesy to do as he asks. Do you hear me?"

He nodded weakly, the sudden return of his strength all at once failing. He sank back into the reaching warmth of the blankets, hearing the dim mutter of Custer's voice asking Major Coates how soon he might expect him to be rational and ready to talk, barely hearing the Assistant Surgeon's replied estimate of four or five hours. Then he neither knew nor heard any further sound.

When he once more awoke, the tent was dark and warm, its only light the faint glow from the smoking wood stove. Such as the illumination was, it was sufficient to make out the lone orderly stationed by the entrance flaps.

"Call the Colonel, soldier, and hop your butt about it. I ain't got all winter."

With the scowling order and the trooper's quick agreement to it, he was out of the blankets and toeing into his stove-dried moccasins. Shortly, the familiar, light, quick step crunching the snow outside the tent announced Custer's arrival.

"Well sir, by thunder this is better. All right, orderly, outside. Now then, Joshua—"

Josh grinned, frost-cracked lips or no.

By God, you just couldn't put this little bantam down. Let him get caught in the wide open with a full field column of green troops by the worst blizzard in ten years and he still had guts and gall enough to rattle on like he was sitting snug and safe back of the stockade at Dodge.

"Yes sir, General." The grin let itself out another stiff notch. "I reckon you want the story of my life with the Dog Soldiers again."

He didn't miss the quick clouddrift of the frown, and wasn't fooled by the peg-toothed grin which supplanted it.

"No sir, I believe I got that before."

With the short nod Custer read it back to him, from Monaseetah's Middle Spring trap to Wasiya's miraculous finding of the Cimarron Crossing camp. The too-bright way he rapped it to you made it sound like some thing he'd read in a Ned Buntline penny-dreadful, and let you know that, scoutwise, you and G. A. Custer had come to the end of the trackline. His own grin died.

"You don't believe it, is that it, General?"

"I *do* believe it, sir. That's the whole trouble. And in the face of it I can no longer trust you with the Cheyenne."

"By God, General, that's not so!"

"I'm afraid it is, Joshua." Custer's contradiction came quietly, Josh noting his voice wasn't high and flighty like it was when he was tempered-up. "It's the girl, you understand? I assume you were taken and held by force and I further assume your complete loyalty to me. But I do not assume the continuing quality of your judgment under the circumstances."

"I don't foller you."

"My entire point," said Custer soberly. "You cannot follow me. You may indeed owe *your* life to Monaseetah and the old chief. But what I owe them and every one of their murdering tribe north of the Arkansas is something else again. You cannot, Joshua, repay your debt to them at the same time you are guiding me in the action I intend taking to collect mine. I'm sorry, sir. California Joe will take the column in from here."

Expecting it or not, the jolt of the dismissal hit a man like the flat of an open hand. Josh shook it off, the apparently easy idleness of his reaction taking Custer off guard.

"General," he might have been speculating on the number of snowflakes crusting the little officer's collar, "how many hostiles you figure you got waitin' for you yonder?"

"Perhaps a thousand, you know that."

"And you got how many troops with you?"

"Eight hundred and fifty, you know that too. What are you getting at, sir?"

The simple bareness of the questioning was beginning to penetrate Custer's impatience, making him hold up and think. Josh stepped softly into the holdup.

"Countin' the full strength of the Dog Soldier Lodge at close to one thousand, you got better than three thousand five hundred hostile bucks squattin' down there in that Big Bend waitin' for you to poke your long nose past it."

"By Heaven, that will do, sir!"

"They'll let you come in on Black Kettle's lodges, pitched like they are on the near side of the Bend." Josh was thinking out loud, ignoring Custer's bristling order. "Then once you get your troops strung out across the open flat of the Bend going for the main Cheyenne camp on the far side of it, the Arapahoe and Dog Soldiers and Stone Calf's hostile Cheyenne will pile in on you from three sides. It can't work no other way, General, the way I got that camp set in my mind. I could draw you a map of it that wouldn't miss six pony steps from bein' accurate down to the last hoss apple."

Custer, quick anger bridled, was listening now, his soldier's mind caught up by the scout's terse detailing of the military picture awaiting him along the one-day distant Washita. His determination wavered, began to fail.

"If I could only be sure of you, man, that map would be priceless. But hang it all, Joshua—"

"Listen, General, you ain't got no choice but to be sure of me. You lead them boys of yours into that camp the way you're aimin' to and you're goin' to get the biggest headlines in them eastern papers you ever dreamed of. Only it's going to be a bad dream, General, and the printin's goin' to be plumb black."

"I've heard enough of your impudence, sir!"

"'CUSTER KILLED ON THE WASHITA,'" he intoned, the dead level of his voice unheeding of the officer's rising tones. "'COMMAND WIPED OUT IN INDIAN TRAP.' 'NO SURVIVORS IN CHEYENNE MASSACRE OF SEVENTH CAVALRY.'"

He paused, shrugging laconically. "How do they sound to you, General? Take your pick."

During the naked seconds of the grim tolling off of the big scout's predictions, Custer's anger had flared, been fought down and brought under control. With no further reaction than an understanding nod, he stepped toward the tent flap.

"Orderly."

"Yes sir, Colonel?"

"I want Major Coates up here, please."

"Yes sir. Right away, Colonel, sir."

With the clearly disgruntled Assistant Surgeon

dragged from his warm billet and crowding in through the snow-billowing flaps, Custer's quiet directions continued.

"Give this man an opiate, Coates. He's more nearly done in than we thought. Not yet rational, you understand? Orderly. Mount a guard detail out front. No one is to come into this tent. Is that clear?"

"My God, General, wait a minute!"

Josh's desperate outburst was countermanded by the quick touch of the slender hand on his shoulder and by the too-ready assurance of the old, bright smile.

"Easy now, Joshua. Take Coates's pill and let that be an end to it for tonight. Let's call that an order, sir." Here, the irresistible broadening of the famous grin. "You've got to rest if you're going with me in the morning!"

With the surprise announcement of the reinstatement, Custer strode from the tent.

Josh, left to the irritated insistences and sugar-coated laudanum tablets of Major Coates, offered no resistance to either.

He was suddenly tired again and tomorrow was another day. Plenty of time yet to make his map of the hostile layout for the General and to sweet-talk him into following it in his approach to the Cheyenne camp. They were still a long day's march from the Washita and the drowsy, warm feel of the blankets and the wood stove smoke-smell was more than a played-out mountain jasper could argue with.

He lay down, letting the leaden ease of the drug push him back and keep him there. Major Coates's face pulled away, got fuzzy, floated around the tent a spell, then drifted peacefully out the flap.

Beyond the thin canvas walls old Waniyetula, the Sioux Blizzard God, still yammered wildly. But in the big Sibley it was close and warm, and the waiting Washita was thirty safe miles away.

Who was there to blame the dozing scout if he failed to hear the sudden, crafty change in Waniyetula's angry howl? The change which put the old devil's harsh voice from frustrated, baffled screaming to sudden mock-hollow laughing. . . .

22. Custer's Compass

JOSH CAME AWAKE. He frowned up at the unfamiliar gray of the tent cover, the lethargy of the opium still slowing his mind. Presently it occurred to him that the gray of that light filtering through the dirty sidewalls was a mite too strong for nighttime. Then, in harsh succession, other things began to cross his quickening thoughts.

That was daylight-gray, well along into morning. Custer wasn't the commander to sleep late on a campaign ride. The storm had let up and it was almighty quiet outside. Way too quiet for a field camp of eight hundred and fifty cavalrymen.

He was at the tent flaps then, sharpening instincts halting him short of ripping them open and blundering out. The big hand parting the flaps moved them no more than a chance breeze.

Outside the air was still, only a powderflake fall of

snow still sifting down. It was nothing like enough to mar a man's eyesweep of the Canadian Crossing campsite.

The overcoated silhouette of the lone trooper patrolling the twenty-foot beat in front of the tent overlay the rest of it. Beyond the trooper's path the story read as clear as the race of a South Park creek.

The long, horse-appled tramplings of the empty picket-lines. The black smudges of the dead-coaled cookfire spots. The silent rows of the parked supply wagons and spare field ambulances. The back-hunched lines of the nosebagged mules. The lonely scatter of the deserted Sibleys. The handful of heavily bundled troopers tending the feeding of the wagonstock. The stark, ironshod staring of the broad path of snow-held horse sign leading into the near side and out the far, of the ice-clogged Canadian.

Add it all up, even in the half-breath it took you to sweep it in. Divide it, multiply it, tot it back up any way you would. It came out the same. There wasn't a Seventh Cavalry saddleblanket in sight.

Custer was gone. And he'd left Josh Kelso behind under armed guard and camp arrest!

The big scout wheeled like an arrowshot bear. Plastering his broad back to the tent flaps, he let the hiss of his held breath go.

Goddam the lousy little scut. Smearing his soft-smiled bullcrap right in a man's teeth. Letting him have the cow-cake of his stinking shoulder-pat and making him eat it too. A man could forgive a lot of things about the General, and forget a lot more, but not this. This a man wouldd remember. He'd remember it as long as he would that buddy-up shoulder squeeze. And then, after that, a hell of a lot longer.

There was only one way a man could go now. That prairie compass had only one needlepoint for a man in his skins. And it wasn't east, nor west, nor north. It was due south.

But it had to be worked so no troopers got shot, and no civilian scouts either! It had to be worked slick and smooth and above all, fast. A man had to have some information first, along with a good, warm issue over-coat. He rolled back into the blankets, let his voice waver out weakly.

"Hey, soldier. Gimme a hand here, will you? I can't seem to make it to my feet."

He heard the answering crunch of the sentry's step on the snow, tried to set himself to look as pale and puny as a hundred and ninety pounds of muscle-tight mountain man could manage.

"Sure, buddy. How you feelin'?"

The trooper's smile was friendly, his behavior hand-made to Josh's urgent order. The boy-simple way he laid that Spencer down when he reached for the expiring scout couldn't have been better planned. Josh had his knee in his kidneys and his arm barred across his trusting throat before the stupefied youngster was aware the blankets had so much as rustled.

"All's fair in war, soldier." His grin came as his free hand scooped up the carbine. "Make certain sure you don't yammer when I ease off'n your windpipe."

He stepped away from him just far enough for the

snout of the carbine barrel to stay embedded in his sucked-in stomach.

"Now then, boy, talk fast and you won't get hurt. How long ago did the General leave?"

"Five o'clock. It's most eight now."

"Where-a-way is his line of march? Dead south?"

"Yes sir!" The boy threw a salute, in his belly-shrinking fluster.

"All right. Good. Where's the saddlemount picket? What's left of it."

"Yonder past that near line of wagon mules."

"You know hosses, boy? To pick one out?"

"Yes sir—"

"Well, pick one."

"The gray mare. She's Major Coates's buffalo pony. He didn't want to risk her down yonder."

"Arab mare? Dishface blaze? Sockfoot, steel-gray?"

"That's her, yes sir."

"By God, that's somethin' anyway. What's left behind here otherwise? How many men? What officers?"

"The Colonel didn't take nothin' but seven wagons of ammunition and one ambulance. There's near thirty of us left here. Only one officer though, Lieutenant Mathis. He's—"

"All right boy, turn around."

His flat interruption brought a hesitating, white-faced obedience. The youth turned carefully with his hands half raised. As his back came around, Josh stepped in. The just-right tunk of the Spencer barrel took the trooper behind the right ear. He went down like a hand-dropped sandbag and Josh apologetically rolled him into the cover of the blankets.

"Sorry, youngster. You won't need this coat. You'll be real cozy here. And just long-quiet enough to get me and that mare clean across the Canadian."

For the first six hours the snow held off, the wind, uneasily down. The clouds were still low, sometimes lying flat to the ground so that a man had to feel his way for a mile at a time. But generally there was light enough to see and Custer's column was leaving a heavy track. Where a man couldn't see it he could smell it, working slow and following the sharp sting of the horse-dropping smell.

Before long he had closed the gap to where a Sioux-trained hand, held close and steady, could detect the radiating core-warmth of the freezing apples. Within half an hour more, he didn't have to squat to put a hand to them. The thin wisps of the bowel-heat smoke, yellow-gray against the white of the snow, told a mountain eye they were only minutes old.

But another mile along the freshening trail and the wind was moving in. A quarter-mile farther, the snow was driving dead level with the flat of the plain. Five minutes more and the rounding snow dimples of the filling hoofprints disappeared. Custer and his eight hundred and fifty men and mounts could have been four hundred yards away and still no nearer than the far side of the Rocky Mountain moon.

Josh felt the sink in his belly.

Son of a bitch. He fought down the fury that rose in him. To have gotten fresh-apple close to them! To miss them by twenty minutes of up-sudden snowhowl!

Or was it snowhowl, by God? The more a man listened to the new noise of it, the less it sounded like howling. And the more like idiot-simple, cracked, crazy laughing.

He set his long jaw, clamping back the unreasonable fear that wanted to come up in him.

Let the old devil laugh. This time Josh Kelso was going to get the last cackle. This time, by God, a man had a trick or two left!

He was riding a fresh horse. The wind, flat and noisy as it was, hadn't switched yet. Old Waniyetula had blown his guts out in his yesterday's try to get him. His bluster was still big and noisy but it didn't have the dead cold in it any more, nor the wild, ever changing swing of the wind. The old villain was trying but a man could tell that he was just blowing and snowing now, and running almighty fast out of real breath.

That wind was coming down off the Canadian as true north as the pole. As long as it held steady he could drift with it and figure he was hitting roughly south. Going that way, if he didn't come up with something else meanwhile, he was bound to sooner or later come up to the damn Washita itself. He could hole up there in the river-bank timber and weather it out, Custer or no Custer.

But what a man actually expected to hit before he hit the Washita was the broad track of the old east-west Indian trail over which the Dog Soldiers had brought him into Black Kettle's camp. Now if he could hit both that trail and Custer too—

Not over half a mile of humpbacked drifting later, the gray mare turned "whiffy."

He brought her up at once and sat watching the work of her muzzle and ears against the crossdrive of the wind.

When a horse that's cavalry-bred and barracks-raised turns all at once whiffy on a man, it isn't that she's smelling Indian ponies or red soldiers. Not when she was as sharp-nosed as this mare. And as eager whiffy. A horse could get scared whiffy too, but any son that had worn out the best part of six leggins' seats polishing them on the cantle of a Texas saddle could spot the difference wink-quick.

This mare was winding friendly. And she wasn't blowing any smell but Seventh Cavalry horse sweat out of her flared open nostrils.

He gave her her head, compounding the generosity with a drive of his moccasins which nearly caved her aft ribs in. Within a handful of snowblind minutes the gray mare had blundered squarely into the storm-turned rumps of Custer's picketlines.

The Colonel had halted his command in a wide snow-filled wash, the low walls of which gave some protection from the wind. Such as this shelter and that of the seven ammunition wagons was, the men of the Camp Supply column were making the miserable best of it.

The one tent, a big Command Sibley, was pitched to the lea of the field ambulance, and toward it now Josh guided the Arab mare. The windrows of huddling troopers seeking the shelter sides of the ammunition wagons or the animal warmth of the picketlines paid him no more heed than had he been one of their own number which, bundled in the high-collared bulk of his late guard's overcoat, he indeed appeared to be.

At the tent he pulled the mare up, grinning his satisfaction.

From the cut and color of the ponies hunching their backs in front of the General's Sibley, a man could rightly guess that a full-out council of war was in progress within. And that the star witnesses and chief hell-getters thereof were California Joe and Apache Bill, along with the rest of Custer's famous string of hired scout-hands.

Stepping off the mare, he paused outside the opening, eying the confirmation of his guess through the slit in the billowing flaps.

If there had been a carpet in that damn tent, his late fellow scouts would have been standing squarely on it. Joe was heading the bunch, backed by the rest of them: Apache Bill, Ben Clark, Jimmy Morrison, the Mexican "Romeo," and old Hard Rope. The General, sided by his brother Tom and by his three field majors and Benteen, was putting the screws to his head-hung scout corps.

"Well, gentlemen," the thin voice was sour as swill, "I suggest that despite your vaunted reputations you've gotten me as thoroughly lost as though I'd hired one of Black Kettle's Cheyennes to do the job. We have left the trail entirely and had it not been for

205

my own use of the compass we would not even know as much as we do, which is simply that we're eight hours south of the Canadian. Any questions on that, gentlemen?"

"None at all, General." California Joe wagged the black brush of his beard soberly. "We're just as lost as Bo-Peep's sheep. Bill and me ain't bin in this Washita country much of late and Ben and Jimmy been up among the northerns pretty much since 'sixty-three."

"That's mortal true," nodded Apache Bill, his own excuse for not knowing the local terrain thinner than any of the others. "Way this cussed Washita country lays, the land so flat and all, a man can't rightly keep long in his head what little landmarks he's got. There ain't a tree high enough for a runt coyote to hoist on, nor a doghill big enough to let a tall gopher see more'n forty yards."

The other scouts nodded wordless agreement with Bill's lament, Hard Rope, the Osage, adding the lone postscript to the majority opinion.

"Me no good, find village," he shrugged. "Me plenty good, *you* find village."

The remark, addressed to the scowling Custer, brought the quick flit of Josh's grin.

The old rascal wasn't talking through his beaver hat. These Osages weren't somehow worth a tinker's damn, come to locating a village of their cousins. But just let a white scout find it for them and they woke up sudden. Nobody could beat them at sneaking in close and spying out the layout of a bunch of lodges. They smelled right to the hostile ponies and even the village dogs wouldn't bark at them.

While he was still enjoying his grin and as he was reaching for the tent flap, a reply to Hard Rope's cryptic observation was coming from the officer group. The nature of that reply, along with its stolid-faced source, checked his hand and shortly widened the spread of his grin.

"Well, Colonel," Benteen's slow voice went to Custer, "here we are. We've got everything but what we came after—Black Kettle's village. And we left the only man who could take us straight to it back there with the baggage wagons. No offense to you other boys," his nod to California Joe and his group was sincere, "this snow is hell. There's no blame on any of you. But I, for one, wish we had Josh Kelso here."

"You ain't wishin' no harder than the rest of us, Captain!" California Joe's fervent affirmative was backed by the soberly agreeing headnods of his fellow scouts. No group of repentant buckskin sinners, mute as they might be, ever echoed a louder or more unanimous "Amen!"

The simple eulogy brought an awkward flush to the listening hero's grin.

A man better get the hell in there and put a stop to those nominating speeches before they had him set to run for President. Especially if he didn't know too much more about where they were than the other scouts did!

But Custer's voice was staying his reaching hand this time, and for a long spell he was glad he'd let it do so. A man was forever selling the little General short, only to have him up and buy his way back into your heart just like he was doing now.

"Gentlemen," the statement was given in one of Custer's rare moods of self-admission, "you can include me in those wishes. But if wishes were horses, we wouldn't need oats along.

"Boys," his short nod went to the scouts, "Joshua was a sick man. I purposely had Dr. Coates drug him so he would not be further depressed by our departure. I believe I regret that action now. I, too, wish we had that thick-headed Mountain Moses here to lead us out of this blizzard's bullrushes. But he is *not* here, and wishing he were is not going to bring him through those tent flaps!"

Josh couldn't resist it. A man could stand outside all winter and never get a better chance to bust in. He took his big grin with him as he bent his tall form through the tent opening.

"Oh, I dunno, General. Depends on how hard you wish—"

His quiet words, preceded by the high flight of the Custerian prose, broke the meeting as wide open as the appearance of any Moses, mountain or biblical, could ever hope to do. In a matter of seconds the backslaps of his fellow scouts and the unabashed handshakes of Custer's worried staffers were completed and the commander ordered the tent cleared save for himself and his prodigal ex-favorite scout.

Josh nodded grimly.

Jealous as always where he smelled the chance for a big decision or a clean-cut military move, the little General was not about to share with his staff any distinction which might result from his scout's disclosures. What Josh might have to tell him about their present location in relation to that of Black Kettle's Big Bend camp, along with any success which might obtain from following up that information, was going to belong to Lieutenant Colonel G. A. Custer, Commanding.

And any history book title or credit for getting the Camp Supply column unlost and heroically led out of the blind gut of that November 26th snowstorm wasn't going to get split up with California Joe, Josh Kelso or any other living soul.

It was going to stay with Custer and his precious compass!

23. The Lonely Hill

THE MARCH OF blundering events put in dangerous motion by Sheridan's notorious General Order of the 15th, now gathered the final speed of inevitability.

It was 5.00 P.M. by Custer's big gold watch, that religiously held instrument which shared the hallowed vestry of his breast pocket with the sacred compass, when the little General ordered his staff to leave following Josh's dramatic arrival. For the next hour the pacing silhouette of the column commander's thin figure moved across the lamplit walls of the big Sibley. In the far corner of the tent Josh's shadow crouched over the Colonel's war chest, the only movement in it the scratchy laboring of the turkey-quill pen.

While the crude map of the Washita grew under the

scout's awkward hand and glass-sharp memory, Custer fired at him an abrupt round of questions concerning the last-minute strength and disposition of the hostile forces.

Was he sure the Kiowa-Comanche camps were largely deserted? Was he convinced the Arapahoe meant to fight? Did he realize that such a gathering of lodges as he described would cover no less than five miles of riverbank? Would house over four thousand Indians? Could he with certainty put the column onto that east-west Indian trail leading into the open side of the camp? Was he positive Black Kettle's lodges were isolated from the main camp? Could they definitely be struck first and, by a bold move, cut off from the others?

To these brief queries Josh's grunted asides provided even shorter answers.

The Kiowa and Comanche were gone, giving the excuse of buffalo-hunting over on Rainy Mountain Creek. The Arapahoe would fight, Big Mouth would see to that. The stretch of the hostile lodges along the Washita reached nearer ten than five miles. There were closer to seven thousand than four thousand Indians clustered up in that Big Bend. He could find the trail. Black Kettle's lodges were right where he was inking them in. They could be cut off in five minutes.

Presently Josh's looming shadow grew tall on the tent walls. The map, the questioning, the answering, were done. Providing the snow eased off they could move with first light tomorrow. Six hours would see them on the Washita. It was up to Custer now.

Seizing the map from his slow reach, Custer studied it for two full minutes which seemed to Josh to crawl on their bellies like snowfrozen molasses. At last the little General laughed, handed the map back to him, the bad-wild light in his eyes beginning to grow.

"Keep it, Joshua. Show it to your children. I've got it now."

Josh took the map², folding it carefully into his coat pocket. He knew Custer's high-voiced excitement was no idle boast. Given half the time he'd used on your rough scrawl, he could six months later draw it for you from memory, not missing a flyspeck nor an inkblot, and drawing it a sight better than you had in the first place.

"I'll get Benteen and the others in now," Custer's tones showed no lowering of his Indian Fever, "and run over the approach with them. You get over to the commissary and put something in that long belly of yours. I won't need you right away, and Joshua," there was that old shoulder-squeeze again, "when you're done, see that you come back here. I won't have you out in this weather. You're sharing the General's tent tonight, you understand?"

He nodded, understanding several things now. Primarily, the business of handing him back the map and telling him to stow it away. No use showing the staff something somebody else had done. Not when Yellow Hair could give it to them cleaner and quicker in his own way, and at the same time make it sound like his personal opinion and private idea.

Moving for the entrance, he found the little officer

there before him, parting the flaps to put in his impatient call for Benteen. The half-frozen trooper outside never got the order. Custer's eyes widened as the flap opening revealed the night sky. Eyes glittering, thin lips suppressing his excitement, he wheeled on the big scout.

"By heaven, Joshua, we've got them now! Look at that sky, man!"

Josh was over his shoulder then, his belly pulling in as his dark eyes narrowed.

As far as a man could see, he was looking at nothing but clear air and clean, black starlight. There wasn't a wind whisper or a snowflake stirring south of the Canadian or north of the Washita. And within two hours there would be moon enough to read a handwritten letter by.

"Don't you do it, General!" He was reading the book of Custer's mind a page ahead. "Your boys have already got eight hours of bad trail behind them. They ain't had no hot food. The hosses is wore down fightin' groundsnow. By God, General, you can't—"

"Orderly!"

"General, for Christ's sake, listen—"

"Orderly. Get Captain Benteen up here. Major Elliott, Gibbs, the rest of them. Instantly sir, you hear?"

"Yes sir, Colonel! Corporal of the Guard ho! On the double!"

"General—"

"By thunder, will you be still, Joshua! You've done your work, man. Now get out and let me do mine. Get out, sir! Do you understand?"

"I understand, General," was all he said, before stepping through the flaps to stand bitter-eyed and silent, watching the wild race of Custer's orders break the huddling camp from its snowbound bivouac.

Within minutes the troops would be on the last, grim southward move. Within miles Josh Kelso and the coming harsh white moonlight would be guiding them toward a trail no mountain man could miss. And within six short, frost-clear hours that trail would have them topping out on the mile-long, naked crest of the last ridge overlooking Moxtaveto's tipis.

The Camp Supply column stood committed. The Washita was waiting, and Yellow Hair was coming.

The light within the lodge came only from the pipebowl's smolder, the alternate rise and fall of its copper glow highlighting the old chief's impassive face. Across from him the girl crouched in thought-held silence. Outside, the wind, quiet for the first time in three days, let the blackened cowskins hang slack and still along the gaunt ribs of the lodgepoles, gave no hindrance to the incessant thunder of the scalpdance drums from the restless camp below.

There was good cause for the silence and the thought-holding.

Two days gone, the last Dog Soldier patrol returning from its pursuit of Plenty Kills had reported hearing rifle fire along the Canadian. Its members had thought, until reaching camp to find theirs the last party in, that it had been one of their own groups shooting buffalo. Last night Red Bird, a loyal Cheyenne, had come back from a scout to report seeing through the snow a long dark line of marching figures south of the Canadian. The light was bad, too much snow. They had looked like buffalo at first but their line was very even. They could have been soldiers. This morning two of White Bear's Kiowa, moving east with a band of stolen Ute horses, had passed through the camp with a tale of having crossed the snowtrail of many ponies wearing iron shoes. And yes, the trail was lying to the south, almost where Red Bird had seen the buffalo.

Black Kettle stirred, palmed the cold ashes from the long pipe, nodded to the waiting girl.

"Bring the ponies now. Tie them outside. I am uneasy. My heart is bad within me."

"Magpie has been on watch since sundown." Monaseetah's words came with her understanding gesture. "It is time he was relieved, uncle. Who shall I send?"

"Double Wolf. He can be trusted. Send him."

The lithe figure of the girl moved quickly through the flaps, leaving the darkened lodge to the last thoughts and long-cold pipebowl of Moxtaveto, the tired Black Kettle of the Southern Cheyenne.

The dry cottonwood logs of the downriver dancefire were piled swiftly higher. *Aii-eee,* cousin! This was turning into *a real* dance!

From the northeast, within the hour, two big parties of new Dog Soldier braves had arrived. Both from Kansas, where they had been raiding even while that senile Moxtaveto had been whining and pleading with the soldier chief at Fort Cobb. Both big for war. Both led by real chiefs. Black Shield, cousin! And Crow Neck! *Wagh!* Real chiefs indeed. And they had white scalps, fresh ones, twenty-three of them. Now they *would* have a scalpdance.

The drums thundered the news. The cracked voices of the old criers, running the village streets of all four tribes, summoned a fresh wave of dancers from the farflung scatter of the hostile lodges. A scalpdance, brother! Come running now! And bring your squaw or sweetheart. This is the time you dance with her.

It was true. In the strict social order of the South Plains tribes, the scalpdance was the sole ceremonial in which the braves and their women were allowed to touch each other's bodies. It was a rare occasion, cousin, and a wild one!

Every warrior old enough to straddle a pony smeared his broad-boned face with the black charcoal paste of victory, seized his chosen one and bound her tightly to him in the folds of a single blanket. A wheeling circle was formed, the paired-off dancers facing inward and shuffling from right to left. Their close-packed shoulders and hips left scarcely room to twist and shift to the quickening throb of the wardrums.

The squaws, their squat features blazoned with ocher and vermilion, their skinning knives or butchering blades belted on the outside of their flaring doeskins, bore proudly aloft the war weapons or hunting shields of their menfolk. The annointed few among them exhibited the matted tangle of the fresh scalps, starkly upheld on slender trophy rods of peeled willow. As they moved, the black-faced braves grinningly bound their rawhide lariats around their bodies and those of the couple next them, that no dancer might quit the circle from the simple excuse of fainting with exhaustion.

Hour after hour, the driving chant of the drums went on. The glaring rise of the Arkansas moon served only to heighten the frenzy of the naked bodies beneath the tight-bound blankets. Ten o'clock came and was pounded under by the drums. Another hour passed. Another began.

On the lonely promontory west of Moxtaveto's lodge, Double Wolf pulled the heavy shroud of his buffalo robe closer. Curse this midnight chill. But then, *wagh!* The dance was going well below and all was still to the west. It was a good clear night and the moon let a warrior see a long ways. All was quiet. There was no use huddling here and freezing. His lodge was only a few steps down the hill. There were the warm embers of a fire in there, and maybe a little of that boiled dog left in the cooking pot. Moxtaveto was an old woman. And it was getting colder by the minute on that cursed hilltop.

Nahooxz! It was time to go home.

Seconds later, only the moonlight guarded the glistening snow of Black Kettle's watchtower.

24. Garry Owen

JOSH KEPT THE GRAY mare close in hand. Beside him, Hard Rope held down the chopping gait of his paint gelding, his slant eyes narrowing as Josh pointed the long ridge ahead.

Behind them a scant hundred yards moved Custer and the rest of the scouts. While another hundred yards behind the little General came the snake-long column of the Seventh Cavalry. The snowsqueak and harness jingle of its cautious advance carried clearly to the tense scout and his Osage companion.

He reined in the mare and flung up the warning signal of his long arm. Custer, catching the prearranged gesture, waved it on to the following troops. The Seventh came to a hoof-shuffling, uneasy halt, the steam clouds from the sweated flanks of its mounts rising arrow-straight in the dead-calm air.

Another wave from Josh and Custer was dismounting the scouts. With them he moved swiftly forward on foot to join Josh and Hard Rope. Leaving two of the Osages to handclamp the muzzles of Hard Rope's paint and Josh's gray, the little group inched up the moonwhite slope of the ridge.

At its crest, belly-flat in the snow, his propping elbow touching Custer's, the big scout let his sidemouth whisper come short and tooth-set.

"You're in luck, General. They ain't even got a sentry posted."

"How can you tell, man? I can see nothing but snow."

217

"That lone hill yonder. The one that sticks up just this way of the main jumble of them ridges. You see it?"

"Yes, what about it?"

"That's Black Kettle's watch-out. They had a sentry on it twenty-four hours a day when I was with them. You can see it's bare as a new baby's butt."

"Good Lord, Joshua, you don't suppose they've gone!"

"They ain't gone, General." He put the frost of his hard grin to the remark. "They just ain't as crazy as you are. They'd never figure you to come down on them in a snow like this."

"I can't believe there's a war camp beyond those hills, sir." He didn't say it like he was asking any questions. He was stating a fact and his next words nailed it down. "We'll move on down the river. You've missed your marks, man."

Josh's rejoinder was to suggest that before ordering a pony-muscle moved, the column commander accompany him, California Joe and Hard Rope to the deserted top of the watch-hill. He added the dry prediction that he's be mortal-happy he had, once he'd shoved his belly across the snowcrown of *that* hill. And he'd be tolerably pleased, as well, that Josh had had him hold the column up back where he had, instead of letting it crunch right up to the last lookout. After all, even "Yellow Hair" wouldn't try to walk eight hundred and fifty iron-shod cavalry horses square up to Moxtaveto's front door across any such loudpoppy snowcrust as they were moving over!

Custer peg-toothed his appreciation of the reminder and put the quick squeeze of his small hand to the scout's bulging bicep.

"All right, Joshua, let's get up there. We can't give the troops time to get on edge."

The four black-furred dots glided down the slope of the ridge, picked their way warily across the open snow of the level separating it and the watch-hill. Within minutes they had again ceased to move, motionless smudges now, on the crest of the distant hill.

The four sets of slitted eyes atop the abandoned silence of Double Wolf's sentry post strained through the puddled darkness of the scene below. Their anxious stares were defeated by the rough tumble of small hills, shelving cutbanks and nebulous blotches of river timber. Custer could see nothing, hear nothing. Josh and California Joe fared little better. But Hard Rope had Indian eyes. And ears.

"Me hear dog bark."

The deep grunt swung the eyes of the listening white men in his direction.

"I didn't hear a living thing." Custer's nervous whisper went to Josh. "And I can't see a living thing!"

"Hold up, General. I got the dog just now. You catch it?"

Custer nodded. There was not only *a* dog barking, there were several of them. And not any mile away either. Those barks were coming out of that right-hand stretch of riverbank cottonwoods, not six hundred yards from where they lay!

"Me see ponies. This side river. You see?"

"Where, Hard Rope?" Custer's glance swung to follow the point of the Osage's arm. "Why, bless you, man, those are trees—or buffalo—yes, by the Lord, they're buffalo! Good heavens, there must be a thousand of them. By thunder, Joshua, you were wrong, sir, you were wrong!"

"There's a thousand of them, all right, General," his voice dropped with the nod, "but they ain't buffalo. And hold your talk down. We can't afford to spook the crazy devils. Happen we work it right, we can gather them in on our way into camp. Happen we work it wrong, the bastards'll stampede and roust out every earpoundin' buck for fifteen miles down the Washita. Let's go, General. *Them's ponies yonder.*"

"I'm not satisfied, Joshua. I remain confident those are buffalo down there, dogs or no dogs. I think your Indians are gone, sir, leaving a few of their curs behind as they always do."

"No buffalo—ponies," grunted Hard Rope.

"If they're buffalo," grinned Josh, "I'd sure as hell like to know who hung the bells on them!"

Custer's quick scowl died aborning. Up from below, tinkle-clear from the ghostly movement of the big herd, came the unmistakable jangle of a grazing bell. It was overlain by the answering music of a second. And a third.

"As you said, Joshua," Custer's light-quick smile fought the moonlight to a standstill, "let us go."

The smile faded in the moment of its flashing, the pale-eyed stare which replaced it putting the gray iron of carbine-close reality to the grim conclusion.

"And may God have mercy on Black Kettle's soul. I shall not!"

Beyond the mile-long shelter of the first ridge, Custer readied his column.

The lean ration of coffee and hardtack for a single day, per man, brought from the base camp on the Canadian, was dumped on the Washita snows, to be followed by the saddlebag of oats each man had brought for his mount. There was to be no turning back, no counting on any source of supply whatsoever. When the troops of the Seventh Cavalry were committed, they were to understand *they were committed.* Each trooper was allowed to carry only his ammunition issue of one hundred rounds and his unbooted Spencer carbine. Even the heavy field overcoats were ordered stripped off and added to the mingling trample of oats and coffee, the huddled men waiting in their issue shirtsleeves for the final "forward ho!"

There was to be no company talk, no shouted commands, no bugles blown ahead of the coming advance. Smoking was completely forbidden and the man who struck a flint or match within the ranks did so in the face of a field-order death sentence.

To Josh, waiting tensely, the sibilant muttering of the hundreds of white tongues sidemounting their frightened whispers in nerve-strung defiance of the "no talking" order to the hand-close comfort of some fellow trooper or perhaps the hard-bitten understanding of a trusted and battle-tried noncom sounded loud enough to be heard in the last Cheyenne lodge down the river.

But a man shook it off, knowing the whole course of the harsh discipline and hand-signaled maneuvering of realigning squads, platoons and companies was going forward with remarkable silence and efficiency. And knowing, too, that when a man knew as much as he did about what was waiting beyond that frozen watchtower of Black Kettle's there was a limit even to his own gut-tough nerves.

He could see the new commands forming up now. Moving the gray mare closer to Custer's staff group, he was able to catch some of the Colonel's low voiced orders.

There would be four attack columns, proper, two of them to move as a unit under Custer. Of the two distinct commands Major Elliott would have one to swing wide around the camp to the south and to come back up and attack from the east. Major Gibbs, or was it Colonel Meyers, there, would have the other, to swing off on Custer's right and between him and Elliott and attack from the south. The third column under Captain William Thompson would move on Custer's left and in direct conjunction with the commander, to attack from the present or western position. The ammunition wagons would be left on the ridge.

Elliott's column moved out first, Gibbs's holding up for fifteen interminable minutes, then following off in planned succession. Custer, sitting his bay buffalo horse in absolute silence, sided by himself and Captain

Thompson, watched the slow crawl of the minute hand on the big gold watch, glanced presently toward the paling gray of the eastern starfields, nodded quietly to young Thompson.

"All right, Captain, let's go. Hold to a walk until we're given away."

The double column of Custer's and Thompson's four hundred troopers split like a snake's tongue around the narrow base of Black Kettle's watchtower. On the far side, they converged toward the dark cone of the single tipi flanking the hostile camp's side of the hill.

Double Wolf's woman, out with the dawn to scrabble firewood for her breakfast pot of pemmican, dropped her cottonwood faggots to stare in unbelieving terror. The next instant she had slipped into the screening brush and was scuttling for the lodge.

Double Wolf, still sleepy from his night's vigil, was rubbing his eyes when the woman entered. He saw her seize their two small children and drag them whimpering through the entrance flap, and heard the warning of her single, guttural growl, "Soldiers!" The next moment he was grabbing his rifle and wrenching back its sidebuilt percussion hammer.

Stumbling outside, still heavy with sleep, he watched the squaw fade into the nearby brush. He turned in time to see the hated silhouettes of the Pony Soldiers topping the rise behind him.

Double Wolf was a "peaceful" Cheyenne. But he had been at Sand Creek and seen his other squaw and four young children ridden down and riddled with carbine slugs. He saw, now, their blood on the snow again, and forgot in its red blindness the insistent order of old Black Kettle to raise the white rags if the soldiers came. Instead, he raised his old percussion musket and fired it with his war cry into the advancing troops.

His twisting body was nearly torn in two by the answering hail of soldier lead. His last memory was of the clarion blare of Yellow Hair's bugler sounding the charge. The instantness of his death spared him the ignominy of hearing the echoing of its blatant signal by the brassy notes of Custer's omnipresent regimental musicians blasting away at "Garry Owen," the war song of the Seventh Cavalry.

The Battle of the Washita was begun.

25. Death of a War Chief

CUSTER'S COLUMN splashed through the waist-deep Washita and sent its horses scrambling up the opposite bank, atop which stood the cluster of perhaps fifty lodges which had chosen to remain camped with Black Kettle. As the General's troopers topped the bank from the northwest, the first of Gibbs's cavalrymen dashed up from the south. Josh, riding ahead of the shouting Custer, saw Black Kettle's squaw run from the big lodge to race for one of the two tethered ponies. A moment later, the old chief ran out shouting and waving at the troopers.

Firing was general now and the few other braves, running half naked from the surrounding lodges, were beginning to go down. Only a handful of these were armed and but one or two of them discharged his piece.

Black Kettle had had no time to seize his faithfully prepared flag of truce. The surprise was too great. The panic memory of the Sand Creek Massacre, too overwhelming. The pathetic tatter of the dirty white feedsack laced to its peeled willowpole was later found within his lodge, trustfully stacked alongside his buffalo-hide war shield and White Horse Lodge ceremonial lance.

Seeing his frantic gestures unheeded, the old man turned and stumbled toward Antelope Woman, the bullets of the laughing, cheering troopers kicking and whining around his heels. The tethered ponies, wild with fear, were lunging and rearing at their halter ropes, defying the efforts of the squaw to approach them. Black Kettle seized the mane of the nearest pony and vaulted to its plunging back. Slashing the picketline with his knife, he whirled the squealing animal toward Antelope Woman, dragging her up behind him and spurring the pony for the Washita.

Josh's shouts of protest to the milling troopers were drowned out by the renewed burst of carbine fire poured after the escaping chief. Custer himself rode him aside in his fury to follow Black Kettle. Fighting the gray mare free of the melee, he threw his glance back toward the lodge in time to see a third red figure dart from its entrance.

Somehow Monaseetah made it to the second pony. She slashed the maddened animal free, made a running mount and drove in a headlong gallop for the screen of the riverside cottonwoods. He had no time to see if she made it clear or not, the converging rush of Gibbs's troops catching him up and sweeping him toward the Washita.

There he was in time to see the miserable end of a Plains Indian era.

Black Kettle's pony, both riders still mounted, had miraculously run the ragged gantlet of the excited troopers' fire to reach the river's edge. And more, had managed to land upright in the shallow stream and keep going for the far side. But that was all.

The pony staggered, hit and ripped from haunch to wither by the simultaneous rupture of a dozen .54-caliber Spencer slugs. He went down in a smother of gray water and bloodfoam. Still he regained his feet, bearing only the squaw now, and struggled on toward the opposite shore. He had not gone three lurching steps when Antelope Woman screamed, threw her hands back to her kidneys and slid off into the water. Her body bobbed and floated, face down, not two yards from that of Black Kettle.

Josh had no time for the nausea and anger which welled up within him. Black Kettle was dead, shot in the back as he fled, weaponless and with his woman mounted behind him, before the senseless fire of the Soldier Chief with whom he thought he had made an honest and honorable peace. As the scout watched, the last miserable coup was struck in the spurious name of that "peace."

Hard Rope, with his fellow Indian scouts, charged

his rattailed pony down off the cutbank and into the Washita. The braves piled off their mounts in midstream. One of them, reaching the sodden body of the murdered chief, felt under the snow-muddy current for the floating tangle of the gray braids, knotted his hand among them to lift the bullet-torn face above the water.

The knife did its shameful work quickly.

The red hand came away, holding triumphantly aloft the clotted honor-token of having counted the final coup on the last war chief of the Southern Cheyenne. Moxtaveto, the Black Kettle, had departed for the Land of his Ancestors, scalped and started up that shadowed trail by a wooden-handled army butcher knife and a vermin-dirty Osage buck who, in Indian life, would not have been fit to feed his poorest pony.

Josh turned from the river, wanting to vomit, and helpless for the moment to do anything but sit and watch the following slaughter.

Custer's military planning had been efficient. Thompson's troops commanded the south bank as well as the entry into Black Kettle's village from the west. To the south, below the camp, sealing it off from the main hostile strength, downriver, stood the two hundred and twenty-five troops of Major Alfred Gibbs.[3]

Yellow Hair had his Indians where he wanted them. And where he wanted them was dead.

The execution proceeded.

In the dead chief's isolated group of loyal lodges there were perhaps a hundred and seventy-five warriors and teen-age boys, with half that many squaws and small children. A group of eighty desperate braves, headed by the ancient Magpie, reached the riverbank, slid over its precipitous edge and began to fight its way downstream. Magpie was killed in the first rush but the bulk of his followers managed to get behind the cut-bank and hold the troopers temporarily at bay. The remainder of Black Kettle's warriors, cut off by Gibbs from their pony herd and by Custer from the river, was trapped.

Custer now stationed Lieutenant Billy Cook with forty sharpshooters on the south bank immediately below the village. He then swung around above the village and drove east through it with his main command. As the braves fled ahead of him, they ran into the withering crossfire of Cook's sharpshooters on the riverbank and Gibbs's troops to the south of the lodges. Those few who managed to win through to the river were mowed down by Thompson's rifles holding the opposite, or north, bank. It was a complete carnage.

Josh's earlier estimate of five minutes for the cutting off of Black Kettle's village could not have been exceeded more than a handful of seconds before the last brave left among the lodges was shot to pieces and the last squaw and child captured.

Custer, with Josh back at his side, now turned his attention to the surviving group holed up along the Washita. Taking Cook's sharpshooters, he led them across the stream and turned their fire into the flank of the Cheyenne. As the trapped braves broke and fled eastward along the bank, Josh counted seventeen red bodies bobbing in the bank shallows or sprawled in the naked clay of the bluff's base.

From the south bank now, and eastward along the Washita in the direction taken by the escaping Cheyenne, came the heavy-throated booming of a full Spencer volley. Custer, light eyes blazing, whirled on Josh with his first words since ordering the bugles blown.

"By the Lord, Joshua, that's Elliott down there! He's got them. Good, good. Let's get down there and give him a hand. That's the last of the red scoundrels, by Heaven!"

"We'd best get down there, all right," the big scout grunted, "but that ain't the 'last' of them, General. It ain't hardly the first."

"Now what do you mean by that, sir?"

"By God, General, I told you there was better than three thousand of them *below* the Bend. We ain't even hit the Bend yet. But Elliott has, providin' that's him firin' down there. He's right on it. Happen he goes a step farther, he's dead. We got to head him off, I reckon."

"All right, let's go, sir." With the words Custer was waving Cook's command forward, putting his bay buffalo horse back into the Washita, grinning back at the following scout.

"But I still think you've lost your touch, Joshua. We haven't yet seen a solitary one of your three thousand 'hidden braves.' "

"You'll see them, mister," Josh muttered to himself,

and put the gray mare to breasting the croup-deep current.

Custer, rejoined on the south bank by his main command, lead the two hundred and fifty troopers down the Washita at a hard gallop, the absence of hostile resistance broadening the grin he flung at Josh. The scout took the grin and kept it, not bothering to give it back. And for a quickly evident reason.

Ahead now, the heavy firing of Elliott's command fell off. Seconds after the impact of this stillness reached Custer, he rode into the rear of Elliott's retreating troops. The column was in good order and a young lieutenant commanding the rear of it informed Custer they had caught and killed thirty-eight Cheyennes in a narrow ravine just ahead. Then the hills to the right and left of them had begun to fill with fresh warriors, apparently from the downriver camps. The lieutenant had not himself seen Elliott, but had assumed the retreat order had been given when the ranks in front of him began to fall back.

Custer, on the point of moving forward to seek out Elliott, felt Josh's big hand on his arm.

"Hold on, General, you'd best hold up here and let me mosey on ahead. I smell a rat here somewheres. Lookit yonder."

Custer, following the point of the long arm, saw the bobbing rows of war bonnets and rifle-barrel flashings beginning to sprout in the morning sun along the nearby hilltops.

"Arapahoe," scowled Josh. "We're in trouble, General. Best let me go on up while you unscramble these boys here."

"All right, sir." Custer's decision came with his second look at the growing clouds of warriors along the encircling hilltops. "Get up there and locate Elliott. Bring him back here at once, you understand, Joshua?"

Josh understood. He wasted no time in spurring the gray mare forward. A man could smell that rat for sure now.

It smelled *dead.*

Five minutes after leaving Custer, he rode into the abattoir in "Elliott's ravine."

He found the thirty-eight dead Cheyennes all right, along with something else the young lieutenant had neglected to mention—half a dozen mutilated white troopers. Among this number one man was still alive. He was off the mare and alongside him instantly.

He didn't bother moving him. A man could see the bullet hole going in through the belly just under the heart, and the three, lower down, coming out through the belly from the back. If that wasn't enough he could take a look at the half-scalped skull, the missing right ear and the lance-gashed thigh and shoulder. If this boy lived long enough to say goodbye, it would be a mortal wonder.

He got his arm under his head, and was rewarded by the opening flicker of the eyes. They were sane and quiet though the youngster couldn't be three breaths short of closing them for keeps.

"What's your name, soldier? What outfit? What happened here? Talk while you can, boy."

The soldier nodded, letting a man know he understood. His voice came clear and easy like a man's sometimes strangely will when he is shot to shreds and shouldn't even be alive.

"Harry Mercer, corporal, Company E, Major Elliott. Some of this Injun bunch here got away on down the river. The Major called for volunteers and went after them—" The boy's voice faltered, his eyes straining to focus on the scout's face.

"You're Kelso, ain't you? The General's scout?"

He nodded, seeing the eyelids sag, feeling the slump of the head across his arm.

"—Funny thing," the trooper muttered, just before the blood came, "them Injuns that made it off—they had that purty Cheyenne gal with them—gosh, but ain't she a looker though—"

This time there was no more movement of the eyes. The hemorrhage welled silently out of the slack mouth, and that was all.

He laid the boy's head down, stepped for the gray mare and swung up on her. There was no hesitation in the sharp turning of her head downstream. A man had his orders. Find Elliott and bring him back. Now he knew where Elliott was. Knew, too, that Monaseetah was still alive somewhere ahead of him down the Washita.

A mile along the river he found them both.

The unmistakable bullroar of the big-caliber Spencers broke on his ears as he rounded the last bluff before the open grass of the Bend. On the west bank of the little creek which was southern tributary to the Washita at the point, Elliott and his little band of volunteers had trapped the last o Black Kettle's Cheyennes. The dozen braves were dead before Josh could get the gray mare up to the creekbank, and the major's men were happily examining their four captives—Monaseetah and three of Magpie's small children.

Moving toward the girl, he caught the warning flash of her scowl.

"Do not speak to me, *Veho!*" she hissed. "The Dog Soldiers are all around us. They must not know. They must not see."

His surprise and any further exploration of it were cut off by Elliott's greeting.

"Kelso, by God. Glad to see you, man. How's the Colonel doing? Where is he?"

"Back yonder past the ravine. He sent me up to tell you to get on back. He's got his hands full of Arapahoe back there and you got nothin' but more of the same plus Dog Soldiers and Stone Calf's Cheyenne ahead of you. You'd best get the hell shut of here, Major."

"All right, Kelso. I believe you're right. I mean to go just beyond this creek to make sure we've cleaned them all out down here. Then we'll head back."

"I wouldn't do that, Major."

The blunt admonition went unheeded. The officer had already turned and was issuing his orders.

"Sergeant Kennedy!" A burly sergeant major moved forward from the gathering troopers. "Take this girl and these children back to the village. We'll follow on as soon as I've had a look across the creek."

"Major, you stay on this side." Josh kneed the mare toward the officer's mount. "I reckon we're already cut off even if we head back now. And don't send that gal off with the sergeant by hisself. He'll never make it in with them, alone."

"Nonsense," responded Elliott shortly. "We'll be right behind him. However," his nod was curt, "you may go along with him if you wish. I'll be all right here."

"I got my orders." He let it come flat and hard. "I was told to bring you in."

"Very well, suit yourself, sir. Here we go!"

Elliott and his eighteen men, Josh counting them across the little stream, forded the creek and pushed out into the open of the Big Bend grasslands. But not far. Just far enough, in fact, to clear the Washita timber and get a good look at what was swarming down off the crossbend hills, north, east and south of them.

Aii-eee! Josh winced, jaw thrust. Here came your three thousand "hidden hostiles," mister. Or at least the best, lousy part of them?

Too late, Elliott saw his situation and called out the order for the retreat back across the creek. As his men reached the banks that last avenue of retirement was cut off.

From the mouth of the little stream's channel through the southern hills, Mad Wolf led his howling Dog Soldiers down its west bank, the bulk of them holding up at its juncture with the Washita, a small band led by Mad Wolf sweeping away to the west to engulf the still visible figures of Sergeant Major Kennedy and his Cheyenne captives.

"We got one chance, Major." Josh's tight words hurried. "Gather your boys and try and ride through them right now. Whatever you do, for God's sake don't stop and hole up here."

"We'd never make it, Kelso. We'll have to stand in this high grass on this side. We can hold them off until the Colonel gets up. He shouldn't be long now."

"I tell you he's likely cut off hisself back there!" The reply was harsh with anger. "He'll never get up to you in time. Why, he don't even have any idea where you are. How the hell's he goin' to get to you?"

Once more the abrupt warnings went unheeded.

Elliott at once reined his horse for the heavy grass of the creekbank, shouting for his troopers to follow him. There he dismounted the men and to Josh's further dismay, ordered their horses turned loose.

Major Joel Elliott would do or die right where he stood.

Josh could not know that as the young officer had dashed off in pursuit of the ravine survivors, he had shouted to his volunteers, "Well, here goes for a brevet or a coffin!" But had the scout heard the famous phrase he could at the present moment have guaranteed the final nature of its grim choice without a second's hesitation.

Major Joel H. Elliott was standing in the shoulder-high side boards of his creekgrass coffin as of right now.

His men could see nothing. Their field of fire was point-blank zero. In the flat of the Bend ahead and to the right of them circled Stone Calf's Cheyenne.

Behind them milled the black-feathered mass of Mad Wolf's Dog Soldiers. To their left the high hill across the Washita was alive with Arapahoe. Sergeant Major Kennedy was dead and with him the last hope of getting word to Custer. Unless—

"Major!"

It was a statement, not a request. He backed it by swinging up on the restive mare.

"I still got my horse and I aim to use her. Give me a burst for cover toward the river. If you can hang on here I'll try and make it to the General. Don't waste lead on long shots, boy. Save it for when they rush you."

He booted the mare out the riverside exit of the creekgrass before the officer could answer, his only remembered view of Major Elliott the bent-double glance he flung back in time to catch the officer's wave of understanding.

It was the last any white man saw or knew of Elliott and his men. All that was ever to be known of the manner and speed with which they died would come years later in the cracked voice of Roman Nose Thunder, one of the Cheyenne survivors, speaking from the time-distant removal of an Oklahoma reservation.

"The shooting was over then. All the soldiers were dead. The fight did not last longer than it would take a man to smoke a pipe four times."

236

26. Yellow Hair's Way

ACROSS THE CREEK, the Dog Soldiers saw the gray dart of Josh's mare streak for the Washita. The burst of wolf howls this discovery sent up among them was instantly stilled by Mad Wolf's barking cry.

"He is mine! It is my vow. I claim the first coup on him. He cannot get away and he is mine alone. Who will deny it?"

Clearly, none of the Dog Soldiers were of a mind to rob their chief of this long awaited honor. It was true what he said, anyway. Ota Kte could not get away. Let Axhonehe have him. Across the creek were plenty of scalps for all!

Mad Wolf, not waiting to hear his challenge accepted or denied, was already plunging his pie-bald stallion into the Washita. Behind him his faithful returned their attentions to Elliott's command. It was perhaps only after three or four minutes of the resumed firing that Yellow Buffalo looked at Big Body and nodded.

The hulking brave returned the nod with loose-grinned understanding. Where Axhonehe went, there went his two lieutenants, whether he ordered it otherwise or not. Only of course it was just the better part of policy not to let him know he was being disobeyed. Unnoticed, the two subchiefs fell back from the lines, caught up their ponies and headed up the Washita after their leader.

But seconds before they departed, another of their relatives had taken the same course before them, and with even less notice.

As Yellow Buffalo and Big Body cursed their ponies forward, Monaseetah had already slipped away from the red ranks of her "rescuers" to swing up on her mare and race westward along the banks of the Washita, following the cross-river course of her white lover by the triumphant wolf howls of the close-trailing Mad Wolf.

Josh had exhausted his ammunition in his brief siding of Elliott's men. He had now between himself and the closing Dog Soldier his guts, his Green River knife, and Major Coates's fast-faltering Arab mare.

In the minutes of his brief race for freedom the deep-throated fire of the Spencers from the creek junction behind him had already begun to fail. Mad Wolf would be up to him in a dozen jumps and behind him not another ten minutes would come the main wave of the big pack now finishing off Elliott. If he managed by some piece of outhouse luck to down the Dog Soldier chief and to get on down the trail ahead of his following lodge brothers, he was still on the wrong side of the river. Ahead of him on the north bank were up to five hundred of Big Mouth's Arapahoe, engaged in holding Custer down. Back of him on the same bank, providing the rest of the Dog Soldiers didn't beat them to him, he had Little Raven and the main bunch of the Arapahoe which were presently helping polish off Major Elliott.

Custer, unless he got to him, was likely to move on

down the Washita and into the same trap the hostiles had closed on Elliott. Monaseetah was with the Dog Soldiers and giving every sign she meant to stay with them. Totting it all up as he threw a snap glance over his shoulder to see that Mad Wolf's studhorse had the chief two jumps off the gray mare's rump, a man had to admit that likely Custer was going under. And for sure Josh Kelso was.

About all a man had left right now was his promise to himself to knock off that axeheaded son behind him if it was his last mortal act. Seeing that it was shaping up to be just that, a man might as well get on with it.

He timed it hair-close enough to suit even his particular mountain tastes.

As his eyetail showed him Mad Wolf's little stallion coming up even with the mare's croup, he threw the slender pony as hard left as he could, pulling her dainty head almost back to the saddlehorn and jerking her front feet out from under her to flatten her like a shoulder-shot elk.

As he felt her go, he flung himself to the right and as far free as he could. He hit the ground hard. But not that hard he didn't see Mad Wolf's stud pile into the mare and go, backside over appetite, right on over her. The Dog Soldier had seen it coming just soon enough to leg off his falling pony and hit the ground in a Cheyenne "shoulder roll." He was on his feet and coming for him before Josh got his senses well cleared.

He had grabbed enough over-shoulder glances during the short chase to know that Mad Wolf had not unbooted his rifle. He knew by that that the red son aimed to try it the hard way.

An Indian never could understand the white man's idea of counting coup with a rifle slug. There was no honor in that, no courage required and no credit coming.

If there was another thing the Indians never understood about their white brothers, it was rough-and-tumble fighting—mountain style.

Josh closed with the Dog Soldier, getting his left shoulder high up under the pit of his upflung knife arm, and knotting his hands behind the small of the brave's back. With the crushing pressure of the South Park bearhug, Mad Wolf's knife hand spasmed. The nerveless fingers lost the blade's haft and the weapon slid harmlessly over Josh's shoulder to the ground.

The big scout stepped back, kneeing his gasping victim out and away from him. Stooping, he seized the chief's knife and sent it whirling into the hand-close Washita.

"Get up, cousin," his grunt came in belly-deep Cheyenne, "I don't want to kill a chief on the ground."

Watching the Dog Soldier regain his feet, he saw the sudden widening of the slant eyes, read their message of triumph, too late. He turned only in time to see the grinning Big Body start the swing of the anvil-headed warclub. His reflex side-twist saved his skull from being pulped, and that was all. The crushing weight of the anvil smashed into his chest and across his shoulder with enough force to drop a buffalo.

The next instant the huge brave scooped him from the ground and barred his sapling-thick arm across his throat. He held him thus, belly out and helpless as a butcher-strung steer, awaiting the mercies of his chief's interrupted coup-counting.

He saw Mad Wolf take the knife which Yellow Buffalo held out for him, and start to move toward him and Big Body. He saw something else too, over there across the narrow channel of the Washita. At the same moment, the grinning Big Body also saw it. But Josh saw it the longer.

The amazed look of discovery was still on the subchief's thick mouth when the neat blue hole of the .44 Henry slug appeared an inch above his unbelieving eyebrow. He was dead instantly.

Twisting violently, Josh broke away from his slackening grasp and knocked up the barrel of Yellow Buffalo's rifle as it leveled on the slim figure of the marksman across the river. The bullet whined harmlessly over the southbank cottonwoods and Monaseetah, kneeling not forty yards away across the Washita, shot the second chief through the belly.

Josh wrenched Yellow Buffalo's rifle from him as the subchief fell. He turned with it in time to smash its barrelswung butt full into the face of the snarling Mad Wolf as the latter came at him with Yellow Buffalo's knife. The Dog Soldier staggered forward, Josh moving aside to let him fall. He hit the ground, writhed over on his side, raised his bloody face with a final blind effort, collapsed and lay still.

By the time he could turn away from him, Monaseetah had splashed the calico mare across the Washita. She swept on past him to catch up the trailing halter rope of Coates' mare, wheeled and galloped the led animal back to him.

"God bless you again, gal!" The awkward English stumbled out ahead of the swollen bruise of the big fist which sought and found her slim hand with the muttered Cheyenne transposition.

"May Maheo bless you, girl. And understand you, too. God knows," here he slipped grinningly back into the English, "Josh Kelso never will!"

"Maheo understands everything," smiled the Indian girl.

With the quiet words, she levered three shots from Black Kettle's beautifully engraved Henry into the belly of the still breathing Mad Wolf.

They crossed the river quickly, putting their horses westward along its south bank through the thick cover of the cottonwoods. Ahead of them in Custer's direction only the occasional black-powder boom of an Indian musket, with its scattered answer of Spencer carbine fire, could now be heard. Behind them, eastward along the Washita toward Elliott's creek, all sound of firing had ceased.

Keeping to the strangely deserted banks of the river they reached Black Kettle's village without incident. Josh at once reported to Custer on Major Elliott's situation and the certainty of its outcome.[4]

For some reason forever a mystery to the scout the little General treated the report with apparent unconcern, simply noting that Elliott was well able to take care of himself and would no doubt join back up in due order. There were at the time, he pointed out, no less than three other detachments similarly missing. Two others, so absent, had just come in to rejoin the main column and there was no valid reason to believe that Major Elliott's and the remaining absentee units would not show up given good time. It was, after all, only just past 10.00 A.M.

The thing now, by Heaven, was to clean up the mess they had right here in Black Kettle's camp, and only then to move on down to pick up Elliott and take care of the rest of the hostiles should any of them be disposed to continue the issue which, in Custer's opinion, by thunder, was highly unlikely!

Josh changed that opinion no sooner than the Colonel had uttered it.

"Take another squint through them glasses, General. Yonder there on the hills where Big Mouth and them Arapahoe has been settin' all mornin'."

Custer raised the glasses quickly, and as quickly put them down.

"By Heaven, Joshua, there does seem to be a considerable number of them moving up onto that hill, at that."

"Not alone *that* hill, General. Lookit over here on the right."

Following the scout's direction the officer swung the glasses toward the southern hills.

"Good Lord! More of them! Aren't those the Dog Soldiers, Joshua?"

"They are." The agreement was succinct. "And they're warpainted just like yonder Arapahoe. These are all fresh hostiles, General, and Monaseetah tells me there's a thousand lodges of them spread for the next fifteen miles down the river. I reckon it's time we went home, General."

While Custer debated the advice, the sergeant left in charge of the abandoned overcoats and march rations beyond the first ridge raced his horse into the camp to report that huge numbers of Indians were swarming in from the west and had overrun the supply dump and taken off in pursuit of the fleeing ammunition wagons.

A momentary grim relief was brought by the present appearance of the wagons around the shoulder of Double Wolf's hill. Their white-faced drivers slid them, brake-locked, down the steep snows of the Washita's far side and dashed crazily into the stream to bring them lumberingly across.

Josh's nod was understandingly short.

Once you got the little General in a real tight, the officer hadn't been commissioned who could outthink him, much less outfight him. If he had a genius for walking into traps, he had an equal one for cool-ordering his way out of them. The big scout relearned that now as he watched the sudden, murderous turning of Yellow Hair's way.

Throwing Cook's sharpshooters and Gibbs's unblooded troops between himself and the threatening thousands of Dog Soldiers and Arapahoes, Custer held them at bay while his own troops methodically completed the rape of the Washita.

His surprise attack on Black Kettle's village had netted him sixty captive squaws and their children. On the icy ground in and around the empty lodges lay the freezing bodies of the Cheyenne dead: a hundred and three warriors, sixteen women, eleven children.

Piled in final total before the big black lodge of the slain chief lay the naked fruits of Indian war: 241 saddles, 1123 buffalo hides, lodgeskins and robes, 82 rifles and revolvers, 425 war axes and lances, 4035 arrows and warbows, 2185 blankets, lariats and buckskin parfleches, 535 pounds of black powder, 1375 pounds of raw lead and molded bullets, and 700 pounds of tobacco plus the untold tons of winter-stored buffalo beef.

Even as Josh noted the wealth of the loot, Custer was putting the torch to it. He had come into the village with nothing but his men and mounts. He was going to leave it the same way. The harsh orders barked out.

Using the captured rawhide lariats, the hurrying troopers began pulling over the lodges and dragging them toward the growing mountain of cowskins east of the already burning loot pile. Shortly, to the flare of two hundred pounds of the captured powder, the winter homes of Black Kettle's murdered Cheyennes were adding their greasy smoke to that of the other camp plunder.

Calling Kelso and California Joe to him, Custer gave the final order—take Hard Rope's Osages and drive in the captured pony herd. There was one last, best chance to break the pressure of the hostile assault building against Cook's and Gibbs's delaying force.

Kill a Plains Indian and two will spring to take his place. Destroy his pony and his heart for war drops dead within him.

There were by this time fully three thousand Arapahoe and Cheyenne clouding the surrounding hillsides. More were riding up by the minute. The situation, already grave, threatened to break out of all hand before the retirement could be begun. As for that retirement, Custer knew, no less certainly than did Josh, that were it not possible to speedily create some major diversion in its face, what might begin as an orderly retreat would become a disastrous rout.

The Indians were driving the holding forces back upon the village. If the movement were not stopped, Custer would join Elliott in his brevetless coffin on the Washita.

As the little General, completely oblivious to the hail of Indian lead, rode the flanks and center of Gibbs's and Cook's failing line, Josh spurred to his side.

"California's got them comin', General. Where do you want them?"

"What's the best place, Joshua? You know these rascals better than I."

"East of camp there," he pointed the spot, "on that clear strip of high ground along the river. The Injuns can look square down on it from them hills."

"Get to it, please." Custer's words were unhurried. "They're pushing us, sir."

Josh wheeled the gray mare to meet the advancing front of the wild-eyed Cheyenne pony herd. "Up on the point yonder, Joe!" The other scout returned his stirrup-standing wave. "Where the red sons can see them go down!"

In three minutes the scouts had the huge herd in a neighing, kicking mill on the high ground of Josh's choice. And in five, the butchering began.

Custer, throwing his entire reserve into the caving forward line, shouted to Cook to pull his sharpshooters out and report to Josh at the pony herd. Joining the scouts, the young lieutenant merely waved his hand in reply to the mountain man's signal. It was a little late in the day for formal orders, given or taken.

For a solid hour Josh's executioners poured their ceaseless crossfire into the screaming mass of the hostile ponies. Watching on the hillsides, the packed ranks of the hostiles grew hushed. The trampled snow around the herd became a fetlock-deep morass of blood slush and acrid, green manure. Still, and interminably, the roar of the short Spencers and the hollow cough of the mountain rifles snarled on.

The Indians were moving now, slowly at first and in small groups. Then more swiftly, by the dozens and the tens of hundreds. Eastward they moved, away and across the silent hills, down and along the crimsoning Washita. Their savage voices were stilled. The barrels of their forgotten rifles cold. Their wild hearts within them, gray and heavy as the river ice.

The war ponies were dead. And dead with them, the wills and minds of their nomad red masters.

No formal count of that pony herd was ever made. But in the minutes of its hurried rounding up, the practiced eye of California Joe had rough-guessed it at better than nine hundred. When the barking volleys of Custer's powder-grimed riflemen ceased, not a Southern Cheyenne pony was standing on the blood-frozen floor of Josh Kelso's Washita slaughterhouse.

Yellow Hair had had his way.

27. *Waniyetula's Blessing*

THE PARTING with Custer was abrupt.

The retreat to the base camp on the Canadian, under forced and fearful march, the men without rations or overcoats in the bone-chill of the Arkansas winter, the horses gaunted from forty-eight hours without feed or any respite long enough for a cinch to be loosened, was completed with nightfall of the fateful 27th.

No sign of follow-up by the overwhelming number of the Washita hostiles developed, Custer's concern they would sweep north around his flanks to destroy his undefended supply train at the Main Crossing proving unfounded. By 9.00 P.M. the last of the hollow-cheeked officers and men and the blanket-wrapped, bitter-eyed Indian women had recrossed Custer's Rubicon.

The following day the retreat was resumed, still under forced march. Camp Supply was reached sometime late in the afternoon of the 29th.

With the surviving regulars gratefully billeted in the long rows of stove-warmed Sibleys, the wounded under delayed treatment in the rough board hospital barracks, and the dead laid in staring-eyed, stiff-limbed state on the frozen dirt floor of a company woodshed, Josh sought out Custer.

His long-striding progress toward the plank door of the commander's sod-roofed quarters was rudely barred by the carbine of a pea-green guard corporal whose sole contribution to the Washita campaign had been the policing of the near-empty stables of the base camp during the Seventh's brief absence.

"Sorry, friend. Colonel's orders. He ain't seein' nobody."

"He'll see me. Tell him Josh Kelso's outside."

"No luck, friend. Sherman and Sheridan are both in there."

"It don't cramp me none if U. S. Grant's in there." The lean jaw moved out. "Tell him Josh Kelso wants to see him. Me and the Injun gal is leavin'."

"Listen, friend," the young trooper's tone turned belligerent, "move along now, see? There ain't nobody less than two stars ranks a break-in on the Colonel right now—"

The corporal's attitude underwent some hasty modification with his feet treading the empty air and the scout's hair-backed fist knotted in the upper blouse but tons of his issue blues.

"All right, mister, all right! You needn't go to gettin' sore about it. I'll fetch your message in to him."

"See you do," nodded Josh. "And don't drag your feet. I ain't got all winter."

The young soldier was back before Josh had more than time to hawk and spit disgustedly into the parade ground slush. His attitude had altered again.

"Colonel says he'll send for you," he smirked. "Says you ain't to worry about your pay, he'll see you get it."

The trooper paused, savoring the tidbit.

"Oh yeah—and he says the Injun gal stays here same as the other squaws. She's a prisoner, friend, and will go east with the others. You got any more billy-doos for the Colonel, friend?"

"Yeah, *friend.*" The big scout's unsmiling grunt came as he turned to go. "Tell him Black Kettle and Josh Kelso said goodbye."

He moved quickly, the full dark of the Arkansas winter night coming down, blackly sullen and heavy, to screen his movement. It was no trick to slip around the huddled guard detail at the loose-stock horse herd. Nor to snake out old Wasiya and the girl's paint mare from under their night-blind noses. After that it got a little thicker.

All the same, he was shortly able to dig their two saddles out of the ruckpile of the Seventh's unloaded wagons. Then to smuggle his own and Black Kettle's Henry repeaters out of the scout barracks and to rummage up a sack of rolled oats and another of hardtack and army dried beef. And finally to get the whole of the borrowed plunder stowed safely away back of the last stable south of camp, without anybody but himself and the horses getting wind of it.

By a quarter of ten he was ready to move.

The captive Cheyenne squaws were being held under a "loose herd" no more humane nor well tended than that of their snow-covered ponies. Their guttering cook-fires dotted the manure-stinking confines of an empty corral just beyond the last stable building.

Getting Monaseetah out of that corral was no more

than a matter of waiting for the three troopers on duty to finish one of their slipshod inspection rounds and return to the comfort of their own fire and battered tin of boiling coffee.

The girl caught his grunting, perfect imitation of a Cheyenne pony whicker. She looked up, returned the rapid movement of his handsigns and slipped quietly away from the tiny fire she was sharing with a dozen older squaws. She joined him bearing the pathetic but eminently practical total of her highborn Plains Indian dowry: two calfskin sleeping robes retrieved from the burning spoils of Black Kettle's lodge.

By 10.00 P.M. the double nightblack line of their pony prints was three miles south of Camp Supply. Eight hours later they had crossed the Canadian and were safely camped in the stormproof shelter of the Antelope Hills.

To the north, sixty miles, Yellow Hair was being routed from the 5.00 A.M. blackness of his conqueror's bed, being unhappily informed that his pet scout and prize Indian captive had departed in the unknown hours. To the south and east, forty remembered miles, Black Kettle was sleeping undisturbed, still and quiet with his faithful woman beneath the winter-calm waters of his native Ouachita.

Above it all, Waniyetula was again laying the thick white cover of his will. But the old God wasn't howling now, nor even bitterly laughing. He was chuckling as he carefully filled the telltale south-pointing hoofprints of the Sioux gelding and the Cheyenne mare. And smiling as he drew the peaceful blanket of his friendly snows over the snug, dry resting place of Ota Kte and Emoonesta.

Bright Hair, his Indian child, had bested him. Even that rascal of a *Veho,* that puny, white-skinned villain of a Pony Soldier scout, had taught him a lesson or two. *Eszenistoz.* Give them a red God's blessing. They were well mated, those two!

Let them dream there under that snug bank. Let them rest now, their grateful voices low and tender with the moment, their tingling muscles easing to the long-sought fullness of the hour's union.

Aye, even hold one's breath a little stiller now, that she might miss no word of the *Veho's* vision. Of the vision of that promise of the endless herd of spotted buffalo he would bring to graze the rich, fat grasses of Moxtaveto's valley. Of how in the moons to come they would prosper, Emoonesta and Ota Kte, brightening the dead chief's homeland with the unfrightened voices of their many children.

And now stop the snow flurries altogether, that the fall of no least, wandering flake should disturb the softness of her answer. Let the listening *Veho* hear its every full-lipped whisper. Let him know that this was the way old Moxtaveto had seen it over the smoke spiral of his last pipe. Let Ota Kte know that this was the way, even exactly as he was telling it to her, that the aging chief had spoken it to Emoonesta that last night within the big black lodge.

Let Yellow Hair come, the old man had said. Let him have his wanton hour of shameful war. Give him the little minute of his willful, bitter pleasure. Then let him go, and let him come no more.

Let there be peace, not war, along the Ouachita. And let that peace come with the growing herds and the smiling, happy children of Ota Kte and Emoonesta.

Yellow Hair had had his way. Now let Black Kettle have his.

Nohetto. Let that be the final end to it.

Endnotes

1. Apache Bill was right. The November 13 meeting with Black Kettle does not appear in the War Department records. Nevertheless, the fact of its occurrence persists both in the first hand accounts of such historical figures as California Joe, and in the tribal lore of the Arkansas Cheyennes and other South Plains bands involved in the campaign of 1868.

2. *Author's Note: Kelso's map of the Washita:* Kelso's map of the Battle of the "Ouachita," drawn for Custer in the field and from memory, contains significant errata: (1) there were no hostile lodges north of the Washita, (2) Custer reported his retreat exactly followed his advance from the east, (3) his own account of the action listed four, not three, attack columns; the fourth under Capt. Wm. Thompson, (4) Col. Edward Meyers, not Major Alfred Gibbs, commanded the column on Custer's right.—C. F.

3. Kelso was in error. These were the troops of Colonel Edward Meyers, not Major Gibbs.

4. Custer always claimed he did not know Elliott was missing until the column had retired from the Washita. It seems at least, viewed in its most charitable light, a peculiar military admission.

Center Point Publishing
600 Brooks Road ● PO Box 1
Thorndike ME 04986-0001 USA

(207) 568-3717

US & Canada:
1 800 929-9108